RECKONING

WOLFES OF MANHATTAN FIVE

HELEN HARDT

RECKONING
WOLFES OF MANHATTAN FIVE

Helen Hardt

HARDT & SONS ♥

❀ Created with Vellum

For my angels

One Wolfe wife is forced into a marriage of convenience to the man she loves desperately.

Another is about to take the fall for a murder she didn't commit.

Time is running out for the Wolfes. Lacey is under arrest for the murder of patriarch Derek Wolfe, and the four Wolfe siblings—Rock, Roy, Reid, and Riley—are still considered suspects. Rock is determined to save his wife, even if it means committing murder himself, while Reid resolves to to discover the truth and avenge his love, Zee, for what she's suffered at his father's hand.

A court order not to leave the state of New York doesn't stop Rock and Reid. Using aliases, they venture out to find the key to this mystery once and for all. Several others are implicated, and an abduction, a death, and a long-lost relative complicate matters and bring new evidence to light.

Rock and Reid will do anything to save the women they love—even if it means neither of them comes out alive.

PRAISE FOR HELEN HARDT

STEEL BROTHERS SAGA

"*Craving* is the jaw-dropping book you *need* to read!"
   ~*New York Times* **bestselling author Lisa Renee Jones**

"Completely raw and addictive."
   ~**#1** *New York Times* **bestselling author Meredith Wild**

"Talon has hit my top five list...up there next to Jamie Fraser and
Gideon Cross."
   ~*USA Today* **bestselling author Angel Payne**

"Talon and Jade's instant chemistry heats up the pages..."
   ~**RT Book Reviews**

"Sorry Christian and Gideon, there's a new heartthrob for you to
contend with. Meet Talon. Talon Steel."
   ~**Booktopia**

"Such a beautiful torment—the waiting, the anticipation, the relief that only comes briefly before more questions arise, and the wait begins again... Check. Mate. Ms. Hardt..."

~Bare Naked Words

"Made my heart stop in my chest. Helen has given us such a heartbreakingly beautiful series."

~Tina, Bookalicious Babes

WOLFES OF MANHATTAN

"It's hot, it's intense, and the plot starts off thick and had me completely spellbound from page one."

~The Sassy Nerd Blog

"Helen Hardt...is a master at her craft."

~K. Ogburn, Amazon

"Move over Steel brothers... Rock is *everything!*"

~Barbara Conklin-Jaros, Amazon

"Helen has done it again. She winds you up and weaves a web of intrigue."

~Vicki Smith, Amazon

FOLLOW ME SERIES

"Hardt spins erotic gold..."

~*Publishers Weekly*

"22 Best Erotic Novels to Read"

~*Marie Claire* Magazine

"Intensely erotic and wildly emotional..."
    ~*New York Times* bestselling author Lisa Renee Jones

"With an edgy, enigmatic hero and loads of sexual tension, Helen Hardt's fast-paced Follow Me Darkly had me turning pages late into the night!"
    ~*New York Times* bestselling author J. Kenner

"Christian, Gideon, and now...Braden Black."
    ~Books, Wine, and Besties

"A tour de force where the reader will be pulled in as if they're being seduced by Braden Black, taken for a wild ride, and left wanting more."
    ~*USA Today* Bestselling Author Julie Morgan

"Hot. Sexy. Intriguing. Page-Turner. Helen Hardt checks all the boxes with *Follow Me Darkly!*"
    ~International Bestselling Author Victoria Blue

BLOOD BOND SAGA

"An enthralling and rousing vampire tale that will leave readers waiting for the sequel."
    ~Kirkus Reviews

"Dangerous and sexy. A new favorite!"
    ~*New York Times* bestselling author Alyssa Day

"A dark, intoxicating tale."
    ~Library Journal

"Helen dives into the paranormal world of vampires and makes it her own."

~Tina, Bookalicious Babes

"Throw out everything you know about vampires—except for that blood thirst we all love and lust after in these stunning heroes—and expect to be swept up in a sensual story that twists and turns in so many wonderfully jaw-dropping ways."

~Angel Payne, *USA Today* bestselling author

WARNING

The Wolfes of Manhattan series contains adult language and scenes, including flashbacks of child physical and sexual abuse. Please take note.

PROLOGUE

I'd felt more with Reid Wolfe—now my husband—than I'd ever felt before.

More than I'd ever wanted to feel.

Yes, I'd fallen hard. But I desperately wanted a husband who loved me as much as I loved him.

My flesh still numb, I walked with Reid back to the Wolfe Building. It was several blocks, and we didn't talk.

We took the elevator up to his apartment. He gathered his staff in the dining room.

"I have some news," he said. "This lovely lady and I were married this afternoon, so you now work for her as well as for me. Whatever she wants, please see to her needs."

Lydia and the others were clearly surprised, but they all simply nodded and then went about their tasks.

I followed Reid to his bedroom. "I'll have your apartment packed up and your things delivered as soon as possible."

"My job..." I began.

"I'll see if you can get an extended leave of absence."

"Mo. The others. They can't afford the rent without me."

"That isn't anything for you to worry about. I'll cover it until they can get a new roommate."

"My job..." I said again.

"I promise I'll take care of all of it," Reid said. "But you'll never have to go back if you don't want to, Zee. I'll see that you're always taken care of, even after the marriage ends."

After the marriage ends...

So the marriage would end, in his eyes.

This was only temporary.

My heart broke in two.

I was in love—and married to the object of my affection.

And it was only temporary.

1

LACEY

everal hours earlier...

Someone pounded on the door to the conference room.

"What is it?" Reid yelled.

"It's me." The voice belonged to Terrence, Reid's assistant.

"What do you want, Terrence?" Reid demanded.

Terrence opened the door. "I'm sorry."

"Sorry for—"

Two uniformed NYPD officers followed Terrence into the room. "Lacey Ward Wolfe?"

My heart thudded. "Yes?"

"You're under arrest for the murder of Derek Wolfe." One of the officers entered and grabbed me out of my chair. Literally gripped my shoulders and forced me into a stand.

Rock stood, his green eyes full of fire. "Hands off my wife, asshole."

I gasped, fear surging through me. I was innocent. *Innocent!* "Rock, please... You'll just get yourself in trouble."

Rock had already been through so much in his life because of his father, Derek Wolfe. This would only add to it.

The officer cuffed my hands behind my back. I was helpless. So helpless.

I hated being helpless.

"Come on," Reid said. "You're really going to parade her out of here in cuffs? The wife of our CEO?"

Would they listen to Reid's words? Would they allow me my dignity?

"I'm only following orders, sir," the blue said.

No, they would not.

"You have the right to remain silent," the other officer began. "Anything you say can and will be held against you. You have the right to an attorney. If you can't afford an attorney, one will be provided for you."

My Miranda rights. The Miranda case was a staple in criminal law class. Anyone who'd ever watched a police drama knew them by heart. Somehow, though, I never thought they'd be directed at me.

"She'll have the *best* fucking attorney," Rock said. "What is the basis for this arrest?"

"Detective Morgan has determined probable cause and the DA agrees," the blue who cuffed me offered. "That's all we know."

Reid glared at Terrence.

We all wondered if Reid's assistant had been behind the phone call made from Reid's office to Rock's landline in Montana three weeks before Derek's death.

"I'm going with her," Rock said. "Don't worry, baby. I won't rest until you're cleared."

"I'm innocent," I said softly.

"We know," Reid said. "We'll prove it."

～

H<small>ANDCUFFED</small>. Like a common criminal.

I sat in the back of the police car, unable to move my arms. Stiff.

Why? Why did this happen to me? I was innocent. As innocent as the day I was born. I was nowhere near Derek Wolfe the night he was murdered. Why would he want to frame me?

Except this wasn't about *me*. Not at all. It was about Rock and his siblings. It was about hurting *them*.

I was a good attorney, damn it. What had I missed?

The squad car stopped at the NYPD Seventeenth Precinct. Rock's driver pulled up behind him, and Rock hurried out of the back seat and walked quickly toward me.

"We've got this, baby," he said. "I swear to you that we've got this."

I nodded blankly as the two uniformed officers led me in. Why hadn't Hank Morgan himself come to arrest me? Was he too good for that? He'd been gunning to make an arrest since the reading of Derek Wolfe's will. Surely he'd want to be the one to bring me in.

Very odd.

The truth will always prevail.

I heard the words in the voice of Leon Huxby, my criminal law professor. They were his mantra. How I'd have liked to believe them, but I hadn't then, and I didn't now. Even though I was an estates and trusts attorney, I'd seen the justice system fail more than one person since I began practicing law six years ago...and that was just for the clients of my former law firm.

Innocent people got convicted all the time. The system wasn't perfect by any means.

I never thought I'd be on this side of it. Did anyone?

Only now was I realizing exactly what was happening. Before, I'd been numb. Frozen and numb. But now? I was arrested. In police custody for a murder I didn't commit.

Lacey Wolfe, you're under the arrest for the murder of Derek Wolfe. You have the right to remain silent...

The officers didn't acknowledge Rock.

I said nothing. I didn't beg Rock to help me, though I was pleading inside. On the outside I was determined to appear strong.

Truth be told, I was scared out of my mind.

Chills spiked along my flesh as I stood facing a camera. Then my profile.

I, Lacey Ward Wolfe, good girl extraordinaire, had a mug shot. A fucking mug shot.

Paperwork. Paperwork. Paperwork.

And then...

A holding cell.

Rock was working on this. I knew that. I'd be out of here quickly, right? He could push this through without an arraignment. But what if he couldn't? What if I had to spend the night here? In a jail cell?

Three other women were in my cell. Two were obviously prostitutes, and the other was a young woman who sat crying in the corner. A toilet and sink sat in another corner.

And then I had to pee. Of course. No way was I taking a piss in front of these other women.

Come on, Rock. Please.

I wasn't wearing a watch, and they'd taken my phone, of course. My purse was back at the office. They hadn't let me bring it when they arrested me.

I sighed, willing back the tears that threatened to fall. This was it. I'd hit rock bottom. Rock bottom, and I hadn't done anything wrong.

You never think it will happen to you.

A guard walked to the holding cell. "Wolfe?"

I nodded and attempted to swallow the lump in my throat. "That's me."

"An attorney is here to see you."

"Hey!" one of the prostitutes said in a raspy smoker's voice. "I never get to talk to my attorney except on Tuesdays."

The guard ignored her, opened the cell door, let me out, locked it, and slapped cuffs on me.

"Is this really necessary?" I asked. "Do I look like I could overpower you?"

"Regulations, ma'am," he said.

I resisted rolling my eyes. I understood rules and regulations. I was an attorney, for God's sake. But I was also innocent!

"Unreal," I said under my breath.

A few minutes later, I was in another room, where Lester Parker, head of the legal team at Wolfe Enterprises, sat. The guard left us.

I held up my cuffed wrists. "Can't you do anything about this?"

"I'm sorry, Lacey. I've tried."

"Call Dane Richards from my old firm. He's the best criminal attorney I know. Rock will pay him anything."

"We're already assembling a top notch defense team," Lester said, "but first things first. I'm working on getting you out of here. We're getting your arraignment on Judge Foster's docket for six o'clock tonight. He's staying late for you."

Baxter Foster, father of my old partner Blaine Foster, never stayed late. That was a known fact. He was near retirement and only put in his eight hours, if that. "Foster?"

"We've made it worth his while," Lester said. "Can you hold out until then?"

I looked around the windowless room. No clock. "I don't have a clue what time it is, Les. I don't have a watch or a phone, and the clock outside the holding cell doesn't work.

"Sorry." He glanced at his phone. "It's two thirty-five."

Two thirty-five. Over three hours. Could my bladder make it until then?

"Do I have a choice?" I asked.

"Not really. We can't just post bail and they let you out. Not on a murder charge."

"Not even for—"

I stopped abruptly. *For a Wolfe?* had been on the tip of my tongue. I was a Wolfe, for God's sake! But I was also accused of murdering a Wolfe.

A Wolfe who was a psychopathic derelict, but whatever. The world was better off without him, for sure, but I wasn't willing to go down for a crime I didn't commit.

"This whole thing is crazy," I told Lester. "I'm the one with the least motive of everyone involved here."

"But you were the easiest to pin it on." Lester cleared his throat, that serious rumbling that only a man in his sixties could make. "All those items stolen from your place. The business cards... Hank Morgan is dirty. I feel it in my bones. There's a reason he's going after you. We just have to figure out what it is."

I huff. "I have to use the bathroom."

"There should be a toi—"

"Yes, of course there's toilet in the cell. I don't want to do my business in front of a bunch of other women. Or a guard who might be getting off on it."

"Lacey, those guards don't watch women take a piss."

"How do you know?"

He drew in a breath. "I know this isn't easy."

"Do you? Do you really know, Les? Have you ever been sitting in one of these rooms in cuffs, across from an attorney, when you know you did nothing wrong?"

"Lacey..."

"Have you ever had to take a piss in front of a bunch of—"

Again, I stopped abruptly, shaking my head. Men pissed in front of each other all the time. That argument wouldn't help me. Hell, none of my arguments would help me. Six o'clock with Judge Foster. That was better than anyone else would get, and I should appreciate it.

I should be thinking about more than the humiliation of peeing in front of others.

I should be thinking...

Damn.

I could be in real trouble here. What if... What if Rock couldn't get me out of this?

What if I went down for a murder I didn't commit?

Then I'd be pissing in front of others for the rest of my life.

2

ROCK

My heart stampeded inside me, as if a herd of buffalo were trampling across my guts.

Why Lacey?

Why not me? Or Roy? Or Reid?

Not that I wanted any of us rotting inside a jail cell, but anyone besides Lacey or Riley. At least my baby sister wasn't in there. After all she'd endured at my psycho father's hands, I couldn't bear the thought of her being locked up.

But Lacey...

My wonderful, brilliant wife.

She sure as hell didn't deserve this. For the first time, I actually wished I didn't have an ironclad alibi. I wasn't in the state of New York when the murder took place. It had been documented. If not, I'd go in there and confess to get Lacey freed. That was how much I loved her.

I'd brought up the idea in spite of my alibi, and Lester Parker told me I was nuts. I'd beg to differ. Just in love with my wife and unwilling to watch her go through this bullshit.

And it was definitely bullshit.

It cost me a hundred grand to get a judge to put Lacey on the docket today. Worth every penny. If my father was determined to punish all of us from his grave, I'd use every last cent of the bastard's money to save us.

The money still meant nothing to me, but for the first time, I was glad I had it. It would help me help Lacey. God only knew what kind of bail would be set. I didn't rightfully care. I'd spend the whole Wolfe fortune to free Lacey, and I'd dare my siblings to object. After all, I'd do the same for any one of them.

I doubted they'd object. Man, I was fired up. Fired up and ready to pounce on something. Anything.

Lester finally emerged from wherever he'd been talking to Lacey.

"Is she okay?" I asked breathlessly.

He nodded. "She's not happy, of course. But she knows the system. She knows she's damned lucky we got her on today's docket."

My phone buzzed with a text. From Zach Hayes.

Where are you?

At the precinct. Les got Lacey on the docket for tonight.

Sounds good. I'm already at the courthouse so I'll meet you both there. You won't believe what just happened.

What?

Your brother married Zee to invoke spousal privilege.

My jaw nearly dropped to the black-and-white tiled floor. My brother? The Wolfe of Manhattan? Married? To Zee? My father's victim?

Where are they now? I texted.

Don't know. I assume he took her back to his place. I guess it's their place now. Morgan interrogated Zee this morning after Lacey's arrest. It wasn't pretty. He wanted her to give info on Reid, so I suggested the marriage.

I can't believe he agreed, I texted back.

I was surprised he did too, but it's better this way.

Good enough. See you over there for the arraignment.

You got it.

Damn. My brother the womanizer was someone's husband. Unreal. But I understood why he'd done it. Not just for himself but for Zee and the rest of us. The less the cops could bother her, the better. The poor thing had already been through enough because of our fucking family.

I'd leave her to Reid. I had my own wife to take care of, and right now, she was sitting in a holding cell, accused of a crime she hadn't committed.

3

ZEE

Reid took my hand. "I'm taking you to dinner. A wedding dinner."

"Shouldn't we tell your family?" I asked.

"Zach is letting them know."

A wedding dinner. Not a reception. Of course not a reception. This wasn't a *real* wedding. "I'm not really hungry. Let's just stay here."

He smiled, and for a moment, I almost saw something more in his eyes. Something real and emotional.

But then he said simply, "All right. Whatever you like. Deirdre can make anything."

"I just said I wasn't hungry." My tone was shorter than I meant it to be.

Then again, maybe not. Maybe I did mean to be short with Reid, my husband in name only.

"You have to eat," Reid said. "I'm going to insist."

"Who do you think you are?"

"I think I'm your husband," he said adamantly. "You haven't eaten well in the last couple days, not since our dinner at Mosaic."

"I've kind of had a lot on my mind." I looked away.

"And you think I haven't? I'm a suspect in the murder of my father, Zee. Lacey is in custody. For fuck's sake, you still need to eat."

I sighed. He wasn't wrong. But my stomach felt like bricks. No way could I swallow any food right now. "Whatever you want is fine."

"Good. It's my fucking wedding night. I want a steak."

"I don't like red meat." I'd told him that at Mosaic, but why should he remember? I was only his damned wife.

"Tough. That's what I'm having. You said you weren't hungry."

True, I did. I turned away from him and faced the king-sized bed. It loomed in front of me like a giant. Why? I didn't know. I'd already slept in it next to Reid. We'd made love in it.

Still, it seemed a stranger to me, nearly as much a stranger as the man I'd just married.

Wasn't marriage supposed to bring two people closer? Instead, an ocean now lay between Reid and me. We were on two separate coasts, a giant body of water separating us.

Reid fumbled with his intercom. "Deirdre, I'd like a steak. Ribeye, rare. Baked potato and something green. Broccoli if you have it."

"Got it. What about Mrs. Wolfe?"

Reid sighed audibly. "Salmon. And a salad with balsamic vinaigrette."

I widened my eyes. He remembered I liked salmon, and that I'd had balsamic vinaigrette on my salad at Mosaic.

Nothing. That proved nothing except that he had a good memory, which any brilliant businessman could lay claim to. It had nothing to do with me.

"I said I wasn't hungry." I still didn't turn to face him.

"Bring in a bottle of Taittinger," Reid said. "Two flutes, and some fresh strawberries."

"Got it, Mr. Wolfe," said the voice of Deirdre.

Taittinger was champagne. Reid knew I didn't drink much. Though I had drunk at the last wedding—Dom Perignon to be exact. Much more expensive than Taittinger. Of course, that had been a wedding where the couples actually *wanted* to get married.

And that, right there, was the issue. I *did* want to be married to Reid. I'd fallen hopelessly down the rabbit hole of love.

"Did you happen to remember I don't really drink much?" I asked with an edge.

"Maybe it's not for you," he said snidely.

Fine. I huffed. I deserved that.

But I loved him. I loved him so much, and this was nothing but a convenience for him.

Though he *had* asked to take me to a nice wedding dinner. He didn't have to do that, and I'd thrown the gesture back in his face. Sure, I wasn't overly hungry, but he'd never fall in love with me as long as I was acting like a bitch. Already I could tell he was losing patience.

"Zee," he said softly.

Finally I turned around and met his gaze. He was so handsome, so very handsome. But his blue eyes were tired. Tired and resigned.

He was a suspect in a criminal investigation, and I was being an immature brat.

"Yes?" I said, this time my tone not snide or bitchy.

"I know this isn't how either of us expected to have a wedding. But this will help both of us."

"I understand that, Reid."

"Do you? Because I wanted to give you a wedding dinner. Then a wedding night. I wanted this to be perfect for you."

"Perfect would be marriage for the right reasons."

He sighed. "I know that. But I'm very fond of you, and you know how attracted I am to you."

Fond didn't cut it. I was in love. So hopelessly in love. No way could Reid Wolfe ever love me. Sleeping with me was one thing. But loving me?

I was damaged goods.

"I'm fond of you too," I finally said.

He touched my cheek, and a spark shot through me.

"Listen," he said. "I'm going to be honest with you, and I want you to be honest with me."

I nodded. "All right."

"I want to give you a wedding night. I want to make love to you all night in that bed. Please."

"It's your right."

"Damn it, Zee." He raked his fingers through his dark hair. "You've got to give me a bone here."

Why was I being a bitch again? I could cut him off. Tell him I wasn't sleeping with him anymore, but I'd be punishing myself as well.

"Today was hard on both of us," he continued. "Morgan was an ass to you. Then you got forced into marriage. This isn't how I wanted to tell you—"

"Tell me what?"

He shook his head. "Never mind. I'll be in my study if you need me. I'll let you know when our dinner is ready."

I plunked down in my leather chair and stared at the papers on my desk. My phone buzzed. Rock.

"Hey," I said.

"She's out. Arraignment is over. Bail was five fucking million."

I shook my head. "Unreal. How is she?"

"Shaken. *Really* shaken. I've got to tell you, bro. I don't think she can take much more of this."

"I feel that."

"I suppose I should say congratulations."

"What for?"

"I got a text from Hayes. He told me about your nuptials."

I sighed. "Yeah. Fuck it all, right?"

"She's easy on the eyes, at least."

"She's...a lot of things."

"No way..." Rock said.

"What?"

"You've fallen for her. For Zee."

"She's a victim. Of our father."

"So? Doesn't mean you can't fall for her."

I could lie as well as anyone. It came in handy during business negotiations. But I didn't have the heart to lie to my big brother. I was just too damned tired. "I guess I have."

"That's great!"

"Except she doesn't feel the same way."

"Then woo the hell out of her, man. You're the Wolfe of Wall Street."

"Manhattan," I said, more rigidly than I meant to. "The Wolfe of *Manhattan*. I swear you get that wrong on purpose."

He didn't laugh. "Yeah, whatever. Babes fall all over you."

"Because of my money. Zee doesn't care about any of that. My money is why she was kidnapped and hunted. Because our fucked-up father had the money to do anything he wanted."

"You're more than your money, Reid. We all are."

God, I was being self-absorbed. Whining to my big brother who'd just had his wife taken away in cuffs right in front of him this morning. "Go take care of Lacey. She needs you. I'm fine."

"I will. But first let me give you a piece of advice."

I sighed. "Okay."

"Don't let her get away. Take care of her. She's been through hell. Show her you can be the husband she needs."

"Yeah." I didn't know what any of that meant. The husband she needs? I didn't know how to be any kind of husband. But I wasn't about to make Rock elaborate, not when his own wife needed him right now.

"I've got to go," Rock said. "I'll check in with you tomorrow. You coming in?"

"I have to. The Vegas thing is still hanging over our heads. Plus I have to take care of Zee's employment and rent for her roommates. Then, of course, there's this stupid-ass case. Fuck..."

"Do me, and yourself, a favor, will you?"

"What's that?"

"Don't think about work tonight. Don't think about the case. Just think about Zee."

Zee and I were in this marriage sham *because* of the case, but I appreciated what Rock was trying to do. "I'll try, bro. Bye."

I set my phone down on my desk.

Just think about Zee.

All I *did* was think about Zee. She was a distraction, and I couldn't afford to be distracted right now, for her sake as well as my own.

But Zee was always there in my mind, since the night I'd first laid eyes on her a mere week ago.

Damn.

My phone buzzed again. "For God's sake," I said out loud without bothering to look at who was calling. "What the hell do you want?"

"It's me, Reid. Nieves."

Fuck. Nieves Romero. Another thing I didn't want to deal with right now. But we needed her cooperation. "Yeah? How's your sister?"

"She'll make it. She had surgery to remove her spleen. They kicked her all over, even broke one of her teeth."

Jesus. "Who did it?"

"I was hoping you could help me find out."

"Nieves, I have my own problems. Rock's wife was just arrested for murdering my father, I'm still a suspect, and oh, I'm married."

"What?"

"Yeah, so no getting back into my bed."

She huffed so hard I almost felt her breath through the phone. "You really think I'm after that when my sister's lying in a hospital bed?"

I sighed. Again. "Sorry. I'll look into it." After all, whoever beat up Leta Romero could have ties to whoever was behind my father's murder. Nieves knew more than she was letting on.

Wait! Man, I *was* tired. I could use that.

"I'll take care of it. I'll find out who did this to Leta, but in return, you have to tell me everything, Nieves. Every last thing."

"I will. I've been scared straight. No more games. I can't lose my little sister."

"All right," I said. "Now start talking."

5

LACEY

My God, I was sick to death of living in Rock's hotel suite. We couldn't move into the penthouse until the investigation was over, and though I itched to get out of the hotel, did I really want to live in a penthouse where a man had died? Been murdered? And I was going on trial for said murder?

Absolutely too much to think about.

I sat in the bathroom now, on top of the toilet seat, my head in my hands. Rock was wonderful. None of this was his fault, but I didn't want to talk. Didn't want to face him.

"Lace?" He knocked softly on the door.

I heaved a sigh. "I'm fine."

"You're not, baby, and that's okay. I'm ordering some dinner. What do you want?"

Damned tired of room service food too. There was a time I would have loved to live in this lap of luxury. Now? I felt imprisoned. Not by Rock or his family. By the situation.

"I'm not hungry."

"Neither am I, but we both need to eat. We won't be any good to each other or anyone else if we don't stay fit and healthy."

He wasn't wrong. I sighed again, rose, and opened the door.

Rock stood on the other side, his green eyes fatigued. We were all fatigued.

"Some fish or something," I said. "I don't know."

He nodded and made the call to room service while I lay down on the bed. I truly wasn't hungry. In fact, I was kind of nauseated. I rubbed my wrists. The handcuffs hadn't chafed me, but I had phantom pain from where they'd been wrapped around my flesh.

Only several hours. Several hours, and I was a huge mess. What if Rock and the lawyers couldn't get me off these charges? What if I went to trial? Was convicted?

Handcuffs would be a way of life. Peeing in front of others would be a way of life.

How had it come to this?

Rock sat down on the bed and placed my hand between his large ones. "We'll get through it, baby."

"How?"

"Don't give up. Not on me. Not on yourself."

"Sometimes it seems like the world has given up on us."

Rock chuckled then.

"Exactly what's so funny about any of this?"

"Nothing, Lace. It's just, I know what you're feeling. The world gave up on me when I was fourteen."

"Oh, Rock."

How easy it was to forget what others had been through. My husband had been sent to military school for privileged boys in trouble when he was not much more than a child. He went through hell. Then there was Riley. And Zee.

"It's okay," he said. "I get it. You've been arrested for something you didn't do. Something horrible. You spent half a day in custody. That would freak anyone out. But I swear to you, you won't go down for this. I'll do whatever it takes."

"I know."

"I'm not kidding. Remember when we were in Montana and that rogue deputy tried to arrest you? I said we'd ride the bike into Canada and never look back. I would've done it, Lace, and I'll do it now if it's what you want."

Temptation loomed. But I was a lawyer. An officer of the court. Becoming a fugitive went against everything I believed in.

"I know you would." I brought his hand to my lips and kissed it lightly. "But where would that leave your family?"

"You're more important than my family."

I believed him with all my heart. He'd do this for me. All I had to do was say the word. But, "I can't. I couldn't live with myself. Someone is going down for this. If not me, then Roy, Reid, or Riley. We can't do that to them."

"You sure?" He thumbed my lower lip.

His touch still sparked need in me, even in my current distress.

"I'm sure. I'm innocent, and there's got to be some way to prove it. Their evidence all seems circumstantial."

"Unless there's something we don't know about," he said.

"They have to supply the defense with all the evidence," I told him. "It's the law."

"Hayes is putting together the best defense team in the state."

"Is Dane on it?"

"From your firm? I'll have to ask him. We're getting the trial in front of Baxter Foster, as well. He's obviously willing to be paid off."

I shook my head. "Is that really what it's come to? I don't want someone to be paid off. I want to get off on the merits. I'm innocent!"

"You are, baby. We all know that. But someone is trying very hard to make it look like you aren't. They're not playing by the rules, so why should we?"

"Because... Because the system is supposed to work."

"Not always."

Had he misunderstood me? Had he thought I said, "the system works"? Because I knew damned well the system didn't always work. *Sorry, Professor Huxby.*

When push came to shove, I did not trust the system when my life was at stake.

This was my life. My life with Rock. We had years and years ahead of us. Maybe children and grandchildren.

"You mean the system *isn't* always supposed to work?" I said.

"No, it's not always supposed to work. There are puppet masters at work, Lace, and sometimes their job is to make sure the system *doesn't* work."

"All right," I finally said. "Do what you have to do."

6

REID

"She was beaten to within an inch of her life." Nieves closed her eyes and two tears squeezed down her cheeks. "This is... It's all my fault."

"What the hell is going on, Nieves?"

"I can't. I can't do this. Look what it's already cost my sister!"

"Wait, wait, wait... You think Leta was beaten up because you're talking to me?"

"Of course I do! And because she talked to you. We had a whole plan. We did. We thought every detail out. We..." She crumpled back into her chair and laid her head on the table, tears falling slowly onto the covering.

I wasn't an unfeeling person. Not at my core. But this? I had no sympathy for her. I didn't wish pain on Nieves or her sister, but they'd fucked with dangerous people, and this was the result.

"Nieves," I said, "there's only one way out of this mess."

She lifted her head far enough to meet my gaze. "What's that?"

"You need to level with me."

I replayed my previous conversation with Nieves in my mind as she stalled again, saying nothing.

Finally, "I can't tell you over the phone. It's too risky."

She'd already taken the risk, and her sister had paid. Her sister might pay again, or Nieves herself. Still, I needed all the information. An innocent woman had been arrested, and the rest of us were still under investigation. I needed the truth from her, and I needed it now.

"That ship has sailed, Nieves. Whoever is behind this already knows you and Leta are talking."

"Then I want...a bodyguard. For Leta too. Twenty-four-hour security."

I rolled my eyes. "Fine." This case was already costing us an arm and a leg. It was only money.

"Get it set up, and then I'll talk."

"Fine," I said again. "I'll get in touch when it's set."

After I ended the call, I automatically called Terrence. Total autopilot. Except I no longer trusted Terrence. He'd altered his calendar the day someone—presumably my father—made a phone call from my office to Rock's landline in Montana.

"This is Terrence," he said.

"Hey there, sorry for the intrusion. I must have butt-dialed you."

"No problem. I hear you got married. Congratulations."

"Thanks. See you at the office tomorrow."

"You got it. Bye."

Shit. Major faux pas. Terrence was out of the loop as of now. He clearly couldn't be trusted. My father most likely handed him a load of cash to keep him quiet about the phone call made from my office. Bummer, since Terrence had connections everywhere. He got things done quickly and efficiently.

Which was a major red flag I should have picked up on much sooner.

I needed an assistant on the inside. Charlie, Roy's wife. I called her quickly.

"Hello, this is Charlie."

"Hey, Charlie, it's Reid. I'm sorry to call you so late, but I have an assignment and I don't want to give it to Terrence for obvious reasons."

"Got it. What do you need?"

"I need bodyguards and round-the-clock security for Nieves and Leta Romero. Leta's in a hospital in Helena, and Nieves is staying somewhere close. I'll text you Nieves's number."

"Sounds good. Do you have a company you prefer?"

"Whoever answers their phone at this hour is fine with me. Get me the details as soon as you can. Nieves is finally going to spill her guts."

"Will do."

"Thanks, Charlie. I know this isn't your job."

"It *is* my job. I'm Lacey's assistant. It's no problem."

"You're a gem."

"Hey," she said, "how are you and Zee?"

"Well, it's my wedding night, and I'm talking to my sister-in-law on the phone. Make of that what you want."

"Oh... Yeah, I'm sorry."

"Don't be. It's on paper only. Zee's fine. She's resting. The interrogation with Morgan took a lot out of her. God, that man's a prick."

"Give her my best," Charlie said. "I'll call you once everything is set."

"Thanks. Goodnight." I shoved my phone into my pocket.

I got up and walked out of my office to my spacious kitchen. Deirdre was plating our dinners.

"Good evening, Mr. Wolfe," she said. "I was just about to let you know everything's ready."

"I'll take it to Zee in the bedroom. Thanks, Deirdre. It smells great."

Actually, it didn't. The words were more autopilot, like my

call to Terrence. The food was beautifully prepared and smelled like steak and salmon, but the usually appetizing fragrance nauseated me instead. I grabbed the tray carrying the plates, utensils, and the champagne.

"You want to use the trolley?" Deirdre asked.

"No, I've got it." The tray was bulky but not heavy as I walked out of the kitchen and through the hallway to my bedroom.

My bedroom that was no longer mine. It was mine and Zee's.

The thought sparked happiness in me, but I tamped it down. She wasn't happy at all, and if she wasn't, I couldn't be. She meant too much to me.

I knocked on the door as best I could without dropping the tray.

"Yeah?" Zee called.

"Let me in. It's me."

The door opened.

She'd changed into sweatpants and a tank top, no bra. Her newly blond hair cascaded over her shoulders, and her face was fresh and devoid of makeup.

She looked gorgeous. I sucked in a breath.

"Why'd you knock?" she asked.

"Because my hands are kind of full." I eased into the room and took the tray over to the table between the two wingbacks, and—

I stumbled over a ripple in the area rug and nearly tumbled to the floor, tray in tow. The stainless steel domes over the plates clattered to the floor, and the steak, salmon, and an array of sides wound up in a mountain of mess on my Turkish rug.

I steadied my stance and looked down at the mess. "Seriously?" I mumbled.

But then, in the midst of my worry, anger, and frustration, a beautiful sound emerged.

Laughter.

Zee was laughing.

And I thought maybe I'd get through this night after all.

7

ZEE

I couldn't help myself. Reid Wolfe, usually so perfectly pressed in his designer clothing, his hair just so, had dropped the tray of food.

In that moment, I loved him even more, if that was possible.

"I'm sorry," I said. "It isn't funny. Are you all right?"

"I'm fine," he replied. "And it *is* funny. I'm not sure I've ever heard you laugh like that before."

"Haven't I? I guess there hasn't been much to laugh about since we met."

He turned to me and met my gaze. "Zee, if that makes you laugh, I'll gladly drop all the food in the place. In the whole city of New York!"

A smile split my face. This, right here, was why I loved him. I hadn't meant to fall in love, but he'd taken such amazing care of me since I'd met him in Las Vegas. He was a good man.

Reid Wolfe was not his father.

"I'll help you clean up," I said.

"I have people to do that."

I shook my head. "I want to. Let me. Please."

"Zee, I don't even know where the cleaning supplies are."

I bent down, picked up the plates, and scooped as much of the food onto them as I could. "I can at least help a little." I got it picked up as best I could without a shop vac or cleaning products.

"That's good. I'll just call Lydia." He walked over to the intercom. "Why don't you stay in one of the guestrooms tonight? I don't want you to have to smell steak all night."

"I don't mind."

"You said you weren't hungry."

As if in response, my stomach let out a hungry growl. "Seems I am now."

"Well"—he picked up the bottle of unopened champagne that had made it through the ordeal unscathed—"I don't dare open this right now, or we'll have an eruption on our hands. If you're hungry, we'll go out, like I originally planned. That will give the staff time to clean the rest of this up."

"I'm sorry. For the waste."

"It's not your fault. You didn't trip me. I tripped myself."

"I know. But you had your chef make such a lovely meal—"

"Which you didn't want."

"I'm sorry." I looked down. "I'm just..."

He tipped my chin, bringing my gaze back to his. "Just what?"

"I don't know. This was all so sudden, and..." I couldn't finish. I couldn't tell him how much I loved him. How much he'd come to mean to me in so little time. For the first time since I fell for him, I asked myself the inevitable question. Was this really love? Or was it just me getting taken care of for the first time in my life?

"And..." he prompted me.

"And...nothing. It's just all a lot to process."

"I know it is." He grabbed me by the elbow and planted a kiss on my mouth.

I opened instinctively, and he deepened the kiss.

What his body did to mine. But my heart was involved now. My heart...and my soul. I was so in love with Reid Wolfe—a feeling I never thought I'd know in this lifetime.

Without meaning to, I sighed softly into him, melting into his lips covering mine, his tongue dancing with mine.

A low growl vibrated from his chest into mine, bursting through me like electric sparks.

He broke the kiss then and met my gaze, his own eyes on fire. "I need to make a call."

"Okay," I gulped.

His gaze didn't stray, though, and in another second his lips were on mine again, and this time the kiss was raw and passionate.

My husband. I was kissing my husband.

Reid Wolfe. My husband who I loved more than anything.

My nipples were so hard, and my core throbbing with heat. I was wet. I could feel it already. So wet, and so ready.

Please, make love to me. Please, Reid.

I wrapped my arms around his neck, slid my fingers through his silky hair. As we kissed, I touched his cheeks, his jawline, memorizing the contours of his face. Then I slid my hands over his broad shoulders, his muscular upper arms.

I wanted to touch every inch of him. Memorize it, because this would end sooner rather than later, and I needed to know every part of him before I was forced back into my old life.

His growl rumbled again, and he lifted me. I wrapped my legs around his waist as he walked toward the bed.

Yes. It was going to happen. We were going to make love.

He laid me down gently—more gently than I wished—onto the soft comforter. He broke the kiss and pushed my tank top to my neck, baring my braless breasts.

"So beautiful," he murmured, and he licked the tip of one nipple.

"Oh…" I groaned, and I arched my back toward him.

He licked it again. My body blazed at his gentle touch, and I yearned for him to just suck the nipple, bite it.

"Please…" I moaned softly.

"Please what, baby?" Against my nipple.

"Suck it. Suck my nipple. Please, Reid."

I arched against him as he pulled the nipple between his lips. He sucked it hard for a moment, and then he let it drop.

I let out a soft whimper at the loss.

"So gorgeous," he said. "I remember you, that night. The night I watched your show. Your nipples were painted red."

"You could see me?"

"Of course. You were the most beautiful girl in the line."

"But showgirls aren't supposed to— Ah!"

He sucked my nipple between his lips once more.

Thought ceased. Emotion overtook me. He sucked it harder, harder, and then closed his teeth around it and bit me.

Electricity charged through me. Through me and over me and under me. The emptiness between my legs ached. I needed him. Needed him so much.

But then he let my nipple drop.

I whimpered softly again. "Reid…"

"I want you, wife," he said softly.

The word wife sent a hot tremor through me. "I want you too." *Husband. Husband.* The word was on the edge of my lips, but I couldn't quite bring it forth. Bringing it forth would make it too real. Would make it hurt all the more when I could no longer call him that.

I readied myself—readied myself for the beautiful assault to my body and mind that would come in a moment.

But—

Reid pulled away from me. "Change your clothes. I'm taking you out for that wedding dinner after all. I'll make that call."

I'd have much rather stayed. In his bedroom. In his bed. But he didn't feel about me the way I did about him, so I nodded, and he left his bedroom. Left his own bedroom, so I could have privacy. We were a married couple, and he left.

I quickly went through my suitcase and found I had nothing suitable for dinner out in Manhattan. I decided on black leggings, an off-white blouse that covered my hips, and the black pumps he'd had repaired for me after I got the heel caught in a grate outside my apartment in Las Vegas. I ran a brush through my hair and applied some blush, pink lip gloss, and mascara.

Ready as I'd ever be.

I left the bedroom, and Reid was in the hallway waiting for me. "Got us a private table at Gabriel LeGrand. Wayne's waiting downstairs."

"Does Wayne ever get any time off?"

"Yeah. He does twelve-hour shifts six days a week."

"That's crazy."

"What's crazy is what I pay him to do it. He's well taken care of. Trust me."

I did. Reid had taken such good care of me since I came into his life. I knew without a doubt that he took care of everyone else.

"Wayne can cut back anytime," Reid continued, "but he's young and unmarried and he wants to put away a nest egg. I'm helping him do that."

"He'll never get married with that schedule. He won't have the time to meet anyone."

"It's his choice, Zee."

I nodded. Reid was right. In fact, I understood. My own schedule was grueling.

Reid took my hand in a chaste way, simply holding it without entwining our fingers. Weird, since we'd nearly made love twenty minutes ago. We took the elevator down and then walked through the mostly empty lobby—which still gave me shivers— to the town car where Wayne was waiting.

My wedding dinner. And then my wedding night.

So it wasn't perfect. Maybe I could be less of a bitch and more of the kind of woman I knew I was on the inside.

Maybe I could make Reid fall in love with me.

The drive didn't take long, as the restaurant was only a few blocks away. Still, traffic was stop-and-go. New York certainly hadn't changed much since I'd been here last.

Which was...

No. I would *not* ruin my wedding night.

Wayne opened the door for us, offering a hand. I took it and slid out of the car, Reid replacing Wayne's hand when he slid out after me. We headed into the restaurant, where the maitre d' recognized Reid right away and led us to our private and secluded table. He held out my chair, and then, after I sat, spread my napkin on my lap for me.

This hadn't happened at our dinner in Las Vegas. I tried to hide my surprise. Even growing up on Long Island, I'd never experienced any of the glitz of the city. My mother couldn't afford it. She'd always thought I'd be her meal ticket, but I'd failed at acting and modeling. She didn't even know I'd disappeared on my way to Smith. It was several weeks later when I escaped, and I had no ID and was apparently catatonic the first few days at the hospital. When I finally told them who I was, she came for me.

The next few months of living at home had been hell on earth. I should have gone to Smith, continued along my path, but I just... I just couldn't. Mom wasn't supportive, though she did help with my medical bills. I never told her what had happened—that a billionaire and the priest who'd given me first communion, among others, had been behind it. I'd signed up for the student health insurance at college, but since I never went, it didn't kick in. Gradually, Mom and I went into major debt, and I turned to meth.

Not my finest hour.

Eventually, I got help, but when I was finally clean, I had to take care of that bill plus others. I also needed to leave my mother. Our relationship had turned from bad to toxic. Nothing other than rock bottom could have made me approach Derek Wolfe. I'd had no other choice.

I perused my menu. The prices were outrageous, worse than Mosaic in Las Vegas. Ridiculous. Seventy-five dollars for cod? Must be a damned good cod.

Our waiter came and went, taking our cocktail order. I declined, but Reid ordered something called Pappy Van Winkle fifteen-year.

"Anything look good?" he asked me.

I folded the menu and placed it on top of my plate. "Not really."

"Order anything. Whatever you want. Your days of eating tilapia with lemon are over."

"Are they?" I asked. "Isn't this a temporary arrangement? I have to go back to work once it's all over."

"Actually"—he took a sip of the amber liquid our waiter had just set down—"you don't."

My heart jumped. Did that mean...? Did he want to stay married...? Hope coursed through me. Could I really be with the man I loved?

"You'll be entitled to spousal maintenance," he went on, "after the marriage ends."

"Oh." A lump emerged in my throat. He'd already said something like that previously.

You'll never have to go back if you don't want to, Zee. I'll see that you're always taken care of, even after the marriage ends.

The words made me feel hollow inside.

I cleared my throat, struggling to hold back tears. "That's not necessary."

He lifted his eyebrows. "Are you kidding? After what my father put you through? You're entitled to a hell of a lot more than that."

"But I—"

He gestured me to stop. "You'll be well taken care of, Zee. You'll have the best of everything, and you'll never have to work again."

The news should have made me ecstatic, especially after the life I'd led for the past ten years. No more destroying my body as a showgirl. No more baring my breasts to the world. No more apartment with three roommates. No more sharing a bedroom with Mo.

It didn't.

It meant a life without Reid. Reid's money wasn't Reid.

I shook my head. "I never asked you for anything."

He smiled. "That's why I'm happy to give it to you. You deserve it. You've earned it."

"That's ridiculous. Maybe I deserve it, but I sure as heck haven't earned a penny of it."

"I didn't mean—"

"It's exactly what you meant. You got to fuck me. Got to see me naked, scars and all. I won't take your money for that."

He sighed and rubbed his forehead. "I didn't mean it that way. You must know that."

I *did* know that. I was being pissy again. Bitchy again. All because to Reid, this was simply a marriage of convenience, while to me, it was so much more. I buried my nose in the menu again.

Reid didn't say anything for the next few minutes. I grew hot, my flesh itching. It wasn't anger or fear. I didn't know what it was. I just had to leave this table.

I cleared my throat again, and he looked up.

"I need to use the ladies' room," I said abruptly.

He nodded. "All right. Do you want an appetizer if the server returns?"

"No." I stood and whisked away from our table.

Once in the ladies' room, I stood in front of a sink letting the cold water run. I splashed it onto my face. Thank goodness I hadn't put any foundation on and my mascara was waterproof. I splashed the chilliness onto my face two more times and then blotted dry with a luxury cloth towel provided by the attendant. A tray with tips sat on the counter. I'd left my purse at the table. I smiled apologetically at the attendant and reached for the door.

"Ow!" I slapped my neck.

Something bit me.

Then...nothing.

8

LACEY

The trout amandine Rock had ordered for me tasted like potting soil, but I dutifully ate all of it, forcing each bite down. I didn't touch the wine. Even Rock only had half a glass with his beef tenderloin.

"What can I do for you, baby?" Rock asked, after he'd moved our room service cart out into the hallway. "Anything within my power, and it's yours."

Let's run. Let's get on your bike, head upstate, and cross into Montreal by morning. So Tempting. Rock's Harley had arrived a few days ago and was in storage somewhere. We could totally do it.

"Nothing. You're so sweet, but nothing. I just want to shower and get all the holding cell yuck off me, and then I want to go to bed."

Bed. My body was ready to collapse. My mind, however, was racing a mile a minute. The sleep I craved wouldn't come. I already knew that.

I headed to the lush bathroom in the suite.

Rock followed me. "I'm going to take care of you, whether you like it or not."

I smiled weakly. "Really, I just want a shower."

He bent down toward the jetted tub. "I think a bath would be more relaxing. Don't you?"

A bath sounded heavenly, actually. I didn't stop my husband from filling the tub with a bubbly wonderland. He peeled my clothes from me then, and though he groaned at the sight of my naked body, he didn't try to coax me into lovemaking. Even though his cock was bulging inside his dress pants.

Rock was the most gorgeous of all his brothers, at least in my opinion. He was tanned and muscled, his dark hair cropped closely. When I'd first met him, his hair had been longer, touching his shoulders. Biker hair.

His most striking feature was his emerald green eyes—the only Wolfe sibling to have them.

God, the Wolfe family... All the Wolfes, including one we hadn't known about until recently. Derek Wolfe had a first wife named Irene Lucent, which factored into all of this somehow, I was certain.

Rock entwined his fingers through mine as he led me to the tub. Steam rose from the woodsy-scented bubbled water.

And still my mind raced. Wolfes. Nothing but Wolfes and the situation we found ourselves in presently. Father Jim. Detective Morgan. Those were my two main suspects, and they both were clean as hell as far as we could tell. Would Morgan bring Jim in for questioning now that Zee had fingered him?

So far he hadn't. Would he bring him in for what he did to Zee? There was no statute of limitations for kidnapping in the state of New York in most cases, but the statute had run out on the assault and battery.

In my mind, Jim had a huge motive. In Morgan's mind, why would Jim off his meal ticket?

I didn't know. But I'd find out.

"Lace?"

Rock's low voice speared into my thoughts. I met his gaze.

"You're a million miles away," he said. "Come on. Get in the tub."

I stepped into the luxurious warm water and lowered my body until I was covered up to my neck. Rock adjusted the inflated pillow under my head.

"Good?" he asked.

I nodded, closing my eyes. Yes, good. But these weren't magic bubbles. They couldn't calm my thoughts. Only my body.

"I'll be in the bedroom if you need me."

I shot my eyes open. "Don't leave. Please."

"All right. If that's what you want." He sat down on the covered toilet.

"That's hardly comfortable. Join me. This tub is big enough for four people, at least."

He smiled. "If I get into that tub with you, I can't be responsible for what my body does."

I returned his smile as best I could. Rock was...well...my *rock*. I needed his hard body next to mine. His presence could calm me more than any bubble bath ever could.

"I'm up for whatever you're up for," I said.

"If you're sure."

"Very."

He disrobed, and I slid forward in the tub. He slid in behind me and pulled me against his hard muscled chest.

I closed my eyes once more. Already his cock was hard against the small of my back. Was it comfortable? Not really. Was it what I needed? Absolutely.

He slid his hands down my shoulders and over my bobbing breasts, tweaking one nipple.

Yes, this was what I needed.

He played with my nipples until they were ultra hard, and though my mind still whirled, my body responded, as always, to my husband's deft touch. He played my body as if it were a Stradivarius, sliding gently across the strings and plucking when necessary.

"Tell me what you want, baby," he whispered against my neck.

"You. Inside me." I turned, splashing some of the water out of the tub, and lowered myself onto his hard cock.

"Fuck," he growled.

Sheer completeness. Always complete, since the first time he'd shoved himself into me in my office during the reading of his father's will. So out of character for me, but Rock planted a seed in me that day—a seed that had matured and morphed into a sexual creature I hadn't known existed inside me.

I rode him slowly, letting the warm water glide over us as I took him inside me again and again. Finally, my mind rested, and my body took over, as I made love to my husband with deliberate movements. We hadn't been together long, but we knew each other. We knew what the other needed. I needed slow right now, and he let me have my way, even though I knew he was roaring to grip my hips and piston into me like a jackhammer.

I leaned into his chest, sliding my breasts up and down as I glided up and down on his magnificent cock. I wasn't after a climax, no. I was after this—this completeness, this togetherness.

This reassurance that I wasn't alone. That I'd get through what was to come.

"I love you, Lacey," Rock said, his voice husky.

I moaned. "I needed to hear that just at that moment. I love you too, Rock. Always."

My words sent Rock over the edge, and this time he gripped my hips, his fingers sliding in the water, and pushed me down on his cock as he released.

His orgasm spurred my own, and it wasn't the normal explosion. This was the opposite. An *im*plosion. Of taking his body with mine, of becoming one, imploding together into a separate being.

Just what I needed.

Perfection.

I melted against him as we came together in the warm bubbled water.

And I knew, one way or another, we'd find our way out of this mess.

Nothing on this amazing menu sounded good to me either. Maybe Zee had a point. This wedding dinner wasn't going to work.

She clearly didn't feel about me the way I felt about her. Who could blame her? The ass who'd sired me had taken her to hell. She only escaped because of an elevator malfunction.

Pure luck.

She'd be dead if not for Roy being in the right place at the right time.

I finished my bourbon.

The server appeared. "Can I get you another drink, Mr. Wolfe?"

I nodded. "Absolutely, and an order of fois gras, please." I could always eat fois gras, even when I was sick to my stomach. It was that delicious.

The server nodded toward Zee's empty chair. "Anything for the lady?"

I shook my head. She wasn't hungry, so I wouldn't feed her. She'd be back soon enough, and I'd insist she order dinner. But I wouldn't force an hors d'oeuvre on her.

A few minutes later, I was nursing another Pappy Van Winkle. Mama's milk. Except my mother's milk, if indeed I'd ever tasted any, would have been sour. I doubted Connie Wolfe had done any breastfeeding. I was the third born, and I was only three when Riley came along. If any breastfeeding had happened, I'd have been too young to recall.

Pappy's was as smooth a bourbon as I'd ever tasted. My drink of choice before this recent discovery was Macallan, a single malt Scotch. No more.

Which reminded me of Nieves Romero. She'd ordered me a Macallan that night at the Wolfe Premiere bar in Las Vegas. The night I'd gotten her drunk on dirty martinis and she passed out. The night she'd promised to tell me everything, but then, the next day, her sister had been attacked.

Can't make this shit up.

Every time I thought I was making some headway, something happened to derail it.

I took another sip.

Nieves and Leta.

Hoss and Manny.

Hank Morgan.

Father Jim.

Terrence.

And now, Irene Lucent.

And Zee. Zee, who I'd fallen hard for. Zee, who could never love me back because of who I was.

How had I come to this? I was the Wolfe of Manhattan, for God's sake. I didn't fall in love.

My phone buzzed. Terrence. I declined the call.

Then, thinking better of it, I called him back. I couldn't allow him to suspect I was onto him.

"Sorry," I said, when he answered. "Couldn't get to the phone fast enough."

"No worries. I hate to bother you on your wedding night, but—"

"This wedding night is a j—" I stopped abruptly. Terrence didn't need to know this was a marriage of convenience. Surely, he already suspected, but I didn't want to say anything that might give him further ammunition to take to whoever he was working with.

Of course, he'd probably been working for my father, who was now dead. How much did he know?

I had to find out. Maybe get Buck to rough him up a little. Though Terrence was big and muscled. Didn't matter. Buck could get anyone to talk. *Anyone.*

I cleared my throat. "I'm sorry. I've got a little sore throat. What were you saying?"

"I hadn't gotten to the reason for my call yet."

"Oh? What is it, then?"

"There's been a security breach in the main office."

"Oh? Then why isn't *security* calling me?"

"I was in there working late, and Dick asked me to get you and Rock in the loop."

Working late? I hadn't given him much to do lately, not since I found the discrepancy on his calendar.

"Always logging the hours," I said. "Why don't you go home now? Take a load off."

"I'm about done here. You want to come down and take a look around?"

He thought I was home, that I could just take an elevator ride down into the office. Maybe he thought I was truly having a wedding night. I was, after all, me.

"I'll just give Dick a call," I said.

"He's pretty busy."

"He's not too busy to talk to me. Thanks for being there and handling this, Terrence."

"No problem. It's what you pay me for. Have a good night."

The day Dick Fallon, head of Wolfe security, was too busy to talk to me was the day he got fired. I quickly sent a call to him.

Rang once. Twice. Then I lost count until voicemail kicked in. "This is Dick Fallon, Wolfe security. Leave me a message and I'll return your call as soon as possible."

I opened my mouth to speak and then pressed my lips together.

First, Dick always took my calls.

Second, if he couldn't, he forwarded his number to one of his subordinates, who always took my calls.

Third, I sure as hell wasn't leaving a message for him. Not when I wasn't sure there was a security breach at all.

I went back over the list I made in my head and added Dick Fallon to it.

He'd been head of security for nearly ten years, so he'd worked with my father.

He was a good man. A family man.

I could use that to my advantage.

The server approached once more with my appetizer. "Here you go. Have you and the lady decided on dinner?"

I looked up at him, and then, at his mention of Zee, looked across the table.

She wasn't back from the ladies' room yet. How long had she been gone?

I glanced at my watch and then at my phone. The call from Terrence had come in fifteen minutes ago, and Zee had left a while before that.

Unless she was sick, she wouldn't be taking this long in the bathroom.

Spikes of chilly glass inched over my flesh.

This was not good.

Not good at all.

10

ZEE

Katelyn. *I'd left her there with two dislocated shoulders. She couldn't possibly survive, but I couldn't save her and save myself.*

Better one of us dead than both of us.

That's what I kept telling myself, anyway.

I was trapped in this bizarre place that seemed like an alternate universe. No windows. Lighting that came and went at someone's whim. It was dark now, and I felt along the walls, the jagged cement sometimes abrading my naked body. Until—

I tripped, nearly stumbling over something on the ground. I steadied myself and then bent down.

My eyes adjusted, and I made out a covered plate. I removed the dome to find a serving of food. It was a meat patty and a potato, still warm. No utensils. I wasn't hungry after the run-in with Katelyn, but I picked up the patty and took a bite anyway. Who knew when I might find food again? For a moment, I considered taking half back to Katelyn, but I had no idea whether I'd find her again. I erased her from my mind—or at least tried to.

I can't save us both. I may not even be able to save myself.

The patty tasted like sawdust, though it wasn't dry. Juices ran down my chin as I ate quickly. I needed to down the food before someone found me.

But the food was still warm.

Someone had left it here, knowing I'd find it.

I was a prisoner, but I wasn't being starved. Interesting.

The potato was also moist, as if it had been slow-baked inside aluminum foil. Without seasoning, it was bland, but that didn't matter. The beef patty, though warm and juicy, had been bland as water. Speaking of which, a bottle of cold water stood beside the plate. I unscrewed the cap and gulped down half. I'd take the rest with me.

Nourished, I crept slowly down the dark hallway until I came to a doorway. I turned the knob and found myself in a more open area. No lights, again, but because it was an actual room, I could see better. A toilet sat in one corner. A tub of antibacterial wipes sat next to the toilet. Interesting. Whoever dropped me here fed me and didn't want me getting ill...but the same group of people had dislocated both of Katelyn's shoulders. I grabbed two of the wipes and used them on the wounds above my breasts. With another, I wiped the beef mess from my chin.

Fear coursed through me before I could think further. I needed to keep moving, so I made use of the facilities before I checked the two other doors. One was locked, so I went through the other, back into another dark hallway.

I was a rat.

A rat in a maze.

Only I doubted I'd find a piece of cheese at the end of it.

I doubted whether an end to this maze even existed.

11

REID

I stood outside the ladies' room at Gabriel LeGrand and knocked on the door. "Zee?"

A woman whisked by me to enter, but I grabbed her arm.

"Hey!" she yelled.

"Please," I said. "Could you see if my wife is inside? She's tall and blond. Her name is Zee."

"Like the letter Z?"

"Just like that. I'm sorry if I frightened you, but please."

"Yeah, sure. Okay." She disappeared into the restroom.

My heart stampeded against my chest. Something horrible was happening. I just knew it.

A few seconds later, the woman emerged. "There's no one in there. I'm sorry."

"Damn!" I raked my fingers through my hair and grabbed my phone.

Where are you? I texted Zee. *What's going on? I'm worried sick.*

She didn't answer, and the lump in my stomach clawed its way up my throat. I already knew she wouldn't respond. I already knew...

She either ran away...or someone had taken her.

God, I hoped it was the former.

I quickly called Buck Moreno.

"Yeah?" he said into my ear.

"My wife is gone."

"Your wife?"

"Yeah. Zee. We got married."

"You *what*?"

"I don't have time to explain right now. She's either on the run or someone has her. Last seen in the women's room at Gabriel LeGrand."

"I'm on it."

"Thanks."

Next call was to Rock.

"Hey, Reid."

"Hey. We've got a problem. Two problems, actually. Fuck. I'm scared, Rock. I'm fucking petrified."

"Easy, bro. We all are."

"You don't understand. Zee is missing."

"Fuck. Find out what you can, and then come here, to the hotel. I'll see what I can find out."

"Thanks." I ended the call and then nearly assaulted the maître d'.

"Is there a problem, Mr. Wolfe?"

"You bet your ass there's a problem. My wife has disappeared. She went to the ladies' room, and now she's gone."

"Perhaps she went back to the table. Maybe you missed her in transit."

Hmm. Maybe. I'd had tunnel vision on my way to the restrooms. I stalked through the dining room until our secluded table was in view.

No Zee.

Damn!

"She's not there," I told the maître d' when I returned to the front of the restaurant.

"And she's not in the bathroom?"

"No. I had someone check. Where's the attendant?"

"Our attendant is off tonight, Mr. Wolfe. I'm sorry."

"A woman can't just disappear into thin air. You remember her, right? A gorgeous blonde? She came in with me?"

"Yes, I recall, but I didn't see her leave. I'm sorry. I may have been showing someone to a table."

"Fuck! I'll never eat at this restaurant again."

"I'm sure she's fine, Mr.—"

I stopped listening and left. I didn't wait for Wayne. I fucking ran to Rock's hotel.

I MET Rock at his suite. Lacey had finally fallen asleep, and he didn't want to wake her or leave her.

"Thanks for coming here," he said, letting me in.

"No problem." I rubbed furiously at my forehead, trying to ease the pounding against my skull. "Buck's on Zee's tail, at least I hope he is. Fuck it all. How the hell does someone disappear from a bathroom?"

"I think," Rock said, "we need to entertain the idea that she may have left on her own."

"She wouldn't," I said. "I promised to take care of her. To protect her."

I'd promised. And either she didn't trust me, or someone else took her, in which case she shouldn't have trusted me. Fuck!

"I know you did, but like you said, how does someone disappear from a bathroom of a busy Manhattan restaurant? It doesn't happen, Reid."

No. No. No. "I love her."

"I know. But she's scared."

"Fuck, Rock. I'm sorry. Your wife spent half the day in a holding cell, accused of a crime she didn't commit, and I'm whining about mine."

"At least I know where mine is," Rock said. "Don't apologize. We all care about Zee. Buck will find her."

I nodded. Rock was right. If Zee had left on her own, Buck would track her down within the hour.

An hour was almost up.

Which meant one thing.

Zee hadn't run on her own.

Zee had been abducted.

I swallowed hard against the nausea crawling up my throat.

"I promised I'd protect her," I whispered, more to myself than to Rock.

"We'll find her," Rock said. "I promise."

I scoffed. "Don't promise. I promised Zee, and look where that got her."

Rock nodded, saying nothing.

We both knew the truth.

And it wasn't pretty.

"I should have told her," I said. "I should have told her I love her. Maybe it would have made a difference."

"Don't play that game."

"It was stupid. So stupid. I was afraid of her rejecting me. Me! Afraid of something so damned stupid!"

"No one likes rejection."

"But I deal with it every day."

"In business," Rock said. "This is different."

Different, yeah. It *was* different. For the first time in my life, something was more important than business. I'd honestly never thought the day would come.

"Jesus Christ," Rock went on. "When will this end?"

I sighed. "It only ends one way. With us finding the truth about Dad's murder. We have to, Rock. We have to."

"You think I don't know that? My wife is set to go down for the bastard, and of all of us, she has the least motive. *No* motive."

"That means one thing," I said. "She was the easiest to frame."

"I know. I should have protected her better."

I sighed. "Believe me. I know exactly how you're feeling."

"Fuck it all." Rock paced around the decadent living area of his suite. "You and I, of all people, should have protected our women better. Damn it!"

"We'll fix it," I said. "We have to."

"Damn right we'll fix it. And if we can't? I'm hightailing it to Canada or Mexico with Lacey. Or that private island our esteemed father allegedly owns."

A light burned brightly above me. The island. Of course!

"Rock," I said, "we have to find that place. I'm betting that place holds the key to what's going on here."

"Easier said than done, bro, when none of us is allowed to leave the state of New York."

"Who the fuck cares? Our old man got away with way more than that. Surely we can grease enough palms to get the hell out of here and solve this mystery. And if we get there and we don't solve it? We fucking don't look back."

"Brother, it sounds good to me."

"You two are forgetting one thing."

Rock and I both jerked our head toward the bedroom door. Lacey stood there, her eyes sunken and weary, wearing one of the hotel's white fluffy robes.

"Baby, what are you doing up?" Rock asked.

"I told you I couldn't sleep. That bath may have relaxed my body, but my mind is going a mile a minute. I fear it won't stop until this ordeal is over, whichever way it turns out."

"It will only turn out one way," Rock said, "with you free and clear."

"And if it doesn't?" she asked softly.

"Then what Rock said. We bail. We fucking bail." I balled my hands into fists.

She shook her head slowly. "Your father's will makes all those stipulations. Rock has to stay here as CEO. None of the major assets are liquid. You'd be walking away from a fortune."

"I don't care," I said. "I only care about Zee."

Lacey gasped. "What's wrong with Zee?"

"She's missing, baby," Rock said. "Reid has his SEAL looking for her. He'll have her within an hour if she left on her own."

I glanced at my watch. "His hour's almost up." My insides ached. My Zee. If they touched one blond hair on that gorgeous head of hers—

Lacey walked into Rock's welcoming arms. "That poor girl."

"Damn it!" I wanted to grab clumps of my own hair and pull them out. Pent-up energy swirled through me with no place to go. "Damn it!" I yelled again.

"We'll find her," Rock said.

"What if someone... If they..." God, I couldn't say the words. "After all she's been through."

"We've been playing Mr. Nice Guy long enough," Rock said. "Have Leif and Buck bring Father Jim to me. I'll fucking kill him with my bare hands."

Lacey scoffed softly. "Then we'll both spend our lives in prison. That's not the answer, Rock."

"She's right," I said. "It's the island. It has to be. Riley's been there. She'll help us."

"Riley's been through enough," Rock said.

"She'll do it. She'll do it for Zee."

"She will," Rock agreed, "but do we want to put her through that?"

"The woman I love is missing! I'm ready to do whatever it takes, brother. I mean *whatever it takes*."

Rock nodded, rubbing Lacey's back in lazy circles. "I understand, but she's a newlywed, and—"

"So am I!"

Lacey pulled away from Rock then. "I agree with Reid, honey. Riley will want to help. She and Matt can have the biggest honeymoon in the world when this is all said and done. Besides, you and I never had a proper honeymoon either. Nor did Roy and Charlie."

"She's got a point, Rock," I said.

"You're right. You're right. I'm just very protective of Riley. I couldn't save her the first time, and now... Now, I can't even save my own wife!"

Lacey kissed his cheek. "We're all doing the best we can. Someone's getting paid off at the DA's office. No way would I have been arrested on anything as circumstantial as some stolen scarves and business cards if this were going by the book."

"It's Morgan," I said. "He's dirty. I feel it."

"I feel it too," Rock agreed. "And behind it all is Father Jim."

"You and I need to pay him a visit," I said. "Along with Leif and Buck."

"Rock..." Lacey began.

"He's right, baby, and you know it. They're not playing by the rules, so we can't either. It's time."

Finally, Lacey nodded.

"Good enough," I said. "We get Riley. We find that island. And in the meantime, we get the information out of Nieves and we pummel Father Jim."

Rock's facial muscles went rigid. "I get the first shot."

"Are you kidding me? He tormented *my* wife."

"I'm going to play the older brother card. Besides, how many biker brawls have you been in?"

He had a point, but, "As angry as I am, I can match you punch for punch any day. You weren't around, Rock, but I learned to fight as well as any biker. I had to, or our father would have killed me."

Yeah, Derek Wolfe would have killed me. He and I were different, I'd told myself over and over

Now, I wasn't so sure.

For Zee, I could kill.

And that scared the hell out of me.

12

LACEY

A knock sounded on the door of the hotel suite the next morning. I opened it to find my sister-in-law, Riley, and her husband, Matt Rossi.

"Come on in," I said. "I ordered bacon, eggs, and coffee."

Riley launched herself into my arms. "I'm so sorry about everything." She pulled back and gazed at me. "Have you slept?"

"Not a bit." I'd already assessed my appearance in the mirror. My eyes were bloodshot and framed with dark circles. I looked as bad on the outside as I felt on the inside.

"Where's your better half?" Matt asked, his blond hair settling over his broad shoulders.

"God, I don't want to think about it."

"What's that mean?" Riley asked.

"It means"—I sighed—"he and Reid went after Father Jim."

Riley's eyes widened into circles. "Oh my God."

"The two of them can take him," Matt said.

"Can they?" I asked.

"Two against one? Of course they can. Either one could take him." Matt rubbed his chin.

Matt was new to our family still. I laughed aloud at that thought. He wasn't that much newer than I was.

"What?" he asked.

"Nothing. Sure. Either Rock or Reid could make pulp out of Father Jim, but he's got Derek Wolfe behind him."

"Derek Wolfe is dead," Riley reminded me. "Good riddance."

"Well, his ghost is wreaking havoc." I rubbed my temples, desperately trying to ease the throbbing. "Who knows what kind of fail safes he put in place for Jim? He was planning to fake his own death, if our theory is right. Surely he'd have protected his partner in crime."

Riley scoffed. "He protected no one. If he had no interest in protecting his own children..." She shook her head wistfully.

"You're right," I relented. "He protected no one but himself. So we have to figure out if protecting Father Jim would ultimately do Derek any good."

"We'll figure it out," Matt said, always the optimist.

No offense to Matt, but he grew up in a small town in Montana where no one locked doors at night. I loved him dearly, but he didn't have a clue.

Riley grabbed his hand and squeezed it, saying nothing. Yeah, she was on my side on this. Growing up in New York City made a person cynical. Being a victim of Derek Wolfe made a person downright negative, and though I hadn't gone through nearly what Riley had, in the end, I was also a victim of Derek Wolfe. I was being framed.

"Are we even sure the guy is dead?" Matt asked.

I nodded. "Believe me, I've had the same thought, but he's dead. DNA analysis was performed on the corpse before it was cremated. Plus, Reid and Roy both identified him."

"Still, things can be manipulated."

I held back a scoffing laugh. "No offense, Matt, but you've watched too many cop shows. Derek's organs were donated, and

DNA was checked on every single one. Even the great Derek Wolfe can't fake that."

"I guess I'm a little naïve," Matt said.

"Don't change that, sweetie," Riley said. "It's part of your charm."

"Naïveté obviously isn't the best trait when we're trying to solve a murder mystery." Matt shoved his hands into the front pockets of his stonewashed jeans.

"The rest of us are cynical enough for you," I said. "And we do welcome your input."

He smiled. Sort of. Crap. I hadn't meant to insult him. But right now I couldn't think about others' feelings. I was ready to go down for a crime I didn't commit. At least New York didn't have a death penalty.

"It's okay," he said. "Plus, I'm sure you're worried about Rock and Reid."

"I am, though you're right. They can take care of themselves. But what if Jim is armed?"

Riley smiled. "You think Rock isn't?"

I dropped my mouth open. Of course Rock wouldn't go anywhere unarmed. My mind wasn't working at capacity, and that had to change. However, it wouldn't change without sleep.

"You're right." I shook my head. "Of course he wouldn't."

"My brothers are the strongest people I know," Riley said. "Our father made them that way."

She wasn't wrong. I never thought I'd be grateful to the asshole, but if Rock and Reid were stronger because of him, I was.

But only slightly.

I jolted at the knock on the door.

"Easy," Matt said. "It's probably the breakfast you ordered."

"Right, right." Man, I was a walking nerve cell. I walked to the door.

Sure enough, it was the breakfast. The server wheeled the trolley into the room, and I scribbled my signature and a healthy tip on the bill.

"Anyone hungry?" I asked.

"I'll just have coffee," Riley said. "Maybe a piece of toast."

"We've got to get you off that modeling diet," Matt said. "Remember in Montana, when you ate Mexican food and pizza?"

"Please," I said. "Help yourself. God knows I can't eat."

"You have to," Matt urged. "You're no use to anyone without sleep and nourishment."

What could I say? He was right. I grabbed a plate of scrambled eggs, bacon, and toast and sat down at the table in the living area of the suite. Matt followed suit, and Riley finally took one slice of bacon along with her toast. It was a start.

Now, the ugly.

"Riley," I said, "what can you tell me about your father's private island?"

13

ROCK

Walking back into St. Andrew's made me want to puke.

We'd been here a little over a week ago for the bastard's memorial service, and we'd sat straight-faced while Father Jim talked about what a paragon of society Derek Wolfe was, about how he'd known him since they were kids, how Derek had steered Jim into the priesthood.

I'd had to hold back retching then, and I had to do so now.

Underneath this parish, we'd discovered—via Reid's SEALS—a system of tunnels and caves, once used for the underground railroad in the mid-1800s. A noble purpose.

Father Jim had bastardized a once noble thing by turning it into a hunting ground.

Why? I'd asked myself that question a million times since Roy'd had his revelation. Why would Derek Wolfe make a game out of hunting women? He could hunt animals. He could fuck as many women as he wanted. Hell, there were men and women out there who'd gladly be hunted for a price.

So why abduct women and hunt them?

We hadn't found any remains. Did he kill them? We were

pretty sure he had, since Reid's SEAL said the underground smelled of rotting flesh. Finding any news of the missing women had taken serious research, and once we found a name, nothing else surfaced, as if the trail had gone dead.

Derek Wolfe had paid off the press as well as everyone else.

Why? Why would he do something so heinous to innocent women?

Then again, why would he molest his own daughter? Why would he ship his own son off to the horrors of Buffington Military Academy?

Which was, in its way, a hunting ground.

Sick, sick bastard.

I followed Reid into the church. The place was beautiful, almost like a mid-century cathedral in Europe, which it was obviously modeled after.

We walked into the sanctuary where a few individuals were seated, praying. One rose, walked to the altar, and lit a candle. Another headed toward the confessional.

The confessional.

Yeah. I was going in.

"He's back there, taking confession," I said to Reid. "I'm next."

"Are you crazy?"

"Hell, no, I'm not crazy. We'll take him by surprise.

"At confession? That's sacrilege."

"Do I look like I care?"

"Yeah, I don't either. Let's do it."

We waited quietly until the young woman left the confessional. I walked in to take her place.

I inhaled, wondering if I should disguise my voice. Nah. Let him know we were here. What could he do?

I cleared my throat. "Bless me father, for I have sinned. It's been...a long time since my last confession." Try nearly three decades.

"What sins do you wish to confess, my child?"

Fuck. That wasn't Father Jim's voice. I should know. I'd just listened to him wax poetic about my dead bastard of a father a week ago.

"Who the hell are you?" I demanded.

"My child?"

"Get on your knees!" Reid's voice came from the other side of the confessional.

"Reid, wait!" I pounded on the panel separating me from the priest. "Oh, fuck it." I left the confessional and ripped away the curtain.

A scared priest was on his knees, my brother holding his hair in his hands.

"That's not Jim," I said.

"I've been trying to tell him. I'm Father Amos. I'm working with—"

"Fuck." Reid let him go. "You're Buck's guy."

"Yeah. Christ!"

"Christ?" I said. "Taking his name in vain? Are you even a real priest?"

Amos glanced around the sanctuary. Luckily, we'd scared away the few people who'd been praying and lighting candles. Nicely done.

"I am," Amos said.

"Then why are you doing this?"

"Taking confession? It's my job."

"For fuck's sake. I mean why are you doing this? For Leif?"

"Because I believe in what I'm doing. I want to take Father Jim down. I want to take all the pedophile priests down."

"Jim isn't a pedophile," Reid said. "That we know of, anyway. I wouldn't put anything past him."

"I know that. But he's as bad. Who the hell hunts women? Frames innocent people? Kills?"

"Good enough. But if you're a real priest, what's with the swearing?"

"Real priests are human beings, Mr. Wolfe. I grew up in Hell's Kitchen. Swearing is in my vocabulary."

I let out a laugh. "Good enough. Now where's Jim?"

"I don't know. He hasn't been in today."

"He lives on-site," Reid said. "We'll find him there."

"Got it. Sorry about the intrusion, Father."

"Hey, I'm here to help. The thing is, I've looked into everything I can, and on the surface, the guy's clean."

"He's far from clean," I said. "We've got an eyewitness tying him to my father's hunting escapades. Reid's wife."

"I know. Leif keeps me up to date." He looked around. "I've been through this place with a fine-tooth comb. Even the underground."

"You've been down there?" I asked.

"Yeah."

"Take us," I said. "Now."

"Sure. No problem." Father Amos smoothed his wrinkled robe. "Be ready to hold your nose, though. Follow me."

He led Reid and me to a staircase. We went down to the lower level, which was divided into classrooms, a large kitchen, and several shelters where homeless people were welcomed.

No windows, of course, but the lighting made it seem a little less like a dungeon.

At the end of one hallway was a doorway. Amos opened it. "Fair warning," he said. "There's no electric lighting beyond this point." He picked up a flashlight out of a basket and then handed another to me and one to Reid. "Let's go."

We went down another staircase to another lower level, which was built out.

"This can't be it," Reid said.

"It's not," Amos replied.

Another staircase, and then another, until we came to a wooden door with a broken lock.

"This is how Leif got in," Amos said. He opened the door and shined his light to guide us.

Anger surged into me. This was where Leif had found Lacey's scarf. Lacey's business card. This was where...

This was where runaway slaves had hidden while their papers were being forged.

Should be an uplifting thought, and it was.

Except this place had more recently been used for sinister purposes. To frame my wife.

And also to...

"Zee," Reid murmured.

"She wasn't here, bro. She was at the other hunting ground."

"Still... Others were here," he said. "Others who didn't make it out."

"No human remains have been found down here." Amos pointed his flashlight. "We've gone through it all."

Only then did I let myself inhale through my nose. "Blech!" Rotten eggs. Sulfur. Nasty-ass meat. And even...burning rubber? With a touch of putrid sweetness? Altogether it was nauseating. I swallowed against the bile in my throat. "I feel like the vultures could descend any minute."

"The bodies aren't here," Amos said again. "Just the stench, and though there's airflow down here from somewhere—there has to be or no one could have lived down here for more than a couple of days—it's not enough to whisk away the odor."

Reid swallowed. "God, it's disgusting."

"Corpses eventually stop smelling, depending on how quickly they're able to decompose. Whatever was down here hadn't finished decomposing when it was removed."

"Is it possible it was some kind of remains other than human?" Reid asked.

"I asked Leif and Buck the same thing, but they swear it's human. They've seen and smelled the worst overseas during service. They should know." Amos held a handkerchief over his nose.

"No flies or anything," Reid mused.

"No bodies," Amos said. "Just the smell."

"The smell ought to attract them."

"How would they get down here?" Amos asked.

"Good point," I said. "Show me where my wife's articles were found."

Amos led us to an opening. "In here."

The place was empty now. All the evidence linking the crime to Lacey had been removed.

"Is this where you found our father's certificate of marriage to Irene?" Reid asked.

"I didn't find it. Buck did. But yeah."

"Interesting. Why would it be down here?" I asked.

Reid rubbed his jawline. "If they were married here at St. Andrew's, it would be here. Churches keep copies of stuff like that. But Buck found the original."

"Which meant Jim had to get it from somewhere," I said.

"Exactly. But it's gone in all the databases."

"Except Dad married Irene before everything was in the databases. A hard copy existed somewhere, and Jim found it."

"Or he had it all along."

"You want to let me in on what's going on?" Amos said.

"Sorry. It's a story with so many plot points, and we're not yet sure how they all fit together. Jim married our father to a woman a couple years before he married our mother. Our mother didn't know about the first marriage, and there's no record anywhere of it being dissolved or annulled. Apparently our mother had some dirty money in a trust fund. Nearly a billion dollars. Dad wanted it, so he married her. Long story short."

"Damn," Amos said.

I couldn't help a chuckle at the priest's language again.

Although none of this was a laughing matter.

"We can go through all the tunnels if you want," Amos said, "but Buck's been through it all and says they're basically clean. Other than the stuff belonging to your wife and the marriage certificate, whatever was down here has been cleared out."

"Which makes me think the other things were planted after Dad's death," Reid said.

"Or before. If Jim got wind of Dad's plan to fake his own death…"

"What?" my brother asked.

"I'm just thinking out loud. Same as all of us. There's got to be a connection we're not seeing."

"Jim," Reid said. "We've got to talk to Jim."

"All right." Amos adjusted his collar. "Let's go find him."

14

LACEY

Riley's face turned paler even than it had been. "I've already told you all I know."

"Do you remember flying there?" I asked.

"Sometimes."

"What do you mean by that, baby?" Matt asked.

She bit her lower lip. "It's like...sometimes I remember being on the jet. But sometimes, it seemed like I went to sleep somewhere else and then woke up there. I think..."

"What?" Matt asked gently.

"He probably drugged me. There were times when things were fuzzy. And there were times when hours seemed to pass in minutes."

"Fucking bastard," Matt said.

My beautiful sister-in-law. How could a father treat his own child the way Derek had treated his only daughter? Drug her? Violate her? The cannonball in my stomach grew even heavier.

"There must be a record somewhere," I said. "Nothing appears on the flight records, so Derek must have a connection at the FAA. We'll need to find that person."

"If that person exists," Riley said.

"What do you mean?"

"People who helped my father had a way of disappearing."

"They did?" Matt shook his head.

"Yeah." Riley rubbed her temples. "I never thought about it at the time. I was consumed with my own issues. I'll never forgive myself for that."

"Honey, you were being used by your own father, and you were in the middle of a budding career. No one would have been noticing surroundings, especially if you were drugged."

"I should have," she said.

"Matt's right." I smiled weakly at Riley. "You had your own problems. When you're trying to survive, the fate of others isn't at the front of your mind. It isn't for anyone."

"I suppose." Though she didn't sound convinced.

"Anything else you can tell us?" I asked. "I don't mean to badger you, but we need to find this place."

"There were always other people there," Riley said.

"Do you remember any of them?"

"Other businessmen in Dad's circle. Sometimes their children."

I shook my head. "I want to leave kids out of this."

"Me too," Matt agreed.

"But the other men," I continued. "Do you remember any of them?"

"Not names. I'm not sure any of them used names. If they did they were probably fake. But I might recall faces. In fact..."

"What?"

"I saw someone on TV a few days ago—it was the morning after our wedding, Matt. I didn't think anything of it because I knew it couldn't possibly be true, but now, I wonder."

"Who?" I asked bluntly. "Who was it?"

"It was Prince Christian."

My eyes nearly popped out of their sockets. "Prince Christian? Of the principality of Cordova?"

"That's the one."

"You think you saw him on your father's island?"

"I think... I think I might have."

"Okay, rack your brain, Riley. Please. Anyone else? Anyone with Prince Christian?"

"I don't know. On TV, they announced that Christian's wife had given birth to their third child, and they showed the family. He's older now, gray hair and all. But when I was younger..."

"How old were you when you saw him?"

"I... I don't know. Like I said, those times are such a blur."

"But you weren't an adult yet?"

"No. I was younger. Really young, actually. Like nine or ten, maybe?" She gasped in a breath of air.

"Easy, sweetie," Matt said. "Take it easy. It's okay."

"Yes, it's okay," I said. "I know I'm rushing you. I'm sorry, it's just—"

"No, I understand." Riley absently pushed her slice of bacon around on her plate with a fork.

"We could talk to Prince Christian," I said. "Though I doubt a prince would take my call."

"He might," Matt said. "You're married to Derek Wolfe's oldest son. The new CEO of Wolfe Enterprises."

I let out a broken laugh and lifted my phone. "Afraid I don't have his number."

"Rock can get it. Or Reid." Matt shoveled eggs into his mouth. How could he eat like that?

"No." I swallowed. "We have to go to him in person."

"How can we," Riley asked, "when none of us are allowed to leave the state of New York?"

"I can leave," Matt offered.

I gave him a weak smile. He was so kind. So wonderful for Riley. But sending Matt Rossi into a foreign country to talk to a prince? Not happening.

"It has to be Rock or Reid," I said. "No one else will be taken seriously. No offense."

"None taken," he said. "I get it. I just wish I could do more. I feel like I'm not really a part of the family."

"Of course you are." Riley linked her arm through his.

"Yes, you are," I said. "I'm sorry if I'm being so blunt. It's just..."

"You're worried," Matt said. "You've been arrested for a crime you didn't commit. You don't have to explain yourself, Lacey."

I nodded. "We need to find the island. If the prince knows where it is, he's our only hope so far."

"I can't even be sure it was him," Riley said.

"I know, but it's our only lead."

"I don't know that it is," Matt said. "Derek Wolfe obviously had a lot to hide. He had to get all his ducks in a row before his supposed death, but then someone killed him. Maybe there's something he didn't get hidden in time."

I smiled at my new brother-in-law. He might be a country boy from Montana, but he'd just uttered gold. "Matt, you're a genius."

Riley's eyes shone. "I always knew he was."

"What did I say?" Matt asked innocently.

"He must have left a stone unturned somewhere," I replied. "You're right. He was planning to fake his death, but someone got to him first. He must have left something undone." My mind raced. "He got his will in order. I know all about that, since I drew it up. What else do you do to prepare for death?"

"You make sure all your assets are liquid," Riley said.

"Which he didn't do," I mused.

"But," Riley said, "the phone call to Rock's landline

happened three weeks before the murder. So we know my father had something in the works at that time. Would he have been able to get everything together in three weeks?"

I shook my head. "Most likely not, but he could have started before then. Way before then. The date of the phone call must be significant. But why? What would or could Rock have done if he actually got that phone call?"

"I don't know," Riley said.

"I do," I continued. "Rock would have said good riddance. He hated Derek."

"Then why make the phone call?" Riley asked.

"I think it's like Rock said. To create a motive for Reid. And also maybe for Rock. But why that particular timing?"

"If we can figure that out, we might be able to piece this thing together," Matt said. "And we might be able to find the stone he left unturned."

15

REID

My Zee.

Where was she?

What was happening to her?

Images swirled through my mind of all the dozens of things that Father Jim's degenerates could be doing to her at this very moment.

"We're not doing enough," I said to Rock as we walked through the rose gardens with Amos to the parsonage on the property where Jim lived.

"I feel the same way," Rock agreed. "But without—"

"Nieves," I interrupted. "You have to get your ex to talk. I don't care what you have to do."

He nodded. "I know. I don't care either, and I'm ready to do what needs to be done. If anyone is spending life behind bars, it's going to be me, not Lacey."

"I didn't mean—"

"Yeah, you did." He paused a moment. "And I agree with you. One thing's for sure, though. If I do spend my life behind bars, I'm damned well going to be guilty of the crime."

were stainless steel, but the Formica countertops were still avocado green from the seventies. "When was this house built?" I asked Amos.

"Not sure. It was added way after the church, though. I think in the fifties, maybe?"

I nodded. Not that it mattered. A carton of eggs sat on the countertop, and a frying pan sat on the stove, empty.

"Looks like he left in a hurry. Like he was getting ready to make his breakfast or something."

Rock nodded and opened the refrigerator. "Maybe not. This fridge is pretty much empty."

"Then this is staged." I touched the carton of eggs. "It's room temperature."

"They can't have been sitting there for too long," Amos offered, "or we'd smell rotten eggs."

"True." Rock began opening and closing cupboard doors. "Plates, glasses, but no food. No canned goods or pasta or anything."

"So he hasn't been eating here," Amos said. "We eat at the church a lot. The church ladies come in and cook for us."

I sighed. "Okay. Interesting point. Do the ladies make you breakfast?"

"Usually just lunch and dinner."

"That sticks a thorn in our theory," I said.

"Still could be staged." Rock nodded toward the egg carton.

"Could be, but like Amos said, it's recent, or we'd be smelling egg."

"Damn!" Rock rubbed at his forehead. "Where the hell is the bastard?"

"Let's check his bedroom." I left the kitchen and walked up the stairway leading to the second floor.

The small abode only had two rooms. I opened the door to

the nearer one. Here was the study we'd been talking about. Rock opened the second door.

"Fuck!"

"What is it?" I ran into the room.

My jaw dropped, and I held back a retch.

We'd found Father Jim, all right.

16

ZEE

I couldn't reach the water no matter how hard I tried.

I saw it. It was sideways. And above me.

In my mind, I stretched my arm toward it, but the arm didn't move. The glass was clear. Half full of water or some other clear liquid.

Half full.

Ironic, that I thought of it as half full, when I...

Where was I?

I swallowed. Except I couldn't. My throat felt like sandpaper. My mouth and lips were parched and dry.

And the water sat there, within my reach.

Move, arm. Come on!

I reached, and I reached...

Why was everything sideways?

I closed my eyes. *Think, Zee. Think.* What happened?

I was... I was with Reid. Yes. We were talking about... It was our...

It was our wedding night. I was married to Reid Wolfe. In love with Reid Wolfe, but to him it was a marriage of convenience.

Then why was I here?

What was going on?

I opened my eyes, and things fell rapidly into place.

My heart thumped wildly as fear snaked along my spine. Yes, fear. Now I was scared.

Because now I knew what was happening.

All over again. *It* was happening *all over again.*

I'd been drugged, obviously. That was why everything was blurry. The glass was sideways because I was lying down on my side. On the floor somewhere. And a glass of water was above me. On some kind of elevated surface. A table or something.

Why only half full? Had I already drunk some of it?

The click of a door opening. Then, "How are you this morning, Ms. Rehnquist?"

Rehnquist. I hadn't used that name in... In...

"Or should I call you Mrs. Wolfe?"

I fluttered my eyes in time with my fluttering heart. Need to turn. Need to move my head to see him. See who's talking to me.

I opened my mouth, but all that came out in my dry croaky voice was, "Water."

Arms lifted me into a sitting position. Hands held the glass to my lips. Lukewarm water dribbled down my chin as the glass hit my lips and water poured into my mouth.

I gagged a bit, but eagerly lapped up what I could. It was heaven to my parched tongue and gums.

"We'll get you better accommodations as soon as possible, Mrs. Wolfe," the voice said.

I squinted. Who was this person?

The voice was deep, but if I had to guess, I'd say it was a female who spoke to me. It had a softness that had been deepened by smoking cigarettes. I knew the type. I heard women's smoke-filled voices all the time in Las Vegas. The star of our show, Candice Hart, had—

"Candice?" I croaked out.

"Who?"

"Who are you?" I asked, though it came out more like "hoo ott doo."

"That's not your concern. I'm not here to harm you."

Perhaps my fear should have eased at her words, but since I had no recollection of getting here on my own, I knew I'd been taken. Again. And people who took other people *always* wished them harm. I should know.

"Your husband will be here soon," the woman said. "We left breadcrumbs for him."

"Where am I?" I croaked.

"The location doesn't matter."

It matters to me! But the words didn't come. They were too complex for my messed-up throat.

"You have everything you need in this room."

Then why am I on the floor?

She helped me onto my feet. "Can you walk?"

I took a step forward and stumbled. At least I could feel my legs. That was something.

"I'm sorry about this," she said. "You must have fallen off the bed."

Bed?

Then a soft mattress cushioned me. My body felt... Not painful, exactly. Not battered, but bruised.

"We mean you no harm," she said again.

"Who...?" The words caught in my throat.

"You can call me Diamond," the woman said. "I'll take care of you as much as I can. The main thing is you must be very quiet, okay? Do you understand?"

"Why?" The word emerged from my tight and dry throat.

"Because if someone else finds you, I might not be able to help you."

Someone else? I swallowed against the lump. Those words would never make it out of me.

"Food is on the way. Quiet, okay? Remember that." Her voice seemed to get softer.

She was leaving.

"No." The word made it past my lips.

But she was already gone.

"Jesus Christ," Rock said. "Is he dead?"

Father Jim lay on his bed, his wrists slit and bleeding. "He's not gray yet. I don't know." I slid my hand over his neck.

Damn. Nothing. Until—

"It's a pulse. It's faint, but it's there. Call 911."

"Or we could let him die," Rock said.

"We can't. We need his testimony. We need to know what he knows."

"You're right." Rock grabbed his phone.

"Wait!" I yelled.

"What is it now?"

"Use your burner phone. We can't have any calls traced to us. I don't want to go down for another murder."

"Right." Rock grabbed the burner. Then, "No, you make the call, Amos. It makes more sense that you'd be here."

"I'm not the one who broke in," Amos said.

"Say you were, then. Say you were worried about... Oh, fuck it all. I'll use the burner. But then we all have to hightail it out of here as soon as they're on their way. Amos, go get some of those Ziplocs I saw in the kitchen."

I found some T-shirts in the dresser drawer and ripped them into bandages. Then I wrapped them tightly around Jim's wrists to stop—or at least slow down—the blood flow. "Jim." I smacked his cheek. "Can you hear me? Hold on. We're getting help."

Amos sat down on the bed next to a bleeding Father Jim and moved his hands in an upward motion.

"What the hell are you doing?"

"I'm doing his last rites."

"For this asshole?" Rock scoffed.

"Even assholes deserve the sacrament." Amos placed his hand upon Jim's head. "Through this holy anointing may the Lord in his love and mercy help you with the grace of the Holy Spirit. May the Lord who frees you from sin save you and raise you up. Our Father, who art in heaven, hallowed..."

I stopped listening.

I understood Rock's dilemma. Part of me wanted to let this asshole die. A big part of me. He'd tormented Zee. My only solace was that he and my father hadn't raped her. Hadn't killed her. But they'd no doubt done those horrid things to many others.

A bloody razor blade sat next to Jim on the night table. I reached for it—

"Don't touch that!" Rock yelled. "Amos, get on with it, and then get the Ziplocs."

Right. Rock was right. I didn't want to be implicated in another murder. Had Jim tried to off himself? Or had someone else done it and wanted to make it look like a suicide?

We wouldn't know unless Jim lived.

Amos finished praying, stood, and headed out of the room.

I touched Jim's neck again. He was cold. But the pulse was

still there. "Hang on," I said. "You're not leaving this planet without paying for what you've done, you fucking bastard."

Blood was quickly seeping through my makeshift bandages.

"How long has he been here like this?" Rock asked.

"Hell if I know. Much longer and he'll be dead, though. We've got to get out of here before the cops get here."

Amos returned with a box of quart Ziplocs. "Here you go. But without gloves, how do we—"

"Use a bag as a glove," Rock said. "Turn it inside out, and then put the stuff in a separate bag. We'll destroy the bags we use for gloves."

I eyed my older brother. Interesting that he knew exactly what to do. I'd ask later. Or maybe I wouldn't. I didn't particularly want to know. I quickly bagged the blade according to Rock's instructions. "Should we take anything else?"

Rock scanned the room. "I don't know. Anything look out of place?"

"He wouldn't be stupid enough to leave evidence, would he?" I raised my eyebrows.

"Who fucking knows? He might, if this is a real suicide. Maybe he's atoning."

My brother raised a good point. I looked around the room quickly. A tattered leather-covered bible sat on top of his dresser. It wouldn't fit inside a quart Ziploc. "I'm tempted to look inside." I placed a Ziploc over both hands and picked up the bible, nearly dropping it because of the slick plastic. Navigating the pages was nearly impossible with plastic bags covering my hands.

Amos took it from me. "I'll do it. My prints on his bible wouldn't be an issue."

You'd better hope they won't be, I said inside my head.

The other priest flipped through the bible. "There are a few passages highlighted, but I don't see anything—"

A small piece of paper fluttered out from between the pages and onto the floor.

"I really wouldn't touch that," Rock said.

Amos nodded, gloved his hand with a Ziploc, and attempted to pick the paper up from the floor, which had, of course, fallen facedown. It took a couple tries. "Next time we bring rubber gloves."

"I sure hope to God there won't ever be a next time for this," I said. "What's it say?"

"It's a number. A phone number maybe?"

Rock looked over Amos's shoulder at the paper. "That's no phone number. Those are GPS coordinates."

My heart pounded. "For what?"

"Do I look like a cartographer to you?" my brother said. "How the hell should I know?"

I regarded Jim. He was still bleeding out, and his pallor had morphed from white to grayish. Not a good sign. I should change his bandages.

Instead, I pulled my phone out of my pocket, walked to Amos, and punched the GPS coordinates into my app.

"I'll be damned."

"What is it?" Amos and Rock asked in unison.

"It's somewhere in the Pacific."

"His island," Rock said.

"That's what I'm thinking."

"What island?" Amos asked.

"Long story," I said.

"Shit!" Rock rushed over to Father Jim. "He doesn't look good, man."

I pushed the palm of my hand back against his carotid. "Fuck. Nothing."

"Whatever he knows is gone with him." Rock looked around.

"What?" I asked.

"Nothing. I was just kind of expecting the demons from hell to come get him, like in the movie *Ghost*."

I rolled my eyes. "You can only see them if you're dead." I paused. "Maybe it *was* a suicide. Maybe he left the coordinates as a clue. Who the hell knows? Maybe he sent us on a wild goose chase and will be cackling at us from the depths of hell."

"We have to consider all possibilities," Rock said. "Now, to figure out how we check out these coordinates without leaving New York."

"I can send Leif and Buck."

"Leif and Buck are good men, but I don't trust anyone on this but family."

"But—"

"Dude, a week ago, you trusted Terrence. Even the most loyal can be turned."

I opened my mouth but then closed it. My brother was right. We had to go ourselves. "So we find Dad's connection at the FAA. No one will know we're gone."

"If only it were that simple," Rock said.

"Maybe it is. Dad had to have left something somewhere. He wasn't planning to die, after all. He was planning to fake it."

"That's still just a theory," Rock reminded me.

He was right. It *was* a theory, but it was a good one. "You're forgetting one thing, Rock. I knew Derek Wolfe better than any of you. I worked alongside him. I learned from him, and I know what's on-brand. Faking his death and screwing over his kids? Classic Derek Wolfe. But putting a hit on himself and having it followed through? *Not* Derek Wolfe. Why would he end his own life? Why would he give up the empire he's built?"

"Good enough," Rock said.

Sirens blared in the distance.

"Shit. Time to go. If we go out the back, is there a way back to the church?" I asked Amos.

"Yeah," he said. "Follow me."

18

LACEY

I sat next to Rock in the conference room in his hotel suite. None of us felt completely comfortable anywhere in the actual office building. Not when an assistant as loyal—or so we thought—as Terrence could be turned.

Rock pushed a new piece of paper with the GPS coordinates written on it toward Riley.

"Ring a bell?"

"Those coordinates?" She shook her head. "I wish I could tell you. All I know is that the island is in the Pacific somewhere."

"Near Hawaii?" Reid asked. "Or Japan?"

Riley bit her bottom lip. "I wish I were more help. I honestly don't recall getting there. It's all a blur."

"She thinks she was probably drugged," I said. "Go easy on her."

"My bastard father," Rock growled.

"Easy," I said.

Rock could be feral when he was angry. Right now, we needed clearer heads to prevail.

"Then there's Prince Christian," I continued. "Or who Riley thinks may have been Prince Christian."

"Two pretty good leads," Reid said. "I've got a call with my contact at the FBI this afternoon. I'm hoping to get clearance for us to fly. We'll use fake IDs and fly commercial. We can't risk taking the jet."

Rock nodded. "Makes sense."

"We just need to find out where the nearest landing field is. We may have to take puddle jumpers or a boat or ferry to the actual island."

"Wait," Riley said.

"Yeah, sis?" Reid asked.

"I have a memory. It's… It's a small boat. I remember puking over the side. Just once. That's all I recall." She paused a minute. "He must have kept me drugged after that, so I wouldn't get seasick."

"So you're saying it was a small boat."

She nodded. "Yeah. Not a yacht by any means, which is odd."

"Not so odd if Dad was keeping the place a secret," Reid said.

Rock cleared his throat. "Okay. Reid, you work on our FAA clearance. I'll research the coordinates and figure out where we need to go."

"Just a minute." I said. "Exactly where are we going to get the necessary identification to leave th—"

Reid's phone buzzed. He took it out of his pocket and glanced at it. "It's Nieves."

"By all means take it," Rock said.

The rest of us murmured our agreement.

"Hey," Reid said into the phone. "Ready to talk?"

His eyebrows nearly flew off his forehead.

"What?" A pause. "Yeah, yeah, yeah. I'll look into it. Keep in touch."

"What is it?" Rock asked.

"Damn it!" Reid scratched at his scalp furiously. "It's Nieves. She's gone."

"But that was her phone number," I said. "Right?"

"Yeah. She left her purse at the hospital, and Leta used her phone to get my number.

"She left her purse?" I asked.

"That's a clue right there," Riley said. "Women don't leave their purses."

"Leta's not sure when she left," Reid went on. "She's in and out of sleep, but the fact that Nieves's purse is still there..."

"Yeah," I said. "Not good."

"This is ridiculous," Reid said. "My Zee is gone, and—"

"Wait," Riley said. "*Your* Zee?"

"Yeah, sis." Reid sighed and rubbed his forehead. "I love her. I want her back desperately."

Riley wanted to smile, but it was clear that given the situation, she just couldn't. None of us could.

"Can we assume that whoever took Zee also took Nieves?" Rock asked.

"We can," I countered, "but it's just as likely they were taken by different people. They've been dealing with different people."

"Wrong," Reid said. "They've both been dealing with us. We're the common thread. I put Zee in danger when I swore I'd protect her."

"We'll get her back, bro," Rock said. "We'll protect our women from harm."

Reid nodded, and an indecipherable look passed between them.

A look that scared me more than a little.

19

REID

My buddy at the FBI, Steve Swanson, sat across from me in a Manhattan diner. He'd taken a train down, and I chose a place no one would suspect. Or even if they did, they wouldn't have had time to place any surveillance equipment.

"I can get you what you need, Reid," Steve said, "but I won't lie. It's going to cost a mint."

"I don't care. We need passports and New York State driver's licenses. Actually, driver's licenses for a different state. Let's say... Nebraska. For Rock and me."

"No one else?"

I shook my head. "It's too dangerous."

"All right. That cuts it down a little, but not much. And I suppose you want all of this yesterday?"

I let out a huff. "Yeah. Yesterday's good."

"I can hack into our files and use the photos in the database. I'll need names and addresses."

"Make it up for all I care."

He nodded. "Yeah, we can do that. Do you want to be brothers?"

"You tell me."

"Normally I'd say no, but the two of you are dead ringers for each other. And for your father."

"Fuck it."

Steve tapped on his laptop. "Shit. Rock doesn't have a passport on file and he doesn't have a New York ID."

"He just moved from Montana."

"Right." He tapped some more. "Yeah, here's a photo. I can use it, but his hair is long."

"He was a biker and construction worker."

"I'll make it work. I can Photoshop it some. What's the most time you can give me?"

"Twelve hours."

"Can't do it. Make it twenty-four and it's done."

Twenty-four hours. It might take that long to get flights anyway. But Zee... The longer she was out there...

Suck it up, I told myself. "Done. I'll wire the money to the usual place."

"Sounds good." He flipped his laptop shut. "I'll be in touch."

I nodded as Steve looked guardedly around the diner, stood, and left. Then I toyed with the fries on my plate.

I wasn't hungry, but what had I told Zee? That she needed to eat. If I was going to be strong for her, I needed to eat as well.

I picked up my burger and took a bite.

It had no flavor.

AN HOUR LATER, I paced the living room of my place when my phone buzzed. Riley.

"Hey, sis."

"I'll come straight to the point," she said. "Matt and I are going to Helena."

"No, you're not."

"It's not up for negotiation. We're going."

"You don't have a fake ID."

"You're wrong. I have *two* fake IDs. Dad gave them to me himself."

Of course. And they were no doubt ironclad, if Dad had arranged them.

"And Matt doesn't need any," she continued, "as he's not under any order not to leave the state."

"Why do you want to go?" I asked.

"Someone has to talk to Leta Romero. Now that Nieves is gone, she's the only one who knows what they were up to."

"She's still in the hospital."

"So?"

"So, the exorbitant amount of money I shelled out for their round-the-clock security was obviously for nothing."

"Not necessarily," Riley said. "Nieves could have left on her own."

"She wouldn't leave Le—" I stopped.

Nieves was first and foremost a mercenary. She might very well leave her sister. Sure, she'd hightailed it out of Vegas as soon as she'd heard about Leta being hospitalized, but that also meant she got to leave before giving me the information I was trying to pry out of her.

"Except," Riley continued, "leaving her purse still doesn't make sense."

"Unless she wanted us to *think* she'd been taken."

"True." My sister paused a moment. Then, "Someone still needs to talk to Leta. In person. Not over the phone. Someone could be standing over her telling her what to say."

"Good point." And one I hadn't thought of, because I'd been too focused on Zee. "In fact, Nieves might not be missing at all. She probably isn't, as I have top notch security on both of them. I don't want you going there, sis. She's up to something."

"I'll be fine. Matt'll be with me, and we'll have security as well."

"Yeah..." Still, I didn't like it. Matt was a great guy, but he was a country boy with a big heart who had no idea what we were dealing with.

"Reid?"

"I'm here." I sighed into the phone. "Don't go."

"I think I already said—"

"Don't. You may have a fake ID, but Matt doesn't, and he's already been linked to you. He's your husband. Where he is, people will look for you, and you're not allowed to leave New York."

"I'll go alone, then."

I held back a scoff. "Did I not just say you can't leave New York? Besides, Matt won't allow that, and neither will I."

"Yeah? Neither one of you is my boss."

"We don't claim to be. Does he even know about this plan of yours?"

A pause.

"Well...?"

"No," she finally said. "Not yet."

"I rest my case."

"Someone needs to get out there," she said. "Soon."

"Agreed. I'll take care of it."

She sighed. "Fine."

"We'll keep you in the loop, sis. I promise."

"You'd better." She ended the call with a short "bye."

Damn. If only Steve could get me those papers sooner, I'd have time to do a hop to Helena and deal with Nieves and Leta myself.

But he couldn't.

I sighed again.

Since when did I let something as silly as no ID stop me from doing something?

Since the fourth of never.

I quickly called Rock. "We're going to Helena."

"Say what?"

"Yeah. You and me. It's on the way to the Pacific, anyway. Sort of. If we head north."

"Why?"

"Because Riley has this ridiculous idea that she and Matt are going to talk to Leta. I talked her out of it, thank God, but she's right about one thing. We need to deal with them."

"I agree. Helena it is, then. But how?"

"Steve'll have our papers in twenty-four hours. He said he can't do twelve."

"Pay him double."

"This is the best he can do."

"Give me his number. We'll see about that."

"Dude, I—"

"Just give me the number, Reid."

I rattled off the number into the burner phone.

"I'll call you back," Rock said.

My heart thumped against my sternum. Rock wouldn't be able to do this. No one could. Twenty-four hours was a godsend.

A few minutes later, though, Rock's burner number appeared on my burner. "Yeah?"

"Done," he said. "They'll be couriered over within the hour."

My mouth dropped open. "What the hell did you have to give him?"

Silence for a moment. Then Rock's voice.

"You don't want to know."

20

ZEE

I awoke again.

This time, I could see clearly. I was in a bedroom. Sort of. It was a room with a bed, anyway. The mattress was comfortable, and the blanket was soft and warm, though I didn't need it. The room was hot. Really hot. My skin was sticky and clammy.

I sat up. A window broke into the wall across from the bed. Sunshine streamed in. The glass was etched, so I couldn't see out and no one could see in. A table sat next to the bed, and on it, a pitcher of water and a now empty glass.

The woman. Diamond. She'd said to call her Diamond.

Interesting name.

I got up. My legs were shaky, but they worked now, thank goodness. I remembered well the feeling of trying to reach for the water but I couldn't make my arm move. Whatever I'd been given was leaving my system now. Of course, someone might come in and force more of it into me.

Two doors. I walked toward one and touched the knob. Locked. The other, on an adjacent wall, was unlocked. A toilet, sink, and shower. Stocked, too. A toothbrush and toothpaste. Soap and shampoo.

We mean you no harm.

Diamond's words. Perhaps they were true. Why else would they leave me personal items? Plus, I was still clothed. Not naked as I'd been when I'd awoken in the concrete room in the sub-basement of the Wolfe building.

Wolfe building.

Reid.

Was Reid looking for me? Or was it good riddance?

No. I shook my head hard. He'd promised to protect me. He wouldn't turn his back on me. I was his wife. In name only, but still...

I used the toilet and washed my hands. Should I shower? No one said I couldn't. I turned on the water and waited until the steam fogged up the mirror. Then I took off my leggings and blouse—the clothes I'd been wearing at the restaurant with Reid—and stepped under the showerhead.

The water scalded me. I jumped out of the spray and worked the knob until it was a temperature I could handle. Then I stood under the rain for a few minutes, letting it warm me and soothe me.

I had no idea what was happening, why I was here.

But Reid *would* come for me. I had to believe that.

I shampooed my hair, cleaned my body, and then stepped out of the shower and wrapped one of the towels around me. They weren't the huge bath sheets Reid used, but they weren't bad. Not threadbare at all.

This was all so strange.

I wrapped my wet hair into a turban with another towel and then walked back into the room.

I gasped.

A trolley holding a tray of food awaited me. Someone had come in while I was showering. I hadn't heard a thing.

Try not to make much noise, Diamond had said.

If I couldn't make noise, whoever was taking care of me probably couldn't either. Or maybe I just hadn't heard anyone come in because of the shower.

The plate held a croissant, a hardboiled egg, and three thin slices of ham. A glass of orange juice completed the meal.

When I saw the food, my stomach reacted with a growl. I was hungry. I hadn't eaten the meal with Reid at the restaurant. In fact... My mind raced. I hadn't even ordered, had I? How long since I'd last eaten?

My tummy was a little queasy—probably from whatever they'd drugged me with—but I could try some of the food. The croissant would be relatively harmless.

I sat down on my bed and pulled the cart holding the tray in front of me. I tore off a piece of croissant and put it in my mouth.

The buttery softness burst across my tongue.

Easy, Zee. Don't eat too much or you might make yourself sick. I tore off another small piece, and then another. Then I swallowed a sip of the orange juice...and found that it wasn't orange juice. It was something tropical. Mango, maybe? It was sweet and delicious. A far cry from the plain meat patty and potato I'd found the last time I was captive.

Captive.

Yeah, this might be a decent room and a nice meal, but I was definitely captive. I'd been taken against my will, the door was locked, and I had no idea where I was or how much time had passed.

I finished half the croissant, one slice of ham, and three quarters of the juice. My stomach rumbled for more, but I wanted to see how it reacted to the food before I crammed the rest of it down.

Would someone come by to collect the cart and tray?

I had no idea.

I had nothing with me. No purse. No ID. No suitcase of clothes. I had only the clothes still on the floor and the two towels covering me. No TV. No books.

Nothing.

All I could do was lie on the bed and wait.

21

REID

David and Michael Bush sat in economy class on an evening flight to Helena. David, the older brother, wore jeans, a Pink Floyd T-shirt, and a New York Yankees ball cap. Michael, the younger, wore beige cargo pants, a plain white T-shirt, a brown beanie, and wire-rimmed glasses.

They were both uncomfortable, being over six feet tall. Coach seats weren't made for people over six feet tall.

No one had glanced their way when they boarded the full flight.

No one glanced their way now.

David sat in the aisle seat and Michael in the middle in row twenty-nine of the aircraft. Settled in the window seat was a gray-haired woman. She'd fallen asleep shortly after takeoff.

I looked over at David, who was, of course, Rock. "She's sawing logs."

He nodded. We'd made a vow not to talk at all on the flight unless it was absolutely necessary.

As far as everyone else in the family was concerned, save Riley, we were on the way to the island in the Pacific.

"I don't like it," Rock whispered.

I nodded. He didn't like leaving Lacey in the dark. Neither did I, but it was the only option. We had to stay under the radar. Even under our family's radar, if we were going to pull this off.

I took off the glasses. They were smudged again. How did people deal with wearing glasses all the time? They constantly got dirty. I wiped them on the edge of my T-shirt and then put them back on my nose. Damn. They were worse than they'd been before. I ached for my contacts.

I heaved a sigh and pulled the airline magazine out of the pocket in front of me.

"Ladies and gentlemen," a flight attendant said over the intercom. "The captain has turned off the seatbelt signs. You're now free to leave your seat if necessary. While seated, we do ask that you keep your seatbelt fastened."

The chair back in front of me came back with a jolt, cramming my knees into it.

I rolled my eyes.

Coach was for the birds.

WE ARRIVED at Helena airport and took a cab to the Holiday Inn. No posh stay at a five-star hotel. We really had to stay under the radar. Again, we talked little during the cab ride. When we were all checked in, we took the elevator to our standard room. Two queen beds and a bathroom. That was it. Not even a damned coffeemaker.

I quickly checked the room for surveillance equipment. "Looks clean," I said to Rock.

"Good enough, Mike."

We'd decided earlier to use our aliases when referring to each other. Just in case.

"We should head to the hospital," I said.

"Agreed. You hungry?" he asked.

"Not overly."

"Me neither, but we need to stay nourished."

"True. What sounds good?"

"Nothing. Let's just grab a burger through a drive-through or something."

"We didn't rent a car."

"Fuck." Rock pulled off his Yankees cap and scratched his head.

"How quickly you've gotten used to the lifestyle, Dave." I couldn't help smirking.

"Fuck off." The cap went back on his head. "We'll grab something at the gift shop, then. A candy bar."

"Nutritious."

"Fuck off," Rock said again.

"Duly noted." I saluted him, beanie still atop my head. "Let's go."

AN ARMED GUARD dressed in black stood outside Leta Romero's hospital room. Muscular but not tall. Rock and I both towered over him.

I cleared my throat. "We're here to see the patient. She's an old friend."

"She's asleep."

"That's okay. We just want to make sure she's okay. I'm Mike Bush, and this is my brother, Dave."

"Do I look like I care?"

"If you're guarding Leta," Rock said, "you sure as hell *should* care."

Mental note—make sure this guy got fired.

"Look, we just want to see her," I said. "Make sure she's okay. She and Dave, here, used to date."

"You tapped that?" The guard was interested now.

"Once or twice." Rock glared at me.

"Tell you what," the guard said. "Go ahead. If you get me her number."

"She's just been through hell—" I began.

"Done," Rock interrupted.

The guard smiled and nodded.

I wanted to sucker punch him in the gut.

But we got into the room.

Leta was, as the guard had said, asleep. Of course Nieves was nowhere to be found. If this guard was indicative of the security I'd hired, that company wouldn't be getting any more Wolfe business.

Leta's face was still swollen, and bruises covered both her eyes. An inch of stitches train-tracked over her jawline. They'd roughed her up good. The rest of her was covered with hospital bedding, but I was sure it wasn't pretty.

"Leta." I nudged her shoulder softly.

Her eyes fluttered open. "Nieves?"

"No, not Nieves. I'm...an old friend of hers."

She squinted. "I'm sorry. Who are you? These drugs keep me pretty messed up."

Drugs. Good. Between the beanie, the glasses, and her drugged-up head, she wouldn't recognize me or Rock. Plus, the only one of us she'd met previously was Roy, when he went to Montana to question her. "You probably don't know me. I'm Mike Bush, a friend of Nieves's."

"Oh."

"This is my brother, Dave."

"I'm sorry. Nieves isn't here."

"We didn't come to see her," Rock said. "We came to make sure you're okay."

"I'm...not okay," Leta replied. "But it's getting better. Slowly. Do you know where Nieves is?"

"No," I said. "Don't you?"

"She went to get coffee or something, but she never came back. That was yesterday. I think. Maybe it was this morning."

She was really doped up. "That's the last time you saw her?"

"I think so."

"Where's her phone?" Rock asked.

"Why would I know that?"

"Didn't you make a phone call with it?" I asked.

She furrowed her brow and then winced in pain. "Did I? I don't remember. Who did I call?"

I eyed Rock. He was the one who'd initiated this line of questioning.

"I work for the cell phone company," Rock said.

Would she buy that?

"You do?" She furrowed her brow again and then winced again.

"Easy," I said. "Don't hurt yourself."

"It hurts whenever I move my mouth or my eyes. Everything."

"I'm sorry."

"It's okay. I don't remember making a call. Her phone's probably in her purse. It's... It's somewhere. Weird that she didn't take it."

"Yes, definitely weird," I agreed.

Rock found a handbag and pawed through it. He shook his head and mouthed, "no wallet, no phone."

Interesting.

"Look around," I mouthed back to him.

He nodded and began to search. I sat down in the armchair

next to Leta's bed, effectively cutting her off from any view of Rock. If she could see at all with the drugs.

"You want to tell me what happened?" I asked. "We're both so sorry about this."

"It's hard," she said. "It all happened so quickly."

"Where were you? Did you get a good look at any faces?"

"They all wore ski masks. Black, except one was brown, I think."

"Where did it occur?"

"I was leaving the doctor's office."

My eyebrows shot up. "Oh? Dr. Manfred?"

"Yeah. How did you know that?"

"Nieves must have mentioned that you see him."

"Did she? She hates him. But he's the highest-rated gynecologist in our area."

"What were you seeing him for?"

She stayed quiet for a moment. Then, "I found a small lump in my breast. He did a breast exam and he thought it was probably normal tissue, but he was going to set me up for a mammogram just to be sure. We never got that far."

"I'm sorry."

"I was leaving his office, and..." She closed her eyes. A yawn split her face. "Ow!" she cried.

That yawn must have hurt like hell.

Man, I should let her rest. But we came here to find answers, and damn it, I was going to get them.

"You were leaving Dr. Manfred's office..." I prompted.

She sighed. "Yeah. I didn't make it to my car. I don't think I did, anyway. It's all a blur after that."

"Can you tell us anything else? We'd really like to help you."

"That's kind of you. How do you know my sister again?"

"She and my brother used to date."

"Oh. What's your name again?"

"Mike Bush. My brother is Dave."

"She never mentioned either of you."

Shit. Shit, shit, shit.

"They didn't have the best breakup. Anything else you remember?"

She didn't reply. I opened my mouth to prompt her again, when—

"Mike," Rock said softly.

"Yeah?"

He shook his head and mouthed the words, "no phone."

Which meant Leta did not make the call from Nieves's phone.

Someone else did.

22

ROCK

"We're renting a car," I said.

Reid furrowed his brow. "We agreed to stay under the radar."

"Do I look like I care? That woman got fucked up after seeing Manny. We've got the fake IDs. No one has recognized us so far. We need a car, man. We need to go see Manny. We'll pay cash."

Reid sighed. "Fine. You're probably right. Taking cabs everywhere would only leave more of a trail. Why didn't I think of that?"

"Because you're not Derek Wolfe. Or a professional investigator. Or a cop. Neither of us is. But we need to start thinking like them if we plan to solve this mystery."

My brother nodded. "You're right."

I shook my head, repositioning the dumbass Yankees ball cap I wore. "In a million years, I never would have suspected Manny of any of this, but now..."

"Money does weird shit to people," Reid said. "I've seen it time and again."

"Hoss skates over ethics sometimes, but Manny? This is

some crazy shit." I clenched my hands into fists. "I'm going to fuck both of them up."

Reid nodded. "Get in line, bro."

"All those years, I lived here. Never asking for a dime from anyone except what I was owed for my labor. What is it with some people?"

"You're stronger than most, Rock. Er...Dave," Reid said.

"Am I?"

"Hell, yeah. You knew what our father was worth, and you turned your back on that life, even when you could have returned to New York when you turned eighteen and made him pay."

"Could I have?"

Reid paused a moment. "Now that you mention it, probably not. It's like Riley said. If we'd known what he was doing to her and tried to stop him, he'd have made *us* pay."

My stomach cramped. My little sis. I *had* known what he was doing to her, and rather than return to New York and try to stop it once I was of age, I escaped to Montana to begin a new life. A life free from Derek Wolfe.

It had cost me my lifestyle. It cost Riley much more.

"I know what you're pondering," Reid said, "and stop it. Even if you'd tried, it wouldn't have worked."

I shook my head. "I still should have tried."

"Water under the bridge, man. Water under the bridge. All we can do is deal with the situation as it is now."

"Right on. We're getting a car, and we're getting Manny."

I DROVE up to Manny's suburban mansion. Being a doctor paid well, of course. Being a mercenary paid even better.

Fucking Manny. He'd crawled right underneath my asshole radar.

Yeah, I could be wrong. But in my gut I knew I wasn't. Manny was involved in this. Hoss probably was too. Somehow they were in it with Nieves and Leta.

Fuck my ass.

"You think he's home?" Reid asked.

"Where the hell else would he be? It's after nine."

"He married?"

"Not that I know of."

"This house screams wife and kids."

"You're not wrong. But I don't see any bicycles or footballs lying around."

"True enough," Reid said. "You want to go in alone?"

"Nah. I can use some backup. The first punch is mine, though."

"Let's get the info out of him before we start throwing punches. He could be innocent."

I nodded. Reid had a fair point, but I'd already convicted Manny in my mind. The man had something to do with this. It reeked of a setup.

And I was going to find out what the fuck was going on.

I parked the Chevy sedan on the street, exited, and walked up the path leading to the front door. I raised my hand and pounded onto the wood so hard it actually hurt.

"There's a doorbell," Reid said.

"Fuck off." I pounded again.

No answer, of course.

"Manny!" I yelled. "Open up!"

"I thought we were staying under the radar," Reid whispered.

"Open up," I yelled again, ignoring my brother. "Open up

this minute or I swear to fucking God I'll break this door down and then I'll break you in half!"

Nothing.

Until—

"Go away. I've called the cops." Manny's voice.

"Good!" I yelled. "I'm sure they'll be interested to hear what you've been up to."

"The cops?" Reid whispered. "If they find out who we are—"

"He's bluffing. If he were innocent in this mess, he'd let me in. He knows I won't hurt him if he hasn't done anything."

"Good point." Reid joined me in pounding on the door.

"You got to the count of three, Manny! Or my brother and I are going to storm in there and take out all our aggressions on you. One! Two! Thr—"

The door opened.

A trembling Manny, clad in green flannel pajamas, stood before us. I pushed him out of the way and walked in.

"Did you really think we wouldn't figure this out?" I demanded.

"Figure what out?" Manny's voice cracked.

I rolled my eyes. "Please don't go there." I looked above to the light fixture in the ceiling of his foyer. "Are we being watched? Listened to?"

He shook his head.

"Forgive me if I don't take your word for it. Have a look around, Mike."

"Mike?" Manny said.

"Shut the fuck up. When I want your input, I'll ask for it." I stood on tiptoe and unscrewed the fixture, shielding my eyes against the blinding light from the naked bulb.

"He probably wouldn't put a camera in the foyer," Reid said.

"Makes sense to me," I replied. "All the comings and goings."

Reid shrugged. "Decent point." He walked into the formal living room and started moving things.

"Just a min—"

"Shut the fuck up!" I said to Manny once more.

He complied. While Reid checked the living and dining rooms, I headed into the kitchen. I wasn't a pro at this, but I was determined to find out if anything was amiss. After a quick scan, I didn't see anything odd.

Still...

"Get in here," I said to Manny. "Where's the back door?"

"It goes out from the family room on another level," he said. "It's a walkout basement."

"Show me."

I followed Manny down a long flight of stairs to a man cave that could only belong to a doctor. I nodded toward his curio cabinet. "What the fuck, Manny?"

"It's a...collection."

"Of what? Sixteenth-century torture devices?" In reality, I knew exactly what the devices were. Who the hell collected that kind of stuff?

"They're speculums. Or specula, maybe. They're used to—"

"I know exactly what they're used for, you fucked-up maniac. For God's sake." I nodded toward the door. "We're going outside."

He shakily unlocked the deadbolt and opened the door. I followed him out, Reid on my tail.

I scanned quickly for cameras and other equipment. I didn't see anything, but just to be on the safe side, I pushed Manny off his redwood deck and out into the yard. Luckily the house sat on a huge lot.

I grabbed his collar. "Time to start talking, asshole."

"Rock, come on," he said shakily. "We're old pals."

"Our friendship ended the day you and Hoss finagled me out

of first class airfare to come to New York to tell me nothing. You're just a mercenary, Manny, and that's how I'll treat you."

"I'm no—"

"Sell it to the Air Force," I said. "Now you tell me exactly what you know about Leta Romero."

"She's a patient. You know I can't—"

"Yes, your ethical duty. That went out the door a while ago, so I call bullshit. The woman got her ass whooped after leaving your office a few days ago. Care to tell me what's going on?"

He gasped. "Is she all right?"

"No, she's not all right. She got the ass-kicking of a lifetime. She's lying in a hospital bed. My question is...who knew she was seeing you that day? Because they jumped her outside your building."

"I wouldn't know."

"Really?" I increased my hold on his collar. "Think hard."

While I questioned Manny, Reid was staking out his yard. He finally joined me. "Looks clean, but you never know."

"We're probably good," I said, "and honestly? I don't fucking care." I turned my attention back to Manny. "Here are your options. You tell me what you know about the Romero sisters, or I'll make sure you end up in the hospital next to Leta."

"Rock, I don't know anyth—"

I pulled back and punched him squarely in the jaw. Didn't even hurt, my adrenaline was surging so powerfully through my veins.

Hurt Manny, though. He crumpled to the ground with a shriek.

"Easy, Rock," Reid said.

"Fuck easy. He knows something and I aim to find out what."

"Fine, fine!" Manny gasped. "I'll talk."

23

LACEY

Rock and Reid had been gone for a while now. I had no idea where they were or where they were going. I didn't even know what their final destination was. They'd have to take a boat to the private island, if what Riley recalled was true.

I didn't know when I'd see Rock again. My rock. My Rock.

I hated this damned hotel suite. I hadn't eaten a decent meal in days, and—

"Shit," I said aloud at the knock on the door.

I wrapped my robe around me and walked to the door, staring out through the peephole. A bellboy. I unlocked the deadbolt and opened the door. "What is it?" I asked sharply.

"There's someone to see you," he said.

Hank Morgan stood to the side, outside the view of the peephole.

"Oh my God."

"We need to talk, Mrs. Wolfe."

"No, we really don't."

"Where's your husband?"

"He's...at the office. Working late." I berated myself inwardly for the pause. Rock was on a plane somewhere, and if Morgan found out...

"Doesn't sound like him."

"You try having your wife accused of a murder she didn't commit. You'd be working around the clock too."

He said nothing. Just stood there. The bellboy edged down the hallway.

"If that's all..." I closed the door.

He glided between the door and me. "It's not all, Mrs. Wolfe."

"I'll call security."

He let out a chuckle. "I'm a detective with the NYPD. I trump hotel security."

I sighed. "It's after ten. What do you want?"

"Just making sure you're here. Not violating the terms of your bail."

"At ten at night?"

"Nighttime is the best time for leaving the city, Mrs. Wolfe."

"I wouldn't know. As you can see, I'm here, right where I'm supposed to be, so if you'll excuse me..."

"I need to talk to Rock."

Chills skittered along my forearms. "Then call him. In the morning. This is ridiculous."

"Maybe I'll stop by the Wolfe building."

My heart nearly stopped, but I kept my facial expression neutral—at least I hoped I did. "Be my guest. But you won't be able to get in at this hour."

He flashed his badge at me. "You sure about that?"

Yeah, I'd overplayed my hand. I was off my game. So damned tired all the time. Tired and worried and ready to pounce on anything, even a police detective who had arrested me for a crime I didn't commit.

Not my finest hour.

Then again, why was he here at this hour?

"I have ample evidence against you, Mrs. Wolfe," Morgan said.

"I know. All circumstantial. Someone above your head wants to make this stick."

"As I've told you, the DA is certain we have the right person."

"And I can assure you that you don't."

"We'll see about that." Morgan took a seat on a chair in the living area of the suite.

What the heck was he after?

"I've been thinking," he said.

"I couldn't imagine what about."

"I might be able to get the charges against you dropped."

I stopped my eyebrows from flying off my face. *Remain cool, Lace. Easy does it. He's playing you.*

"Oh? Charges that have no basis in fact in the first place? I'm sure you could. Anyone could."

"Someone wants you to go down for this crime," he said.

"That someone seems to be you."

Morgan gave a slight smile. "This goes way higher than my pay grade."

"I get it. My father-in-law was a first-class psycho creep who bought everyone off. And you're saying you can change this situation? Because if his own children can't, I can't see how you could."

"I have connections."

"Better connections than the Wolfes?"

"Better? I don't know. Different? Maybe."

I sighed. "How much will it cost?"

"Do you think I'm asking for a bribe, Mrs. Wolfe?"

I couldn't help it. I burst into laughter. Fatigue and fear and hunger had taken their toll. "Yeah, Mr. Morgan, you are. You are *definitely* asking me to bribe you. I suppose now you're going to tell me it's against the law to bribe a police officer. Of course I know that. I'm a lawyer, for God's sake. But what does it matter? I'm already going to trial for a murder I didn't commit. What's bribery? It's a fucking mosquito. A nuisance. A distraction and a pain in the ass, but nothing, basically."

"Unless it's carrying West Nile virus," Morgan sneered.

I plopped down into the chair opposite Morgan. "Touché. Now," I began again, "what will it cost?"

"May I speak frankly?"

"By all means."

"I want to get out of here. I'm sick of this game. I'm sick of the corruption in the force and in the DA's office."

Seemed he was a big part of the corruption, but I kept that to myself. "Welcome to New York."

"You seem to think I want you to go down for this murder."

"Don't you? You're the one who arrested me. You're the one who's been subjecting all of us to ridiculous interrogation again and again when we've told you all we know. You know damned well you don't have any real evidence against me, so don't try to tell me you do. Neither of us are that stupid, Hank."

He lifted his eyebrows at my use of his first name.

I didn't care. It was nearing eleven p.m., and all I wanted was to escape this hell. If I could pay him off to do it, I might be talked into it.

I wished Rock were here. He'd know what to do. Or even Reid.

Me? I was a good girl. But it had become increasingly clear that in the world of the Wolfes and the NYPD, the good finished last.

I had no intention of finishing last.

"So what are you asking for?" I continued. "A new life somewhere else? You want money? You want a new ID? What?"

"You could do that for me?"

"*I* can't do a damned thing for you, Hank. I'm only asking what you want."

"I want out."

"You're going to have to be more specific."

"Fine. I want ten million. Cash. I'll get the charges dropped, and you'll never hear from me again."

I nodded, smiling.

Rock had done something a few days previously. I'd balked at it, but in the end, he did it anyway. This moment changed my mind.

Never had I been so glad that my husband had installed video and audio recording in our suite.

I held back the smile I wanted to give to Morgan.

Gotcha.

Diamond didn't return. I wished she would, since I'd been so out of it I had no idea what she looked like. Her voice had been smoky and husky, so I imagined she was an older woman, but perhaps she wasn't. Candice was only a little older than I was, and her voice was similar.

I'd often wondered how Candice kept in such good shape being the chain smoker she was. She could move nonstop for an hour during a show and not even be winded.

The show...

Reid had said he took care of everything, but no doubt my job was gone at this point. Did I even care? Yeah, in a way. It wasn't the easiest way to make a living, but it was *mine*. I'd earned it. All those dancing lessons my mother dragged me to when I was a kid. I'd put them to good use.

Why was I even thinking about all this? My current problem was that I was being held captive. At least no one was hurting me.

Not yet, anyway.

Hours had passed, and no one had brought more food. The hard-boiled egg lay on the tray from this morning. Night had fallen, and stars shone like blurs through the etched window in my room.

A knock. I jerked upward off the bed. "Yes?" I said meekly.

The doorknob turned and the door slid open. A woman entered. Her face was worn and slightly wrinkled, though her deep-set brown eyes, high cheekbones, and full pale lips indicated she'd once been beautiful. She wore island garb—a tent-like dress with a bright orange floral pattern over black. Her feet were bare and tanned.

"Diamond?" I said hesitantly.

She nodded. "I'm sorry I couldn't come sooner. I've got another meal for you."

Couldn't come sooner? Why?

Was I allowed to ask?

"Thank you." My stomach had settled from whatever they'd poured into my system, and I was actually really hungry now. Fear be damned. I had to eat if I wanted to get through whatever was coming.

Diamond wheeled in a food trolley. She eyed the other cart that was still in my room. "Not hungry this morning?"

"I was a little queasy. I ate the croissant and one slice of ham. And the juice. What kind of juice was that?"

"Mango and passion fruit."

"It was delicious."

She nodded but didn't smile as she removed the cover from the plate of food sitting on the trolley. "All I could get you is a chicken breast and some veggies tonight. A few slices of bread."

"That's fine. I don't really eat red meat anyway."

"We don't serve any red meat here."

I arched my eyebrows. "What is this place?"

Diamond bit her lip. "I shouldn't have said that."

"Is this some kind of hotel or something?"

She didn't reply.

"Why am I here, Diamond? Why was I taken?"

Again, no response.

"Please. I'm supposed to be somewhere else. There are people who need me to—"

"I can't tell you anything else." Her tone was soft yet abrupt. "You need to stay quiet. Please."

"Diamond, I'm begging you. At least tell me where I am."

"I can't…"

"Zee. My name is Zee."

"I know who you are."

"Then why do you want me? I'm a nobody." That wasn't exactly true. Not anymore. I was the wife of Reid Wolfe, and I had a story that could take down Derek Wolfe's accomplices.

"Listen," she said quietly. "I want to help you. I really do. You have to keep quiet and stop asking questions, okay? That's all I can tell you right now."

"I've been taken against my will—"

"We all have!" she whispered harshly.

I dropped my mouth open. She was once beautiful, but was now an old woman. Not old so much as…used. She looked used. So very used.

"I'm sorry for whatever you've been through, but—"

"Quiet. That's enough for now, Zee. I'll tell you more when I can. In the meantime, you need to stay here, stay quiet, and eat your food. That's your only job."

REID

"Rock."

My brother turned to me. "What?"

"He said he'll talk. You're going to have to unclench your fist from around his collar."

"Why should I?"

Good question. I found I had no good answer.

Turned out Rock didn't need an answer. He let Manny go, and the other man crumpled to the ground.

I looked to the sky, mesmerized. Montana, even in a big city like Helena, looked vastly different from Manhattan. I could actually pick out the Big Dipper as if it were flashing in neon. It was that visible.

"Start talking, Manny." From Rock.

"Can we go sit on the deck?" Manny asked. "I'd like a chair."

"Nope," Rock said. "You might have audio set up on the deck. We'll talk out here. In the open air."

"I swear to God. No audio. Nothing."

I rolled my eyes. "Sorry, I'm with Rock. We basically don't trust you."

Manny gulped. Rock and I stood over him. His pudgy face was visible under the starlight. No flashlight necessary. Unreal.

For the first time, I understood my brother's love affair with Big Sky Country.

"You'd better start talking, Manny," Rock said. "I have no problem with kicking a man while he's down."

"Yeah, yeah. Okay." Manny coughed, clutching at his throat.

"Save the dramatics." This from me.

"He just tried to choke me," Manny gasped. "Give me a minute, will you?"

"Nope." Rock kicked him.

"Jesus!" Manny clutched his side.

"Start talking," Rock said again, "or more is coming. From both of us."

"Not a fair fight," Manny said.

Rock let out a low guffaw. "Fair fight? You've been fucking me over, and you talk about fair? I ought to pummel you for that comment alone."

I said nothing. I wouldn't undermine my brother in front of Manny, but if Rock pummeled him, we'd get nothing out of him. I hoped Rock could put aside his anger to realize that on his own.

Instead, he gave Manny another kick to the gut. "Last warning. Spill it."

"All right. All right." Manny managed to get himself into a sitting position on the grass. "It started with Nieves."

"We know that, asshole. Give us something new, or I'm going to open up a can of whoop-ass on you like you've never imagined." Then Rock growled. Seriously. He *growled*.

"Nieves knew Hoss and me from the biker bars. She and Hoss had worked together before, and—"

"Say what? Nieves worked with Hoss? On what?"

"Nieves had run a credit card scam and she got caught. She

knew Hoss was an attorney, so she went to him, and he got her out of it."

"Back the fuck up," Rock said. "The Nieves I know wouldn't go near either of you."

"The Nieves you know isn't the real Nieves," I said softly. "Did you ever think she'd go into your place after you broke up with her?"

"Good point. She slid right under my radar, just like you and Hoss did, you prick." Rock kicked Manny again.

"Fuck!" Manny doubled over.

"Easy, Rock," I said. "He's starting to talk."

"Yeah, yeah. Keep talking." Rock adjusted his Yankee cap.

"Anyway, Hoss got her out of the mess. I'm not sure of the details, but knowing Hoss, she probably had to sleep with him."

"Oh?" Rock lifted his brows. "Not buying. Nieves told me point blank she wouldn't let either of you near her."

Manny let out a laugh. "So Nieves is a liar. Are you really surprised?"

Rock said nothing. Manny was right, and we both knew it.

"Keep going," Rock finally said.

"A while back, Nieves intercepted a message on your answering machine."

"We know all that," I said. "Get to the new stuff."

"How the fuck am I supposed to know everything you know? Jesus."

"Just keep talking, ass-wipe." Rock raised his knee. "Or you want another kick?"

"No. No more. Jesus." Manny cleared his throat. "Nieves went to Hoss with this information. Evidently the two of them had a deal."

"A deal?" I asked.

"Yeah. After he took care of the credit card fraud for her. Part of his payment was that she'd come to him with any possible moneymaking ventures. I guess she thought this message had potential."

"Of course she did," Rock said. "Since Derek Wolfe was worth billions."

"Yeah," Manny went on. "She thought you"—he nodded to me—"must be in on this hit on your dad somehow, and that maybe we could blackmail one of you to keep quiet about it, or whatever."

"Except none of us was in on the supposed hit," I said.

"Right, but we didn't know that. As far as Nieves knew, the information was good, and she'd intercepted it instead of you, Rock. So we had leverage."

"Leverage to do what?" Rock demanded.

"Hoss came to me with Nieves and Leta in tow," Manny said. "They wanted to brainstorm about how we could potentially get a payoff with this info."

"And where did that brainstorming lead?" I said harshly.

"Nowhere I ever wanted to go." Manny said. "You've got to believe me."

"Does it really matter what we believe?" I asked. "Actions speak louder than words. Now what the fuck happened?"

"Hoss wanted to contact Derek Wolfe himself, but the three of us were against that."

"Good choice," I said.

"Then we talked about going to you." He met Rock's gaze.

"You didn't come to me, though," Rock said.

"No, we didn't."

"Why not? You knew me. Knew where I was. *Who* I was."

Manny looked down. "We also knew you didn't have any money."

"Ah..." From me. "Not surprising."

"Hoss took the lead, and we came up with a plan. We'd

contact the NYPD with the evidence we had and ask for compensation for the information."

I laughed this time. "You really thought the NYPD was going to give you money?"

"Hey, it was a good plan. The Helena PD offers rewards for information all the time."

"New York ain't Helena," Rock said.

"Yeah. Well, we found that out. Turned out someone at the NYPD already knew about the hit, or at least they said they did. They weren't interested in this information, and they basically told us to fuck off."

"But you didn't fuck off, did you?" I said.

He shook his head. "I wish we had."

"Keep talking," Rock prodded.

"Nieves went back to your place one day while you were at work," Manny said. "That's when she took your gun."

"Why the fuck would she take the gun?" Rock demanded.

"The rest of us didn't know at the time, but someone had contacted her, asking what kind of guns you had. She didn't know, so she went to your place. The Glock happened to be out of the safe, and she didn't know a handgun from a shotgun, so she took it. Then she gave the information to the person who contacted her."

"Who contacted her?" Rock demanded.

"He didn't give her a name, but he promised a hundred grand would be sent as soon as the deed was done."

"And was it?" I asked.

Manny shook his head. "Nope. Never."

Rock laughed uproariously. "All this shit, and you didn't even get paid! That's classic."

"Question," I said. "How did Nieves know our father had been killed an hour before it actually happened?"

"The dude she was talking to let her know."

"And you never bothered to find out who it was?"

"He wouldn't say. And before you ask, yeah, we've looked at Nieves's phone records. The number changed each time."

"Burner phones," I said. "At least he's not sloppy."

"The only sloppy assholes are Manny, here, Hoss, and the Romero sisters."

"Leta came to me later, under the guise of being a patient. She was scared. She wanted out of the whole thing. So did I. But Nieves and Hoss still thought there was money to be made."

"You wanted out, huh?" Rock shook his head. "Too little too late. I hold all four of you responsible for this. You let information about the hit leak to the NYPD, and my dad had all kinds of moles there. He also probably had people there who hated him and who decided to capitalize on this information. His fake hit turned into a real hit. You set this whole goddamned thing in motion, Manny, and now my wife has been arrested for my asshole father's murder. I ought to—"

I pushed Rock away from Manny before he brought his foot down on his head.

"We need him. He hasn't told us everything yet."

Rock let out a slow breath. "You were supposed to be my friend, you fucked-up psycho."

Manny said nothing.

"You'll pay for all of this," Rock promised. "If I have to go down for murder myself, I swear to God, you'll pay."

26

LACEY

organ finally left, and I squealed with glee. Literally twirled around in that damned hotel suite giggling. For a moment, the past forty-eight hours disappeared, and I was on top of the world.

We had him. *We had Morgan asking for a bribe.*

I had no idea where Rock was at the moment. Still en route to the Pacific, and no way could I reach him. Ditto Reid. Texting Riley or Roy this sensitive information wasn't a good idea either. It would have to wait until morning when I could talk to them in person in a safe place.

Rock had shown me how to access the video and audio from my laptop, so I fired it up to save a hard copy. That had to be done quickly, for once Morgan realized he'd been set up, he'd make the evidence disappear.

I couldn't help smiling as I accessed the footage on the computer. I grabbed three blank thumb drives from our stash of hundreds. I hadn't used a thumb drive in years, but I didn't trust this information to the cloud.

I wanted it in my hot little hands.

And there it was, in black and white.

"Do you think I'm asking for a bribe, Mrs. Wolfe?"

"Yeah, Mr. Morgan, you are. You are definitely asking me to bribe you. And I suppose now you're going to tell me it's against the law to bribe a police officer. Of course I know that. I'm a lawyer, for God's sake. But what does it matter? I'm already going to trial for a murder I didn't commit. What's bribery? It's a fucking mosquito. A nuisance. A distraction and a pain in the ass, but nothing, basically."

"Unless it's carrying West Nile virus."

I plopped down into the chair opposite Morgan. "Touché. Now," I began again, "what will it cost?"

"May I speak frankly?"

"By all means."

"I want to get out of here. I'm sick of this game. I'm sick of the corruption in the force and in the DA's office."

"Welcome to New York."

"You seem to think I want you to go down for this murder."

"Don't you? You're the one who arrested me. You're the one who's been subjecting all of us to ridiculous interrogation again and again when we've told you all we know. You know damned well you don't have any real evidence against me, so don't try to tell me you do. Neither of us are that stupid, Hank."

"So what are you asking for?" I continued. "A new life somewhere else? You want money? You want a new ID? What?"

"You could do that for me?"

"I can't do a damned thing for you, Hank. I'm only asking what you want."

"I want out."

"You're going to have to be more specific."

"Fine. I want ten million. Cash. I'll get the charges dropped and you'll never hear from me again."

Bingo.

I saved the whole conversation to three separate thumb drives. One I placed in the safe in our suite. Tomorrow, another would go in Rock's safe deposit box that he'd opened as soon as he became CEO of Wolfe Enterprises. The third? I giggled as I imagined hiding it in my pussy or my ass. Rock would love that.

The third I'd keep on me for now. In my bra, not my ass. Which meant sleeping with a bra on tonight, but that was no big deal. I'd done it before.

If only I could get hold of Rock and tell him!

This was great news.

We were on our way now.

27

REID

"That's it," Manny said. "That's all of it."

"Bull," Rock said.

"I'm with Rock." I adjusted the brown beanie on my head. Damn, my scalp itched after wearing the thing most of the day. "First of all, where the hell is Nieves?"

"I honestly don't know," Manny said. "Maybe Hoss would know. This was their baby. Leta and I were just along for the ride, like I said."

"Bull," Rock repeated.

I nodded. "I agree. You were all involved so you're all equally responsible. Now where's Nieves?"

"I told you. I don't know. Check with Hoss."

"Man, you are cruisin' for a bruisin'." Rock hoisted Manny to his feet. "Get on the horn, and get Hoss and his skinny ass over here. Now."

"He won't come at this hour."

"You make him come. Don't take no for an answer. Tell him you have sensitive info. Tell him you want to suck his dick. Tell him whatever it takes!"

Manny trembled. "My phone's in the house."

"Then by all means." Rock gave him a push. "Let's go get it."

~

AN HOUR LATER, Hoss drove into Manny's suburban driveway. Rock and I were waiting behind the front door when he knocked.

I pulled the door open, and Rock swept in for the kill. Except not literally. He grabbed Hoss by the collar, jerked him inside, and then forced him through the house and out into the backyard. I led Manny along like a lost puppy.

Hoss gasped the whole way, trying to speak but not able to get any words out.

Finally, Rock let go of him and pushed him onto the ground. "Nieves," Rock said. "Where the fuck is she?"

"She's gone?" Hoss rasped out.

"Don't even think about playing dumb with me. Manny here already spilled everything. How the four of you were trying to make money off my father's hit. It might interest you to know that he planned the whole thing. It was you who made it a reality."

I shook my head slightly at Rock. He was talking too much. At this point, our father orchestrating it was still just a theory. A good theory, but we hadn't proved it yet. Though we were certainly close.

"Sorry, man," Manny said. "They roughed me up."

"You damned pussy." Hoss scowled at Manny.

"You want a little?" Rock said. "It'll take a lot less effort for me to put your skinny ass down."

"I wouldn't provoke my brother," I advised. "He's got a hot temper. Now start from the beginning. Nieves came to you with a credit card problem."

"Attorney-client privilege."

Rock landed a kick to the side of Hoss's head. "That ship has left the harbor. It's so far out that it can't be seen by the naked eye."

Hoss cried. Literally. Tears fell from both eyes. Very visible in the shine from the starlight.

"Just level with them, Hoss. Maybe we can make a deal."

I laughed then. Really laughed. "You think you hold any cards here?"

"Of course we do," Manny said. "Hoss here knows where Nieves is, don't you, bro?"

Hoss didn't answer.

"Do you, asshole?" Rock demanded. "Here's the deal, then. You tell me, and I *don't* beat you bloody."

Hoss looked up at me, pleading.

"Seriously?" I said. "Whose side do you think I'm on here? I may not be a brawling biker like my older brother, but I'm just as strong and just as mean. So don't even think you can gain my sympathy. Right now we're all suspects in our father's murder. All of us, and Rock's wife has been arrested. All because of you four manipulative cunts."

"Fuck, Manny. You told them everything?"

Manny didn't reply. Just looked sheepish. Though the swelling of his jaw spoke volumes.

"Doesn't prove anything," Hoss said, his voice cracking.

"It proves plenty," I said. "We can trace this to your call to the NYPD. They were tipped off, and someone who wanted my father dead for real took advantage of it."

"Why would anyone on the NYPD want him dead?" Hoss asked.

Rock kicked his gut. "You really want to go there? You want us to believe you're *that* naïve?"

Hoss didn't reply. He was too busy gasping for air.

"You may want to take it easy," I said to Rock. "He's half the man his pal is. Literally."

"Fuck it." Rock ripped off his ball cap, smoothed his hair, and then replaced the hat. "Where the fuck is she, Hoss?"

"I don't know," he gasped.

"And I don't believe you. Manny already intimated that you know. Hmm, let's see. What would make you talk? How fond are you of your balls?"

Hoss sucked in a breath while Manny visibly trembled next to me. Whatever Rock had in mind, I wanted no part of it.

"I'd talk if I were you," I said.

"I don't know where she is," Hoss rasped. "She disappeared."

"Nice try. She also faked a phone call from her sister from her phone." Rock slapped Hoss's bald head.

"How's her sister doing?"

Rock laughed. "So you know that much. Your partner here claims that was a surprise."

"Jesus Christ, Manny." Hoss shook his head.

"Hey, don't blame me," the other man said. "I didn't know what I was supposed to tell them."

"Everything," I said. "You tell us everything, or I'm going to let my big brother there remove your balls one by one."

Manny let out a squeak and a shudder.

"How much did you tell them, Manny?" Hoss demanded.

"About the deal with the NYPD, and how it didn't work."

"Your stupid-ass phone call cost my family—specifically my wife—everything," Rock said. "You'll never be able to make it up to us. I could finish you both off now, and I swear to God, no one would ever find the bodies."

Easy, Rock. I didn't say the words, but the last thing we needed was his threat recorded anywhere. This yard was most likely safe, but my big brother sure had a mouth on him. I didn't doubt for a second the truth of his words.

"Can you blame us for wanting to make a buck?" Hoss asked.

"You unethical son of a bitch. Preaching ethics to me at that meeting in New York, when the whole time this was all your fucking fault. That call you made to the NYPD let some corrupt officer in on my father's plan to fake his death. Gave him an easy way to make it a reality."

"Why would the NYPD want to off your father?" Hoss demanded.

"How the fuck should I know? Everyone wanted to off my father. He was a psycho prick." Rock stomped in the grass. "He had enemies everywhere."

"Find the guy at the NYPD, then," Hoss said. "None of us did it. We were all here in Helena."

"Can you prove that?" I asked, holding my temper in check.

"Of course we can," Manny said.

"Can you really?" I asked. "I imagine it wouldn't take much to forge some evidence placing all four of you in Manhattan at the time. Throw in the phone call that Nieves intercepted at Rock's place, and you'll look even guiltier."

"You can't do that," Hoss said. "It's not legal."

I chucked softly, shaking my head. "You really don't want to play that card, asshole."

Hoss looked at his feet. No, he didn't want to play that hand at all.

"Tell us where Nieves is," I said. "And you can keep your balls."

Hoss sighed. "Fine. She made the call from her phone, pretending to be Leta."

"We pretty much already figured that part out," I said. "Go on."

"We thought we could throw you off track if it looked like someone took her."

"You think you're pretty smart, don't you?" Rock said to Hoss.

"Except Nieves's purse is still in Leta's hospital room, but her phone isn't. And Leta has no recollection of making a call from the phone."

"Yeah." He cleared his throat. "We figured Leta's still so drugged up we could blame any lack of memory on that."

"Except you didn't think about leaving the phone in her room." Rock laughed. "You dumbass."

Hoss looked for a moment like he was going to retort, but then he seemed to think better of it.

"Who beat the shit out of Leta?" I asked.

"We don't know," Manny said. "That's the God's honest truth."

I drew in a breath. "We find the person who put Leta in the hospital, then," I said to Rock, "and then we can trace him to whoever's behind this whole thing."

"I sure thought it was Father Jim," Rock said. "Except he's dead."

"Who's Father Jim?" Manny asked.

"Never you mind, shithead." He turned to Hoss. "Where's Nieves?"

"She's staying at my place."

I rolled my eyes. That was an image I didn't need.

Rock gripped Hoss by the shoulders and hauled him to his feet. "I'll let you keep your jewels for now, but know this. You're being watched. Every fucking move you make. I have eyes and ears everywhere."

28

ZEE

A pitcher of water sat on my nightstand. I poured a glass and drank it down. My flesh was sticky. I was somewhere tropical. Las Vegas in the summer was dry. The air was cool in my room, but still humid. I felt like a sheen of sweat covered me all the time, even after a shower.

I found, surprisingly, I was hungry again. No food, though, so I went into the shower. Yesterday, breakfast had miraculously shown up while I showered.

The warm water was soothing, but I showered quickly anyway. I didn't want to tempt fate. If I was supposed to be quiet, running the water for too long could be a problem.

Sure enough, my breakfast was waiting when I left the bathroom clad in a towel. I wished for clothes. My black leggings could probably stand on their own by now.

If only I knew where I was.

If only I could get in touch with Reid.

He must be worried sick!

He'd promised to protect me. And I'd believed him.

I ate more this time. The whole croissant and the whole portion of scrambled eggs. Only one slice of bacon, but I drank the entire glass of that delicious mango-passion fruit juice. Once I was finished, I set everything back on the tray and wheeled the trolley closer to the door. Just for fun, I checked the doorknob.

Still locked in.

Then a soft knock. I jerked, being so close to the door.

"Yes?" I said softly.

The lock clicked, and the door opened. Diamond walked in, glancing over her shoulder. She held what looked like a straw beach bag.

"You ate," she said. "Good."

"I was hungrier today."

"I'm glad. I'm sorry you're in this situation."

"It would help if you could tell me what's going on."

"I will when I can. In the meantime, I brought you some clothes. Go ahead and change, and I'll make sure the ones you have on get laundered."

I nodded. I wasn't going to give up a chance for clean clothes. I grabbed the bag from her and headed into the bathroom.

Inside, I pulled out a pair of shorts with a drawstring waist, three pairs of plain white panties, two white T-shirts, and a one-size-fits-all island dress similar to what Diamond wore. I still felt clammy all over, so I chose the shorts and one of the T-shirts. In the bottom of the bag was a pair of white socks and a pair of rubber flip-flops. She'd obviously guessed at my shoe size. They were slightly small.

I put the socks and flip flops in the bag. Why not go barefoot? I was far from cold, and I wasn't going anywhere anyway.

I gathered my soiled clothes, left the bathroom, and handed them to Diamond.

"Put them back in the bag," she said.

"Oh. Sure." I went back to the bathroom, dumped the socks, flip-flops, panties, and T-shirt onto the floor, and handed her the empty bag.

Diamond quickly threw my clothes in the bag. "Sorry there's no bra. I wasn't sure of the size."

"No problem." She probably had no idea I was used to going braless much of the time.

Or did she know? She'd said she knew who I was, but did she know everything about me?

"It may be a while until I can get back here. Is there anything you need?"

"I'll get hungry at lunchtime," I said.

"I know, and I'm sorry about that. It would look odd if I took more than a meal's worth."

"Look odd to whom?" I couldn't help asking.

She shook her head. "I've said all I can. Stay quiet. I'll try to get you some non-perishables. Don't count on it, though."

I nodded. What else could I do? I was stuck here. Why hadn't I saved the extra slices of bacon off my plate?

"I'll do the best I can." She lifted the bag. "I'll bring your clothes back as soon as I can."

"Thank you."

Thank you. All I could say. And though I was here against my will, I *was* thankful. I wasn't being mistreated, and I knew what it felt like to be mistreated.

I wanted to beg her to stay, just so I'd have someone to talk to.

I wanted to ask if she could contact Reid, but I already knew the answer.

She'd told me he was coming. That they'd left "bread-crumbs." Whatever the heck that meant.

I lay down on the bed and closed my eyes.

Reid, where are you? Will I ever see you again? Will I ever be able to tell you how much I love you?

Why hadn't I told him?

Simple. I'd been afraid he wouldn't return my sentiment.

Foolish vanity. I no longer cared if he returned my feelings. I wanted him to know how hard I'd fallen for him. How much I yearned for him. How he made me feel emotions I'd thought were dead in me forever.

All I could do was lie here.

No phone. No books. No TV. No nothing.

Just lie here and contemplate what might be going on outside this small room.

And how it could all go bad very quickly.

29

REID

Manny and Hoss in tow, Rock and I drove to Hoss's house, where Nieves was supposedly hiding out.

"Your place wired?" Rock asked.

Hoss shook his head.

"Mine isn't either," Manny said. "We could have talked in the house."

"You idiots," I said. "Just because you didn't wire your place doesn't mean someone else didn't."

Manny gasped. "What a...!"

"Violation?" Rock said, scoffing. "Yeah. No shit. You've fucked with our lives. How's it feel to have someone fuck with yours?"

Neither replied.

"Where's the bitch?" Rock asked.

"She's inside."

"Let's go, then." I opened the passenger side of the car and stepped out, grabbing Manny out of the back seat.

Rock took care of Hoss.

We entered from the back, as his front door was lit up like Vegas.

Hoss's suburban mansion was even bigger than Manny's.

"Check for surveillance," Rock said to me.

I nodded and began my search.

I'd learned a lot from my father, but how to sweep for hidden bugs and cameras had never been among his lessons. I'd learned that after his death. After my siblings and I had been implicated.

From my father, however, I'd learned to trust no one.

And I didn't.

Looked pretty clean, from what I could tell, though I was no expert. If Leif or Buck were here, they'd be able to ferret out the most cleverly hidden device.

My gaze finally fell on a vase of carnations—looked like one of those cheap bouquets the New York street vendors sell.

"Never pegged you for a floral type," I said to Hoss.

"Got them for Nieves," he said.

I eyed the flowers closely.

Sure enough, hidden among the blooms was a tiny listening device. I grabbed it and crunched it beneath my sneaker-clad foot. "Nice try."

"Hoss?" Manny asked.

"Hey, can't blame a guy for the attempt."

"Easy enough to spot," I said. "If someone else bugged your place, it's professionally done. I don't see any evidence to the effect, but—"

"You fucking lied to us?" Rock grabbed Hoss by the collar.

Manny went rigid.

"And here I thought you valued your balls," Rock continued.

"Hey, what—"

All heads turned toward the woman's voice.

Nieves Romero stood in the entrance to the kitchen, clad in a long satiny red nightgown.

Rock released Hoss, who crumpled to the floor. "You little—"

"We know what's going on," I interrupted. "We know everything. You're something, Nieves, leaving your sister alone in the hospital after such a trauma and then faking a phone call from her."

"What are you talking about?" Nieves asked innocently.

"Don't even try. Your two cohorts here spilled it all." Rock looked around. "We should go outside."

"I think it's clean," I said, "but I agree. Outside is best."

"I'm not going outside in this." Nieves looked down at her gown.

"Uh...yeah. You are." Rock grabbed her by the arm.

She whisked it free. "You don't have to manhandle me. I'm going."

Hoss had a concrete deck complete with enclosed patio and hot tub. Way better than Manny's smaller redwood deck. I looked farther into the yard. Fucker had a built-in swimming pool too.

Breaching ethics apparently paid well.

Nieves pulled her long gown off, revealing her near-perfect body. "We should all take a dip. The tub's big enough for five."

"You've got to be kidding me." Rock picked up Nieves's gown and shoved it at her. "Cover yourself."

Yeah, no shit. We'd both seen Nieves in her glory, and while the sight was pleasurable indeed, I had no desire to see Manny and Hoss in their birthday suits. That'd be an image I could never unsee.

Nieves, to my surprise, obeyed and put her gown back on. Manny and Hoss's gazes never strayed from her. If they started drooling, I wouldn't be surprised.

Rock didn't miss it either. "Stop staring, assholes." He pushed Hoss and then Manny off the concrete and onto the grass. He steered clear of the pool, as well. Clear of anything where surveillance equipment could have been installed.

"You sit down," he said to Nieves.

She dropped to the grass, pulled her gown up, and sat cross-legged.

She was determined to show skin. Did she really think Rock and I thought with that head?

Apparently.

Hoss and Manny clearly did.

"Time to get real," I said. "Who the hell beat up Leta?"

"We don't know," Manny said. "I've tried to tell them."

"And you..." I eyed Nieves. "You left her alone in the hospital. What for? To come here? Are you kidding me?"

"It got you here, didn't it?" Nieves said snidely.

Rock shook his head. "It's a good thing I draw the line at hitting women. You'd be mincemeat by now."

"Do you forget we were once in love?" she said.

"I never loved you."

"Well, I loved *you*, Rock. If we'd stayed together, none of this would have ever happened."

"Are you kidding me? Of course it would have. You've shown your true colors, Nieves. You follow the money. Somehow you'd have tried to get your hands on my old man's money."

"You don't know that."

"Sure I do. That's what you've done here. You tried your best, but it backfired, and it got me, Reid, and the rest of us all implicated in the bastard's murder. I swear to God, I won't let my wife go down for this."

Nieves rolled her eyes. "Your precious wife. That uptight attorney?"

"You mention her again, and I'll have no problem breaking my rule about women."

I needed to take control of this situation before my big brother did something he'd regret. "We're all here. Is there anything you haven't told us? You seriously don't know who attacked Leta?"

"No," Manny said. "We don't. At least *I* don't."

Hoss darted Manny a glare. "You think I'm keeping things from you?"

"I think you and Nieves might be. Leta and I were along for the ride here. You two were the brains behind this whole stupid thing."

"You didn't think it was stupid when there was money involved," Hoss retorted.

"For the love of God..." I rubbed at my forehead. "Rock and I have places to be, so let's get this settled. Now."

"Reid's right," Rock agreed. "You tell me right now who attacked Leta. And why."

"We don't know," Hoss finally said. "We don't know why, either, though we've speculated that it was because she met with your brother a few weeks ago."

"Now why don't I believe you?" Rock said sarcastically.

"I'm with my brother," I added. "The two of you"—I gestured to Hoss and Nieves—"are still hiding something."

"You ran out on me in Vegas when Leta was attacked, Nieves. But now you left her alone in the hospital? Doesn't jibe."

"Sure it does. She's going to be fine."

"She's still drugged up for the pain!" Rock roared.

"I know, but her life isn't in danger. To be honest..."

Rock scoffed. "You've never been honest a day in your life."

"For God's sake, would you let me speak?"

I nodded slightly to Rock. We needed every piece of information out there. If we let Nieves talk, she might slip up and reveal something.

"Fine," he said. "Go ahead."

Nieves cleared her throat. "Hoss and I... We talked after Leta was attacked. We admitted that we'd gotten in over our heads. I knew if I disappeared, that would draw you out here, Rock."

"You're still deluding yourself that I have feelings for you?"

"You're here, aren't you?"

"For fuck's sake." Rock advanced toward her.

"Okay, okay," she said. "We figured it would get *someone* here. We need your help."

This time I laughed. Seriously just burst into bellowing laughter. "You'll get no help from us."

"You might want to rethink that position," Hoss said. "If Nieves and I tell our stories, the focus will come off the two of you and onto someone at the NYPD."

"Right," Rock said. "And I have some swampland in Florida that I think you want to buy."

"Not only that," I added, "the two of you will be hauled in for questioning and possibly charged. After all, how else could you get a phone call that the deed was done before the crime was committed, Nieves? And you..." I turned to Hoss. "You're an attorney, for God's sake. You know what will happen."

"I think I can get a deal for immunity for the two of us," Hoss said. "We have info the police don't."

"Except you don't," I said. "All you did was leak the phone call our father made to Rock pretending to be me. They already know that."

"But if we cooperate—" Nieves began.

"They know who you are already," I said.

"Maybe they don't." Hoss rubbed his jawline

"They do. How else do you think they got to Leta? If they wanted anything from you, they'd have brought you in already. You have nothing to offer us."

"But—"

Rock kicked Hoss in the jaw to shut him up. "No buts. This is over."

I stifled a jerk when my burner phone vibrated in my pocket. The only person who had this number was Buck.

I walked out of earshot of the others and put the phone to my ear. "Yeah?"

30

LACEY

I couldn't wait with the information. I called a night meeting with Riley, Matt, Roy, and Charlie. They met me in our hotel suite.

"I've got Morgan." I held up the thumb drive.

Roy looked to the ceiling. "You sure it's safe here?"

I nodded. "Rock had this place wired while I was locked up. His guys didn't find anything else while they were here."

Roy breathed a sigh of relief. "Good deal."

"Morgan's dirty," I said. "I've got proof. He's setting me up, though I still haven't figured out why. But I've got him dead to rights asking for a bribe right here." I hooked the thumb drive into my laptop and played the video.

"Nice job." Riley smiled. "Is this really over now?"

"Unfortunately, no," I said. "We can prove Morgan's dirty, but that doesn't make the case go away. Someone else will take over, but the fact that the evidence against me is purely circumstantial will help. I believe Morgan must have fabricated evidence to get the DA to go along with the charges against me. Either that or the DA is in on it too."

"Don't they have to tell you what they've got on you?" Matt asked.

"Technically, yeah." I shook my head. "But we're dealing with people who don't think the rules apply to them."

"I can't believe Morgan actually came to see you," Charlie said.

"I was skeptical myself. He was looking for Rock, and I was shaken for a minute."

"You hid it well," Matt said. "You looked cool as ever in the video."

"I'm glad I pulled it off. Now, though, we have to figure out who's on the up and up at the NYPD that we can take this to."

"I'll check that out in the morning," Charlie said. "I can get Jarrod on board."

"No, not Jarrod."

"I thought Terrence was the leak," Charlie said.

"Terrence is definitely not clean," I said, "but Jarrod used to work for Derek, so let's leave him out of this. Plus, he and Terrence are good friends."

Charlie nodded. "Got it." She made some notes on her phone.

"I wish Rock and Reid were here," Riley said. "They'd know exactly what to do with this info."

"Should we wait for them?" Charlie asked me.

I shook my head. "I don't want to wait. We have no idea how long they'll be gone, and I don't want to sit on this. If Morgan's asking for bribes, he's antsy. He could up and disappear, and then we're sunk."

Charlie nodded. "Got it."

"I've been thinking..." Riley cleared her throat.

"What?" I asked.

"I'm the only one who's ever been to that island of Dad's. I should be with my brothers."

"Baby"—Matt grabbed her hand—"they'll be fine. They want you here. Safe."

I drew in a breath. "I can't say I'm not worried about Rock, but if anyone can deal with this, he and Reid can. Reid knew Derek better than anyone, and Rock..." I couldn't finish. Rock could be a hothead, and that scared me more than a little.

"Let's go through what we have," Roy suggested.

"Okay," I agreed. "One. The gun used to kill Derek had Rock's fingerprints on it, but Rock wasn't in New York when the murder happened. His gun, the exact same model as the one used, was stolen from his place before the murder took place. However, the serial numbers don't match."

"Except the serial number on the murder weapon was tampered with," Roy added.

"True," I said. "Still, though, we've proved Rock wasn't in New York at the time and couldn't have killed Derek."

"We've got me," I continued. "No alibi, but I *was* in my apartment. Of course, the video from the surveillance that would show me leaving and entering is missing from that time period."

"We've got Zee," Roy said. "Except now she's missing as well. All of our evidence seems to fly the coop."

Riley bit her lower lip. "I'm so worried about her."

"I know, baby," Matt said. "We all are."

Roy went on. "Then there's Nieves. She got a phone call saying Derek had been killed an hour before he actually was killed. The number of the person who called her is untraceable."

"And," Charlie added, "she's far from innocent. Her sister, for some reason, told Manny what was going on during a gynecological exam. That still doesn't sit well with me."

"Me either," I agreed.

"Then there's the man who seems to be at the center of all of this. Father Jim."

"And he's dead," Matt said.

"Yes, apparently by his own hand," I said. "And he left the GPS coordinates to what we assume is Derek's island for us to find."

"Do you think Father Jim was trying for redemption?" Charlie asked. "Offing himself and giving us the clue we needed?"

"Could be," I said. "Or someone could have made it *look* like a suicide and planted the coordinates to send us on a wild goose chase."

"He was a priest, after all," Matt said. "Maybe he had a crisis of conscience."

Riley didn't look convinced. "Honey, I've been around degenerates my entire life. They can't have a crisis of conscience."

"Why not?" her husband asked.

"Because they don't *have* consciences. It's like they're born without souls or something. A good man can do a bad thing and feel regret. A bad man... Well, he's just bad. He can't feel regret. He doesn't have it in him."

"Still," Charlie said, "if Jim wanted to go into the priesthood, he must have been a good man at some point."

Riley shook her head. "No. Remember, he and my father were friends from childhood. If there was ever any good in Jim Wilkins, my father choked it out of him."

"Why would he go into the priesthood, then?" Matt asked.

Riley sighed. "It's a good cover, I guess? I mean, how many news stories have there been about priests abusing children? It's disgusting and sick."

"This entire situation is disgusting and sick," Roy said, grimacing.

I nodded. "At least we have Morgan. Thanks for coming at this time of night."

"It's not like any of us are sleeping well anyway," Riley said. "Not with this hanging over all our heads."

"You got that right." Matt kissed Riley's cheek.

I looked around at my new family. Wonderful people, and not one of them deserved what was going on.

We were making progress, but not quickly enough.

And Rock was gone. He and Reid were en route to some vague coordinates in the Pacific.

The thought I'd been suppressing nudged into my brain.

They were walking into danger.

And I might never see my husband again.

31

REID

"Got some startling news," Buck said.

"Don't keep me in suspense."

"That priest? Father Jim? Turns out he's *not* dead. They fucking revived him."

I nearly lost my footing. Had I heard him right?

"Surprised the hell out of me," Buck continued. "You sure he was dead when you and Rock left his place?"

I racked my brain. "Yeah. Yeah, he was. But he had a faint pulse when we got there. He was unresponsive, though."

"And you guys left before the squad got here?"

"Hell, yeah. We had to. We couldn't let them find us there."

"If he'd only been dead a minute or two, they could have revived him. Or maybe he wasn't dead. You just couldn't feel his pulse."

Possible. I wasn't a damned doctor. He'd sure felt dead to me, though.

Was this good news or bad news? Father Jim being out of the picture had taken one person off our radar, but if he was alive, he could answer questions.

If we could get to him.

"Where is he?" I asked.

"He's at Memorial in ICU."

"I need you to get in to see him."

"I figured you'd say that. I'm already working on it."

"I don't know when Rock and I'll get back. You'll need to coordinate with Leif."

"What about your other siblings?"

"Riley's been through enough. She and Roy are both newly-weds. If we can leave them out of this, that'd be best."

"Right, but isn't Roy the one who actually *saw* Father Jim with your father when that showgirl escaped?"

I cleared my throat. "He is. But if you can do this without him, do it."

"Gotcha. I'll be in touch. Anything else?"

"Nothing." At least not at the moment. No one knew Rock and I were in Helena, and I meant to keep it that way.

"Good enough. Later."

I shoved the burner phone back into my pocket and headed back to where Rock was holding court over Nieves, Hoss, and Manny.

"What's the good news?" I asked my brother.

"I actually have a little," he said.

I lifted my eyebrows.

"Nieves here let something slip that she shouldn't have."

Nieves's pale cheeks were rosy under the starlight. Yeah, rosier than usual. She'd fucked up.

Good.

"Do tell," I said.

Nieves bit her bottom lip.

"Tell him," Rock said. "Or I will, and you won't like my version of the events."

"Okay, okay," she said. "The phone call I got the night your father was killed."

"We already know about that," I said.

"Except your little Freudian slip," Rock said. "Keep talking, Nieves."

Nieves chewed on her lip again.

"I'm fucking ageing here." I darted a glare to her.

"All right. The phone call. I know who made it."

"Oh? The number was untraceable."

"Your brother," she said. "Your brother made the phone call."

My eyebrows nearly flew off my forehead, and my stomach did a flip. Roy? No way.

"Yeah," Rock said. "She flubbed up her story. I was interrogating her about the voice on the other end of the line when she stole that message from my answering machine, and she said it was Roy who made the call the night of the murder. Funny thing happens when you lie, Nieves. You have to keep all the stories straight, and it gets more and more difficult, especially under duress."

"Dumb bitch," Hoss said.

I looked around at the three people. Hoss. Manny. Nieves. If someone asked me who I hated most out of the three, I wasn't sure I could give an answer. I hated them all for different reasons.

My mind raced. We had only Nieves's *claim* that the call was made by Roy. She hadn't met him. Hadn't ever heard his voice. Maybe it was my father pretending to be Roy, as he'd pretended to be me when he called Rock's landline.

Which was still all just a theory...

"Just how the hell do you know it was him?" I demanded.

"He identified himself," she said timidly.

"And this was something you've kept from us this whole fucking time?" I was beginning to see Rock's point about going back on that promise to never hit a woman. "So all we have, then, is you *telling* us it was him. You claiming he identified himself."

"Yes," she said, looking down at her bare feet.

I shook my head. What could I say? Nothing.

I turned to my brother. "Are you thinking what I'm thinking?"

"That our father made that call? Yeah, it's crossed my mind."

I kneaded my temples, trying to ease the throbbing. "He couldn't have done this, right? He couldn't have actually had *himself* killed."

"I don't know, man." Rock rubbed at his stubbled jawline. "At this point, I'm ready to believe just about anything."

"I've considered it," I said. "Going out on his own terms. It's very Derek Wolfe. Maintaining control at all costs. But actually *dying*? Not being able to enjoy the empire he built? That's very *not* Derek Wolfe. What *is* Derek Wolfe is him faking his own death and then living out the rest of his life on a private island in the Pacific."

"Agreed," Rock said.

"Which means," I continued, "our theory that he put this in motion, intending to go out with a bang and then live out his life in paradise makes more sense. Then someone at the NYPD got involved, thanks to these three clowns"—I gestured—"and someone took advantage of what our father had put into motion. Dear old Dad had already made sure the four of us were suspects, so there you go. Easy plan. Derek dies, and we fry for it."

"Right on," Rock said. "That's a lot more believable, and we already know the NYPD got involved thanks to these jerks."

"So why, then," I asked, to myself as much as to Rock, "would Roy—or Dad—call Nieves and tell her he was already dead? It doesn't make any sense."

"What exactly did he say to you?" Rock asked Nieves.

"I don't remember."

"Uh...yeah, you do," I prompted.

"Fine." She huffed. "He said, 'This is Roy Wolfe. It's done.'"

No way. I yanked the stupid beanie off my head and threaded my fingers through my now greasy hair. Roy was not involved in this. Absolutely not.

"It was an imposter," I said. "Roy did *not* make that phone call. He would have told us."

"Bro," Rock said, "Roy has always been kind of a closed book."

"No." I shook my head vehemently. "Don't you see what's happening here? It's our fucking father. He's pitting us against each other from beyond the grave. Motherfucker."

"There is that phone call Roy got, though." Rock paused a moment. "Remember when he called us all to that pub? I'd forgotten about it, because I found Lacey there with that massage therapist who wanted her to pay for his dinner. Fuck it all."

"Right." My mind raced again. "Neither of us took him seriously. We both had other shit on our minds. He was uptight that night. Something was really bothering him, and neither one of us took him seriously. Fuck. Not Roy."

"He's married now," Rock said. "And he's happy. We have to protect him."

"If it was even him. My best guess is still that Dad called Nieves and pretended to be Roy. If not Dad, someone else."

"Who, though? Who would do that?"

"Jim, maybe? Morgan? Someone else at the NYPD who was taking advantage of the situation and wanting to pin it on one of us?"

"Another fucking loose end." Rock twisted his lips. "Man, I could use a drink. What do you have in the house, Hoss?"

"You think I'm giving you any alcohol?"

"I think you'll do whatever my brother wants," I asserted. "We've got you by the balls, remember?"

Rock grabbed Hoss's arm. "I'll take him in and bring back the alcohol. You keep watch on the other two."

I nodded.

One more loose end.

We had to talk to Roy to tie this up, but how? We were supposed to be on our way to the Pacific.

And Zee.

Where was my sweet Zee?

Even with all of the shit raining down on us, she never left my mind for a moment.

I'm coming, I called silently to her. *I'm coming, baby.*

R*eid. I love you so much. I need you. Please come for me. Please!*

The words formed in my mind independently of thought now. Two nights had passed since I'd been brought here. I hadn't left the room, and now it was the middle of the night again.

Reid consumed my thoughts.

He was searching for me. I was sure of it. But would he find me? Diamond had said breadcrumbs had been left, whatever that meant.

So much I hadn't had time to think about since the Wolfes came into my life, and ironically, now I had nothing to do but think.

A conversation I'd had with Riley slid into my mind.

"What did he do to Reid?" I asked.

Riley sighed. "I don't fully know, and even if I did, his story isn't my story. You'd have to ask him."

"I can't. I don't even know him. Yet you're asking me to tell my story."

"Zee, this isn't about us or even about you. It's about clearing all of our names. None of us are willing to go down for his murder when we're all innocent."

I adored Riley. Truly. But her words had been untrue. It *was* about them. About all of them. Proving their innocence was about *them*, not about me.

So much time for my thoughts to invade me.

So much time…

I didn't know Riley's story, but my imagination had conjured up vivid images of Derek Wolfe doing horrid things to his only daughter. And my Reid…

Had he been abused? Hunted?

No. I doubted it. Neither he nor Rock had been. They were both strong as oxen and twice as tough on the inside. Roy was a bit of a question mark, but I doubted it also. He and Charlie seemed deliriously happy, and if he were dealing with some sort of trauma—other than his recent memory of his father's hunting ground, which had led to my rescue—surely I'd be able to see it in his actions.

Sometimes, though, abuse and trauma made a person stronger.

Again my thoughts flashed to Reid, as they always ended up doing.

Riley hadn't known what, if anything, Derek Wolfe had done to his youngest son. Reid had been Derek's right-hand man, so Derek would have had to prepare him for that.

And Derek Wolfe had no problem using physical force. I knew that as well as anyone.

Had he hit Reid? Beat him? Abused him physically? Sexually?

The thoughts raced at me like a stampeding herd of buffalo. Every possible scenario flashed in my mind's eye.

My Reid. My sweet Reid.

What had happened to him?

Then I jerked upward in bed.

The doorknob was clicking.

No. Just no. Diamond said no one would harm me.

I darted my gaze around the dark room. Where to go? Hide in the bathroom? There was no lock on the door. I stood quickly, ready to fight with all I had.

I heaved a relieved sigh when Diamond walked in carrying a tote bag.

"Shh," she said. "Don't talk."

I nodded as she set the bag down and left, clicking the lock in place.

What had she brought? I hurried to the bag and lifted it. It was heavy. I had no light to turn on except for the moonlight streaming in through the etched window.

My stomach growled when I pulled out a loaf of bread wrapped in plastic. Underneath were some fruit and pudding cups in plastic. Then a jar of peanut butter and some—I had to stop myself from squealing—bars of Belgian dark chocolate. At the very bottom was a plastic knife and spoon along with my laundered clothes.

Bless you, Diamond.

Middle of the night or not, I couldn't help breaking into the chocolate. I opened one bar and broke off a bite-sized piece. Its smooth deliciousness melted against my tongue. I'd read somewhere that chocolate was supposed to ease depression.

I wasn't depressed so much as just chronically worried. About Reid. About myself. About pretty much everything.

The chocolate was velvety, but when the flavor dissipated, I found myself no less worried.

No less alone.

At least tomorrow I wouldn't starve between breakfast and lunch.

Who was Diamond, anyway?

For the first time in a while, I said a prayer. For Reid. For his family. And for Diamond.

33

REID

Dave and Mike got on a plane to Honolulu at three a.m. Coach again, and Rock had the aisle seat, damn him. I found myself pushing my feet against the floor of the plane, trying to get there faster.

Of course, I had no idea whether I'd find Zee once we got to the coordinates.

I had to believe we would, though. If I let myself think otherwise, I wouldn't be able to go on.

"Fuckers," Rock muttered under his breath.

After Rock and I each took a shot of Hoss's shitty bourbon, we'd left Nieves, Hoss, and Manny, quickly calling Buck to get eyes on them twenty-four-seven, which we should have been doing this whole damned time. Not one of us had foreseen their involvement. Hell, Rock had thought the two weekend bikers were his friends.

Nothing pissed me off worse than people sliding under my radar. Derek Wolfe taught me better than that.

And now...Roy.

Did I know *any* of my siblings?

Rock had been sent away when I was only nine years old,

and I spent most of my childhood and early adult years envying Riley for the attention our father heaped on her. I'd been wrong about both of them.

But Roy...

I never knew him, really. He was such a recluse. He spent most of his time in his room when he was home, and though he took some of our father's abuse, most of it was saved for me.

I didn't let myself think about it most of the time, but damn...

I'd taken a lot of physical abuse from the man.

His hand. His belt. A yard stick once, and not just a regular yard stick, but a thick one. He beat me over the ass and back with it, leaving marks.

The marks had faded over time and were now hardly visible.

Even now, I remembered the pain.

Remembered biting my lip to bleeding to keep from crying out, determined he'd never hear me wail.

I hadn't always been successful, but most of the time I was able to hold back.

It just pissed him off more, and he took it out on my hide.

It was a miracle I didn't have more scarring than I did. Just a few marks on my back that looked like nothing more than stretch marks from a growth spurt during adolescence. Most people never noticed them, and if they did, I gave them the stretch mark story.

I didn't dare make any of this public now. Only gave me more of a motive to have him done in. Same reason why Riley hadn't gone public—not that she'd want to anyway. What she went through was intensely private and I honestly didn't want to know. My imagination was bad enough.

And Zee...

Those scars at the top of her breasts. I still didn't know her whole story, and...

Damn.

I had to find her. I just had to. She couldn't go through more.

If only I'd let her be.

She'd be home now, in Vegas, in her bed but possibly still awake after her ten o'clock show.

Why hadn't I left well enough alone?

I wouldn't know the love I feel, but she'd be safe. Safe and sound and free of all the shit I'd piled on her.

As God is my witness, when I find you, Zee, I'll let you go. Let you live your life. And I'll take care of you. You'll have whatever you need and want for the rest of your life, and if part of that is to never see me again, I'll grant it. Anything you desire, Zee. Anything.

Even if it breaks my heart.

Rock nudged me out of my thoughts.

"Yeah?" I whispered.

"Do they still have those credit card phones on planes like they did back in the early two thousands?"

"They discontinued that service in 2006. Where've you been?"

"In Montana, dude, and not having a lot of cash to be flying places."

I nodded. How easy it was to forget where we'd all been a mere fifteen years ago, when so much had happened in our lives in the last month.

"We need to call Roy. Find out if what Nieves said is true," Rock said.

"In an emergency, the flight crew can make a call for us," I said, "but we don't want to draw attention to ourselves. It'll have to wait until we land."

"Fuck." Rock inhaled sharply.

"I know. I think she's either lying, or whoever it was used Roy's name. It definitely wasn't Roy." I wanted to believe my words. In fact, I did. Sort of.

"Something doesn't sit right with me," Rock said. "It couldn't have been Dad. I know that was our first thought, but it couldn't have been, right? Not when he was dead an hour later."

"Don't know." I let out a sigh. "I just don't fucking know."

"I don't think Nieves is lying," Rock said after a pause. "We've got her good and scared. Remember when I told you I was sending someone in to frighten her? She disappeared before he got there."

"Why do you think she's scared, then?"

"Just the look on her face tonight. She's usually confident as all hell, but now she's in over her head."

"I'm wondering..."

"What?"

My mind raced. "If we can find a way to pin this whole thing on her and Hoss. Manny, too."

"What about Leta?"

"She's been through enough."

"You know," Rock said, "Leta and Manny may have just been along for the ride, but they're every bit as responsible as Nieves and Hoss are."

I nodded. Rock was right. We couldn't go soft.

"I can't believe what I'm about to say..." Rock went on.

"What?"

He shook his head and adjusted his Yankees cap. "They're cunts, all of them, but they didn't kill our father. Pinning it on another innocent person isn't the answer."

I sighed. He was right, of course. At least Zee had an ironclad alibi. She was safe from charges.

But was she safe from everything else?

I was on my way to her. I had to believe that. Those GPS coordinates had been left for a reason. The question was...did Father Jim try to kill himself? Or did someone else make it look like he had?

We could find the answer. He was alive.

But we were far away from him at the moment.

Rock was right. We needed to contact Roy. Buck would take care of Father Jim.

Right now, all I wanted was to get to Zee.

I'd go down for a murder I didn't commit if it meant saving the woman I loved.

34

LACEY

I jerked upward in bed.

Had I actually slept? One of my burner phones—I had three—was buzzing and vibrating against the nightstand. Only Rock had this particular number.

I grabbed the phone. "Hello?" I said breathlessly.

"Hey, baby."

"Rock! Thank God! Where are you? Are you all right?"

"Shh. Calm down. Reid and I are fine. I'm in the Honolulu airport, using a pay phone."

"With a credit card?"

"Yeah, but don't worry. It's in my alias's name. We're good."

"Thank God. When did you get in?"

"Just a few minutes ago. I need you to do something for me."

"Of course. Anything."

"I need to talk to Roy."

I glanced at the clock on the night table. Six-thirty a.m. "He was just here a few hours ago. That reminds me! I have some incredible news!"

"What?"

I filled him in quickly on Morgan's attempt to bribe me.

"That's awesome, baby."

"What should I do?" I asked. "Obviously, I'd take it to the NYPD in a normal situation, but it seems half the force is dirty these days."

"Reid has a guy. Buck Moreno. Give it to him. He'll know who to trust on the force."

"How do I get in touch with him?"

"Just a minute."

I waited while Rock presumably conferred with Reid. Seconds seemed to morph into hours, until finally...

"Jot down this number."

I hurriedly grabbed a pen and wrote down the digits Rock repeated.

"Use a burner, not this one. Tell him who you are and what you have. He'll come to you. He knows how to make sure he's not followed or watched."

"Good. Good."

"Now, I need you to get Roy for me. Bring him to the suite, and then call this number. I'll be waiting."

"Why didn't you just call him?" A bad feeling squirmed in my gut.

"I want him at the suite, where I know we can speak freely."

"He's probably asleep. I called everyone here in the middle of the night to show them the video."

"He'll wake up. This is important."

"What do you want me to tell him?"

"Just tell him it's important. That Reid and I need him. He'll come."

"Okay." I gulped. "I'll get him here as soon as I can."

"We'll be waiting. Reid's talking to the captain of our private plane now—the one that will take us to the coordinates."

The coordinates. Rock and Reid could be walking into mega danger. But I couldn't let myself think about that. Not now.

"How long do I have?" I asked.

"As long as it takes,' he said. "But make sure it doesn't take long. We want to get moving on the Pacific as soon as possible."

"Got it. And Rock?"

"Yeah, baby?"

"I love you. I love you so much."

"I love you too, Lace. More than you'll ever know."

"Come back to me. Please."

"You can count on it."

After the call ended, I called Roy on another of my burners. It rang several times, and just when I was sure it would go to voicemail, he finally answered.

"Roy, it's Lacey. I need you to come back to the hotel suite."

"Charlie and I finally just fell asleep."

"I know. I'm so sorry, but it's important. Rock and Reid are in Honolulu, and they said they have to talk to you before they get on the plane to go to the coordinates."

"Fuck."

"What is it?" Charlie's voice.

"We have to go back to Lacey's suite."

"Why?"

"Hell if I know."

"Please," I said into the burner phone. "It's important."

"Yeah, I know. We'll be there as soon as we can."

ROY AND CHARLIE arrived an hour later, looking like they'd both just rolled out of bed. I quickly scanned the hallway.

"No one followed us," Roy said.

"Are you sure?"

He nodded. "Trust me. We've both been on high alert since this shit started."

"Good. Have a seat." I grabbed the burner phone and called the number Rock had given me.

"Lace?" he said.

"It's me. Roy and Charlie are here."

"Does that burner have speaker?"

"I have no idea." I took it from my ear and checked. "Yeah it does."

"Good. Put it on speaker."

I pressed the button and sat the phone on the coffee table. "It's on. Can you hear me?"

"Yeah," Rock's voice came through clearly but softly among the hustle and bustle in the background. I understood. He was in the middle of the airport, but still, ears were everywhere.

"I'm here, Rock," Roy said. "Charlie's with me. What's going on?"

"Bro," Rock said, "I want you to know, before I ask you what I'm going to ask you, that Reid and I trust you implicitly. Got it?"

Roy's face went pale. "Uh...okay. What the hell is going on?"

Rock cleared his throat. "Did you call Nieves Romero the night Dad was killed?"

Roy's eyebrows rose, as did both Charlie's and mine. What was Rock talking about?

"Uh...no. I didn't even *know* Nieves Romero at that time. You know that."

"Here's the thing," Rock said. "You know that call she got an hour before Dad was killed? The one we can't trace?"

"Uh-huh." Roy swallowed.

"Nieves says the call was from you. That whoever called identified himself as Roy Wolfe."

Roy's jaw dropped. He said nothing.

I spoke up. "What else did she say?"

"That's it. She said the whole conversation was, 'This is Roy Wolfe. It's done.'"

"She's lying." From Roy.

"That was our first thought," Rock said. "We knew you hadn't made that call, but we had her scared, Roy. We think she's done lying."

"Which means," I said, "whoever made that call was pretending to be Roy."

"Why?" Roy asked. "I had nothing to do with Dad."

"We know," Rock said, "but whoever put this sequence of events in motion wanted all of us as suspects. Dad had already set it up that way, but this supposed phone call makes you more of a suspect."

"I was at my place that night," Roy said. "You all know that. I was alone. Painting. You know I paint at night sometimes."

"He does," Charlie confirmed.

"Hey, we're not questioning you," Rock said. "We believe you, but we wanted to let you know about it and also ask you point blank."

"So a part of you *didn't* trust me," Roy said, sighing.

Silence on the other end, but only for a moment.

"We trust you, Roy," Rock said. "But you were freaked about all this at first. Remember when you called Reid and me to that brew pub to tell us you'd gotten a phone call?"

Roy said nothing.

I remembered. It was the night I had dinner with that massage therapist, Brent. Man, he'd been a flake.

"Yeah," Roy finally said. "Whoever it was never called again. It was a guy's voice, but that's all I know."

"We're not sure," Rock said, "but it was probably someone on the inside of the NYPD. You got freaked because you were dealing with that memory of Dad and Zee."

"True enough," Roy agreed.

"There's no way to find out who made that call to you," Rock said, "but can you tell us anything that you haven't already told us?"

"Rock—"

"Don't take this the wrong way, bro. We trust you. But you were a mess before you remembered that day in the elevator. Part of you wasn't thinking straight, so maybe you left something out."

Roy furrowed his brow while Charlie entwined his fingers with hers.

"It's okay, babe," she said. "Just tell them."

Roy shook his head. "I would if I could. There's nothing. I swear."

"Good enough," Rock said. "Just know someone impersonated you on the phone, so watch your back."

"I always do. Charlie and I are just living one day at a time. Damn. When will this be over?"

"Soon," Rock said. "It has to be. We need to get Lace off the hook, and we need to find Zee. It all has to happen quickly. Reid and I won't let you down."

"We know that," Roy said. "Charlie and I won't either."

"Anything else we need to know before we become unavailable somewhere on the Pacific?" Rock asked.

"Lacey told you about Morgan, I assume," Charlie said.

"Yeah. She's going to give the info to one of Reid's men."

"Then I can't think of anything else," Roy said. "But guys, be careful. Please."

"Yes, please," I echoed.

"We will. We'll find Zee, and we'll put an end to all of this. Love you all. Bye."

Then the click of the receiver.

A feeling of pure dread shrouded me.

Would that be the last time I ever heard my husband's voice?

35

ZEE

I jerked upward once more.

Darkness streamed in through my one window.

I gasped at the shadow standing over me.

Before the scream left my throat, a hand clamped over my mouth.

"Shh. Don't make a sound. I'm not here to hurt you."

A woman's voice. Diamond's voice. I nodded jerkily.

"I was planning to drug you to move you," she continued, "but I don't want to do it. So I need you to cooperate. Understand?"

Again, I nodded.

"I'm going to move my hand now. Promise me you won't scream."

I nodded for the third time, and Diamond slowly unclamped her fingers from around my mouth.

"Don't talk," she whispered. "I'm moving you to a nicer place, but it's even more imperative that you be quiet."

"Where?" I asked.

"I said don't talk!" she whispered harshly.

I bit my lower lip. It was the middle of the night. I still had no idea where I was. Only that it was most likely someplace tropical.

"Please," I whispered. "You have to tell me something. It's not fair. I'm here against my will, Diamond."

"I know that. I know…"

"Please…"

"I wish I could. Now quiet. I don't want to have to use this." She pulled a syringe out of her pocket.

I clamped my mouth shut. No drugs. No. Not again. Whoever brought me here had drugged me, and I didn't want to be under any influence again. Not after all I'd done to get clean years ago.

"Stay here a minute." Diamond left the room and was back a moment later with a wheelchair. "Sit down."

"I'll walk."

"No. You're not even supposed to be here. Please, just do as I say."

I sighed softly and sat down in the chair.

"Close your eyes. Pretend like you're out of it. I'm going to put you in the back of a van. It's a short drive."

I nodded, closed my eyes, and dropped my head. What about my things? My clothes? The food supply she'd provided? Would she bring it all? I wanted to ask, but I didn't. I couldn't risk her injecting me with some unknown substance.

I stayed still and quiet as a mouse as she wheeled me out into the darkness. I ached to open my eyes, to get some idea of where I was, but I didn't dare.

She wheeled me down a ramp and across an even but slightly bumpy surface, and then I tilted as she presumably wheeled me up a steeper ramp and into the van.

"Stay still," she whispered. "I can't belt you in, but I'll drive carefully."

I didn't nod. Didn't dare to.

I kept my eyes shut during the drive, pushing down every urge to look. I'd only see the back of a van in the dark of night, so why risk it?

Reid, where are you? I love you so much.

After what seemed like an hour or so—I'd lost all track of time—Diamond stopped the van. A few seconds later, she opened the back. I heard her set down the ramp, and then she wheeled me down.

She moved her head so close to my ear I could feel her breath. "Don't talk," she said so quietly I could barely hear her with her lips at my ear.

I didn't dare nod. I stayed quiet.

She wheeled me up a slight incline and then inside. I could tell because the humid air was replaced by the dry cool of air conditioning. I listened, trying to hear anything that might give me a clue about my surroundings.

Nothing.

No noise at all.

Not overly surprising, since it was the middle of the night.

Finally, the click of a door.

A moment later, she whispered, "We're here. Be very quiet. Get out of the chair, and lie on the bed."

I opened my eyes. The room was dark, but already I could see that it was bigger than where I'd been.

"Where—"

"Shh. You're supposed to be out cold. Remember?"

I nodded and lay down on the bed. This one was bigger. Queen-sized at least, compared to the narrow twin in the first room.

"Go to sleep," she said. "I'll bring your breakfast in the morning."

She whisked out with the wheelchair and clicked the door locked.

I wasn't sure whether I should be frightened or relieved.
I was both.

36

REID

My brother looked green.

Seriously green.

We'd taken a puddle jumper from Honolulu to an unnamed island that was used only as a gateway to the privately owned islands in a small cluster about four hundred miles south of Hawaii.

A private ferry would transport us to the coordinates.

We still used our aliases and paid for everything in cash except where a credit card was required. Then we used the cards in our alias names.

The ferry. The waters weren't rough today, but my older brother still looked like he was about to hurl. I couldn't help a chuckle.

"What's so fucking funny?"

"The great Rock Wolfe is seasick."

He swallowed hard. "I'm fine."

"Dude, there's no shame in being seasick. You've never been on a boat before."

"And you have?"

"Dad's yachts, of course."

"Poor me." Rock grimaced.

"It'll pass once we get to solid land," I said. "In the meantime, try to focus on something on the horizon."

Except that there was nothing on the horizon. Shit. Were these dead coordinates? Was Father Jim leading us to some point in the water that had no meaning to anything?

"Okay." Rock gazed toward the endless ocean depths. "I see it."

Sure enough, a sliver of land appeared in the horizon.

"It won't be long now," I said.

"If I can make it without losing my lunch."

ROCK DIDN'T LOSE his lunch. The boat docked at the island recognized by the GPS coordinates. Several uniformed workers got us docked, and a jeep waited for us.

"What is this place?" I asked our driver.

"You mean you don't know?" The driver was pale-skinned but had a definite Pacific Islander accent. "How did you get here if you don't know where you are?"

"We're here on business," Rock said.

Sure. Good enough. When in doubt, say you're on business.

Of course, we were still wearing our very non-business clothes—Mike and Dave Bush's clothes. Who cared? Maybe they were travel clothes.

"What kind of business?" the driver asked.

"The confidential kind." Rock dug a hundred dollar bill out of his wallet and handed it to the young man. "Take us somewhere where no one will know we're here."

He nodded and drove into what appeared to be a luxury resort. No sign indicated the name of the place, though. Surely

Derek Wolfe would have put the Wolfe branding somewhere, but not that I could see. At least not yet.

The driver stopped at a large mansion built of stucco and red clay shingles.

"Hey," Rock said. "This is hardly a place where we can keep a low profile."

"I was instructed to bring you here."

"Instructed?" I demanded. "Who the hell are you? Who knows we're here?"

"Diamond," he said. "She's been expecting you."

Diamond?

What the hell?

"Her son left for the US yesterday," the driver said. "He's the one you need to be concerned about. Diamond is on your side. Most people here are on your side, but we still have to be careful."

"Who says there's any side?" Rock said, trying—but failing—to remain calm.

"There is," the driver said, "Mr. Wolfe."

Fuck. Whoever this guy was, he already knew who we were.

"Who the fuck are you?" Rock demanded.

"My name is Remy. I'm a friend."

"I'll be the judge of that. And you've got my identity wrong. I'm David Bush, and this is my brother Mike."

"As you wish. Follow me, please."

Rock and I had armed ourselves before we left Honolulu and paid off the pilot of the puddle jumper to let us on. I knew how to shoot, but I was depending on my big brother if push came to shove. He'd had a lot more experience than I had.

We followed Remy into the house where an older woman was waiting.

"Thank God you're here," she said.

"Who the hell are you?" Rock demanded unceremoniously.

"I'm called Diamond," she said, "but my real name is Irene."

My eyebrows nearly flew off my face. "Irene Lucent?"

"Irene Lucent Wolfe. Yes."

"So you *do* exist," Rock said.

"I do, though your father kept me hidden."

I looked around tentatively. The house was beautifully furnished in a Pacific island theme. "You live here?"

"I do."

"Remy mentioned a son," I said, putting two and two together in my mind. If she had a son...

"Yes. Your father's son. You have an older brother."

I steadied myself before I lost my footing. Rock, though, was steady as...well...a rock.

"What's going on here? You need to start talking now, lady. Where's Zee? And what is this place?"

"Easy," she said. "Jordan—that's your older brother—is in the states. That's why we planned this for now." She turned to me. "Zee is here."

My heart nearly jumped out of my chest. "She's here? Where? Is she all right?"

"She's fine," Diamond said. "Just a little shaken."

"Why?" I demanded. "Why did you bring her here?"

"To get *you* here," she said frankly.

"Then you're the one who left the coordinates in Father Jim's bible?" Rock said.

Diamond furrowed her brow. "Father Jim's bible? No. We left a napkin in the bathroom where Zee was taken. Didn't you find it?"

"No," I said softly.

"We also left a voicemail on your work phone with coordinates," Diamond went on.

"We haven't been using our work phones," Rock said. "We think they're probably tapped."

"Which means someone else might know we're here." I shook my head. "Damn."

I took the dreaded beanie off my head for the last time and riffled my fingers through my hair, which now stood on its own and needed a good wash.

Diamond and her son no doubt had a story to tell us—one we needed to hear. Quickly, too, because others may well be on their way here.

All of this was important. Our lives depended on it.

But only one thing pervaded my mind.

I grabbed my pistol out of its shoulder holster and pointed it at Diamond.

"Take me to Zee," I demanded. "Now."

37

LACEY

A t Rock's and my attorneys' request, I wasn't venturing anywhere. I stayed in the hotel suite, which monitored my every move—along with anyone else who came in contact with me.

I wasn't expecting anyone, so I jumped at the knock on the door.

I checked the peephole.

Moira Bancroft, one of the Wolfe staff attorneys.

The attorney in whose office Zee had found my pink handkerchief and a stack of my old business cards.

I sighed. Why not open the door? If I could get her to talk, I'd have it all documented.

I opened the door. "Good morning, Moira."

"Mrs. Wolfe."

"Lacey, please. Would you like to come in?"

She nodded and walked into the living area of the suite.

"Can I get you anything? Coffee?"

"No. I won't stay long, but I do need to talk to you."

"Of course. Have a seat." I gestured to the sofa and chairs.

She took the sofa, so I, rather than sit next to her, sat in a chair across from her. "What's on your mind?" I asked.

She cleared her throat and fidgeted, lacing and unlacing her fingers. "I just wanted to tell you face to face... I did *not* steal your handkerchief or your business cards. I hope you can believe me. I have no idea how either of them got into my office."

"Relax," I told her. "You're an intelligent woman and an excellent attorney. If you had stolen them, you certainly wouldn't have left them out in plain sight."

"Yes." She nodded, her eyes wide. "But I didn't steal them."

"I want to believe you. Do you have any idea how they got there?"

"I don't, but I've been asking around. Henny recalls finding Terrence outside my office while Detective Morgan was questioning Zee. I don't want to accuse him without any hard evidence, but that's the only clue I've found so far."

I nodded. Terrence. Yes. Terrence who faked a personal day on his calendar the day someone—presumably Derek—made a phone call to Rock in Montana from Reid's office line.

Moira was right. This wasn't hard evidence, but the evidence the cops had used to arrest me wasn't much better.

All circumstantial.

"Are you sure there's nothing else?" I asked.

"I hate being a..." She shook her head. "Well, for lack of a better word, tattletale. But that's all I've found. I've questioned everyone close to my office."

"I'll make sure someone asks Terrence what he was doing over in the legal department, but of course, as Reid's executive assistant, he could easily have a reason."

"He and I haven't been working on anything together, though."

"He could have just been walking by."

She nodded. "All Henny could tell me is that he was outside the office."

"She didn't see him arrive?"

"No. She was in the restroom, and he was there when she came back."

Hmm. Convenient. He could have been waiting for Henny to vacate her post. "Was he standing there? Or just walking by?"

"I asked her the same thing. She wasn't sure, but as soon as he saw her, he nodded to her and walked on."

"I see." The information wasn't overly helpful, but it was enough for me to question Terrence myself.

Except I couldn't.

My attorneys wanted me here. I could call Terrence over, but he'd ask about Reid and Rock. Right now, the official party line was that they were working round the clock on the Wolfe Cinquieme contract issues and couldn't be disturbed.

On the other hand...

I was a skilled attorney. If Terrence came here, maybe I could get something out of him.

It was tempting, but no.

I needed to continue to lie low. If we didn't get this solved, I could be going down for a crime I didn't commit. The DA was already pressuring my attorney to strike a plea.

No way in hell.

"Moira," I said, "I appreciate your candor. You have to admit, though, that those items didn't just appear by themselves. Didn't you notice them?"

She shook her head. "I don't look on the top of my file cabinet a lot. In fact, I can't remember the last time I did, but if I had, and if the hanky had been there, I'd have noticed. As for the business cards, I do open the top drawer to my desk quite a bit to grab the tube of lip balm I keep there. I'd have noticed them, which makes me think Terrence—or someone else—planted them during Zee's interrogation."

I was thinking the same thing, but I didn't want to agree too wholeheartedly with Moira just yet. Let her think she might be in trouble. It would keep her watching her back, which meant if she was in this, she might slip up.

"Is there anything else you can tell me, Moira? Anything that seemed out of place to you?"

"Anything?" she asked. "Or any*one*?"

I lifted my eyebrows. Interesting differentiation. "Either."

"Just Terrence on that day." She met my gaze, her eyes unreadable.

Did she want me to continue to probe? She was a good attorney. She had a good poker face.

"Just Terrence that day," I echoed. "What about any other day since Derek Wolfe was killed? Did anything—or anyone—seem out of place?"

"Only once," she said, "but it was only a day or two after the murder."

"I'm listening."

"I don't see how it could be related, but Mr. Wolfe's lady friend was in a heated conversation with Terrence in the hallway."

"Mr. Wolfe's lady friend?"

"Yeah. The supermodel. Fonda Burke."

Fonda Burke. She'd been at the reading of Derek's will, and she'd left in a huff along with Connie Wolfe when they both found they hadn't been provided for.

I'd thought nothing of it at the time, but...

She had an alibi. The police had ruled her out almost instantaneously. She'd been out of town, and she provided documentation. None of her fingerprints had been found near the scene of the crime.

Which in itself was odd, since she and Derek were involved at the time. Her fingerprints showed up at other places in the penthouse, of course. Derek's bedroom. His bathroom. The kitchen.

But in the living room, where Derek was killed, Fonda's prints were noticeably absent.

How had we let her slip through our fingers?

I shook my head. Easy enough. We'd all been dealing with Morgan's ceaseless interrogation and clearing our own names. And...we'd been led on a different path. Nieves. Hoss. Manny. All of whom were involved, but none of whom were guilty of the actual crime.

Yes.

Yes, indeed.

We'd been manipulated quite well.

We'd been played like an ace up the winner's sleeve.

Fonda had all but disappeared after the reading of the will. Why hadn't any of us taken notice?

Fonda. Terrence. Both were involved somehow.

But how?

38

ZEE

"**B**aby. Oh my God!"

I jerked out of sleep and opened my eyes.

A figure loomed above me. A voice. *I'm dreaming. I must be dreaming.*

"Zee, baby. It's me."

I reached toward the mirage, expecting to feel only air.

Instead, my fingers met a stubbly cheek. I traced the nose, the jawline. The image was still a blur, but...

"Reid?"

"Oh, baby. Thank God you're okay. We're going to get you out of here." He grabbed my shoulders and pulled me against his hard body. "I'm so sorry. I'm so sorry."

"For what?" I choked out.

"That I didn't protect you. Whatever they've done to you, they'll pay. I promise you. They'll wish they'd never been born."

"But..."

He squeezed me so hard, I nearly lost my breath.

"Reid..."

"Yeah? What is it, baby?"

"They... They didn't hurt me. I mean, other than taking me against my will."

He pulled back a little and whispered in my ear. "You're okay? You're really okay?"

I nodded against his cheek.

"Still, they'll pay. They took you from me. How?"

"I...don't actually remember."

He pulled back farther so our gazes met. "They drugged you."

"Yes. But that was the only time. They haven't drugged me since I got here. And they've fed me. Gave me a warm bed, some clothes, a bathroom."

He shook his head. "And this all seems okay to you?"

Did it? None of it was okay, but it had been a heck of a lot better than the previous time I'd been taken against my will. No one had hurt me this time. No one had forced me to run for my life.

"Not okay," I said. "Just... Well, lots better than the last time."

He pulled me against him once more, kissing the side of my neck. "My Zee. My baby. You deserve so much more than to think this is okay because they haven't hurt you. This is *not* okay, and whoever is responsible will pay."

"Diamond..."

"Yes. I promise Diamond will pay."

"No." I shook my head against his shoulder. "She took care of me. She's been nice to me."

He pulled back, met my gaze. "She has?"

"Yes. Please don't hurt her."

"Then she'll be well taken care of," he said.

Then his lips were on mine, and everything around us stopped. Time suspended itself as Reid kissed me. I eagerly returned the kiss. *I love you!* my heart sang.

I had to tell him. Had to tell him my true feelings. He was here. Here rescuing me, just like Diamond said he would.

I had to tell him. Had to...

But the kiss mesmerized me. Took me away, to a place I'd only visited in my dreams. Those few dreams that weren't nightmares.

I melted into him as he deepened the kiss. Where was I? I still didn't know, and for the first time, I didn't care.

Only Reid existed. Reid and me, in this perfect bubble of sweet arousal. Our lips slid together, our tongues tangled, and lust radiated through me.

Nothing mattered. Nothing except Reid and this moment.

Too soon, he pulled back when someone entered the room. "What?" he yelled.

"Reid, she's okay. We need to—"

Reid moved gently away from me, and then stood, all gentleness gone from his demeanor. He was now a tropical storm. "Get the fuck out of here, Rock."

"Look, I know you're glad to see her—"

"Glad to see her? That doesn't even begin to define how I'm feeling."

"Dude, I know. I know the feeling. But we have to deal with this woman. With our newfound brother."

Newfound brother? What were they talking about?

I didn't know. Didn't care. I just wanted Reid's lips back on mine. His body inside mine. His soul entangled with mine.

His love. I wanted his love.

But even if he could never give me his love, I wanted to give him mine.

Now. Right now.

"Reid?" I said.

He turned away from Rock and met my gaze. "Yeah, Zee?"

I inhaled deeply. "I love you. I love you, Reid."

His lips parted, and his eyes... They widened slightly. Was he surprised? How could he be? Who in her right mind wouldn't love him?

That suspension of time during the kiss? I wanted it to resume. Really. He didn't answer. Just stared into me with those beautiful blue eyes.

Say something!

"Baby?" he finally said.

Did he expect me to repeat it? If he wasn't going to return my sentiment, no way was I saying it again.

"You love me?"

I nodded. I still was determined not to repeat the words. Never, unless he could say them to me.

"How? After all my father did to you? How could you love me?"

Really? *This* was where he was going?

How should I respond? I weighed my options. Finally I decided on, "You're not your father, Reid."

He smiled then. "No, I'm not."

Still no return of the words. I pressed my lips together. I knew this was a possibility going in. I was okay. I wanted him to know how I felt, even if he could never feel the same way. It was okay. *I* was okay.

He closed the door on his brother then and walked back to the bed where I sat. He pulled me to my feet and cupped both my cheeks, making shivers run through me.

"I never dreamed you could love me, Zee. I never did. I gave up hoping."

I didn't reply.

"I love you too. I should have told you when I married you. I should have told you at dinner, before they..." He shook his head. "I should have protected you better. I should have protected what I love more than anything."

My heart raced and my skin warmed as I stared into his eyes. I looked for something—anything—to negate his words.

But all I saw was love. Pure love.

Reid Wolfe loved *me*. Troubled and broken me. *He loves me.*

His lips claimed mine once more. We were alone in this room, and I wanted it. I wanted it all. I wanted his cock inside me, his lips on every inch of me. And I... I wanted my lips on every inch of him as well.

But Rock... And Diamond...

I pulled away and broke the kiss.

"What is it, baby?" he asked.

"Where am I? And what am I doing here? So many questions, Reid. And Rock is right outside."

"Fuck Rock. And fuck everything else."

"No." I shook my head. "As much as I love you and want you this instant, we need to see to business. Right? What is this place, and why did someone bring me here?"

He pressed his lips to my cheek. "I think I just fell in love with you even more."

Then a knock on the door.

Reid groaned, stood, and opened it. His brother stood in the doorway.

"Hey," he said. "Diamond says her son won't be back here for a few days. She's going to show me around this place and give me the scoop. Remy will drive us. So...you two will be alone. For a few hours. But that's it, Reid. That's it. So make it fucking count."

"I should go with you."

"For Christ's sake, bro, I'm trying to help you here. Just take the gift, all right? Take it, because when I come back, we're going to get to the bottom of this."

Reid nodded and murmured, "Thanks," before closing the door. "Does this thing lock?" he asked me.

"It does, but only from the outside. Diamond locked me in."

"She did?" his cheeks reddened.

"She did, but she was protecting me."

He inhaled deeply, as if trying to calm himself down. "I hate the thought of you being imprisoned like this."

"I'm not fond of it either, but no one harmed me. I swear to you."

"So we can't lock ourselves in."

"No."

He gripped my shoulders. "I'm going to make love to you, Zee. I'm going to fuck you hard. Then I'm going to fuck you slow. Then, I'm going to start all over again and again until Rock knocks on that door. And since we can't lock it, anyone can walk in on us at any time. Are you good with that?"

Not only was I good with it, the idea turned me on, though I had no idea why.

I nodded.

"Tell me," he said. "Tell me you want me to make love to you. To fuck you. To cover every inch of your body with my lips, teeth, and tongue. Tell me, Zee. I want to hear you say it."

"Yes," I sighed softly. "I want all of that. All of that and more. I want every part of you touching every part of me. I love you, Reid. I love every part of you."

"God, I love you too. So fucking much." He tangled his fingers in my hair. "Your hair is so soft, so beautiful. God, I've missed you. I was so afraid... So afraid I'd never see you again. Never get to tell you—"

And his lips came down on mine once more.

39

ROCK

I owed my brother a good fuck. He'd found his love, and if the tables had been turned and I'd found Lacey, nothing and no one would have stopped me from being with her.

I sat in the front seat with Remy, and we were ready to depart to God knew where, when my burner phone buzzed with a number I didn't recognize.

"Yeah?" I said.

"Rock?"

"Who wants to know?"

"This is Buck Moreno, Reid's PI."

"You're the SEAL. Why aren't you calling him?"

"He gave me this number and said to call you if he ever didn't answer."

Yeah, I bet he didn't answer. "He's indisposed at the moment. What can I help you with?'

"I've got some sensitive intel. Is this line secure?"

Yeah, the line was secure, but I still didn't trust Remy and Diamond. They seemed okay, but appearances could deceive. I knew that better than anyone now, thanks to Hoss, Manny, and Nieves.

I turned to Remy. "I've got to take this. Give me a few minutes." I exited the jeep and walked about a hundred yards away.

"I'm here," I said into the phone. "What have you got?"

He cleared his throat. "Father Jim Wilkins is dead."

Was I supposed to care? Maybe. I wouldn't be able to pummel him for information. "What happened?"

"A few hours after I left him, an air bubble somehow got into his IV. Stroked him out."

"After you left him?"

"Yeah. But I got some intel. Unfortunately, now that he's gone, it'll be hearsay."

"Whatever, man. What did he say?"

"I didn't even have to threaten him. He sang like a fucking bluebird. Said he was sorry for everything. Of course I made him tell me what everything was. Whether he's telling the truth or not, who's to say?"

"Yeah, yeah, yeah. Get to the good stuff, man. Did you record it?"

"Of course I did. I'm no novice. You want me to play it for you?"

"How long is it?" I looked back at the jeep. "I want to hear it, but I've got some shit to do."

"What the hell is more important than this?"

He had a point. "Give me a minute."

I walked swiftly back to the jeep. "Hey, this is going to take a while. I need some privacy. Can we do this tour thing later?"

"Sure enough," Remy said. "I'll take Diamond back in.

Back in. Shit. "Could you give my brother and his wife some privacy, please? Maybe stay out here?"

"It's a big house," Diamond said. "We won't disturb them."

"For Christ's sake. All right." I walked back to the secluded area. I was glad to be outside, where there was no chance of surveillance. "You there?" I asked Buck.

"Yup."

"Have you made copies of the recording?"

"Of course I have. All are in safe places."

"Ten-four. All right. Play the damned thing."

The recording cracked through the line.

Father Jim: Who wants to know?

Buck: I already know. I've seen your chart.

Jim: Who are you?

Buck: Never mind that.

Pause.

Jim: How'd you get that in here?

Buck: Never mind how. It's here, and I know how to use it and to use it quietly. I need some answers, Padre.

A sigh.

Jim: Okay.

Buck: Did you try to off yourself or did someone do it for you?

Jim: Both, I guess.

Buck: What the fuck does that mean?

Jim: It means I considered it, was ready to do it, when someone else came and helped me along.

Buck: Who?

Jim: I honestly don't know. It was two people. Masked.

Buck: Male? Female? Big? Small?

Jim: Male. I assumed, anyway. They didn't talk. One held me down and the other cut me.

Buck: Cut your wrists.

Jim: Yeah.

Buck: Is that how you were planning to off yourself?

Jim: Nah. I hate blood. I was going to hang myself.

Buck: You hate blood?

A sarcastic laugh.

Jim: Yeah, hate the stuff.

Buck: Yet you watched your pal Derek Wolfe cut a young lady's breasts open.

No response.

Buck: And a hanging? Funny. I don't recall seeing any rope at your place.

Jim: I was going to use a belt. A leather belt.

Buck: What's a priest doing with a leather belt?

Jim: We have to keep our pants up the same as the next guy.

A loud scoff.

Buck: Whatever. Tell me about Derek Wolfe.

Silence for a few seconds.

Jim: He's dead.

Buck: I know that, genius. Tell me about you and him. Your hunting games.

Silence again. Finally,

Jim: I regret all of that.

Buck: Too little too late, Padre.

Jim: Why do you think I wanted to end my life? Now that Derek's gone, I no longer have to do any of his shit.

Buck: So it was his idea, you're saying?

Jim: Of course it was. I'm just a lowly priest. He had all the money and all the pull. How'd you get in here anyway? I'm not supposed to—

Buck: Shut up. I'm asking the questions. Me and my friend, here.

Another pause. Mostly likely he gestured to his gun.

Jim: Derek wasn't always so messed up. He was a good guy before.

Buck: Before what?

Jim: Before Connie. And her money.

Buck: Yeah? Tell me about Irene Lucent.

Jim: You know about her?

Buck: You left their marriage certificate in that underground play-

room of yours. Stop trying to fuck with me. I know you wanted us to find it, along with all that shit implicating Lacey Wolfe.

Another pause.

Buck: Save the innocent act, Padre. I'm not buying.

Jim: I'm not messing with you. I didn't put any of that there. I haven't even been down there since...

Buck: Since when? Since Derek was killed?

Jim: Well. Yeah. A couple weeks before. And we'd just cleaned it out.

Buck: Right. Moved the bodies.

Jim: What bodies?

Buck: Save it again. I know the lingering stench of human flesh when I smell it.

Another pause. A long one this time. I began to wonder if the conversation was over, when—

Jim: I think I want a lawyer.

Buck: Do you?

Jim: I have that right.

Buck: You do. If a cop is questioning you. I'm not a fucking cop.

Jim: I'm done talking.

Buck: Are you now?

Jim: Okay, okay. Put that thing away.

Buck: I think you're more apt to talk with it pointed at you.

Jim: Someone's going to walk in. I've got a call button.

Buck: Try it.

Another long pause.

Jim: What the...?

Buck: I don't leave anything to chance, Padre. No one's going to come in here until well after I'm gone. As I've told you, I can shoot you dead and be out of here before anyone's the wiser, so don't even think you're calling any shots. You don't get to ask questions, and if I have to tell you again, you're not leaving this place alive.

Jim: Then I won't be able to tell you anything.

Buck: I have other ways. Now keep talking. We're on Irene Lucent.

A heavy sigh. Then,

Jim: She was Derek's first wife. They were high school sweethearts, except they didn't go to the same school. Derek and I went to this fancy prep school, and Irene was a Hell's Kitchen girl. Through and through.

Buck: How'd they meet, then?

Jim: Some youth thing through St. Andrew's. It was a charity car wash or something.

Buck: A car wash. In New York City. Right.

Jim: Yeah, it was. We washed a lot of cabs.

Buck: I'll pretend I believe you.

Jim: Why would I lie? You've got a fucking gun pointed at me. Plus, I already know I'm headed to prison. I know all about that showgirl who told her story. No way am I getting out of this. Why the hell do you think I wanted to kill myself?

Buck: We're on Irene, Padre.

Jim: Right. Right. Derek loved her. Always did. That's why he refused to divorce her.

Buck: So he was a bigamist.

Jim: He was, though he erased everything about Irene.

Buck: Why didn't he just divorce her?

Jim: I just told you. He loved her.

Buck: Give me a break.

Jim: He did, man. I'm not kidding. Once he got his hands on Connie's billion, he bought this island and set Irene up there. She was...

Buck: She was what?

Jim: She was pregnant.

So. My esteemed older brother, Jordan. That was how he'd begun. On this very island.

But Riley had said she'd been here... Why would he bring...?

Unless...

Shit, I wasn't listening to the recording. "Buck. Rewind just a little, will you?"

"Sure thing."

Buck: She was what?

Jim: She was pregnant.

Buck: So he's got another kid? Who wasn't mentioned in the will?

Jim: Oh, the kid's doing fine. The whole island was left to him, along with all its amenities.

Buck: What amenities might those be?

Jim: It's a resort. Sort of. For well-to-do guys who can spend a million dollars per day to stay there.

My eyebrows shot up. *Keep listening, Rock.*

Buck: What kind of place?

Jim: It's a hunting ground. A real one.

Buck: Wait, you're telling me...what, exactly?

Jim: The hunts we did here in New York, they were tests. For the women who could make it through. Those who did were guaranteed a job for life on the island.

Buck: A job doing what exactly?

Jim: A job as prey.

Buck: So for life you mean...

Jim: Yeah, exactly what I mean. For life...as long as they could stay alive.

40

REID

I undressed my wife in a flash. I wanted to go slowly, truly I did, but my dick had other ideas. Happiness flowed through me like rainbows. God, how sickening, but no less true. All I could think about was getting inside her.

Inside my wife.

And I realized...

This would be the first time I made love to her as her husband. We hadn't had our wedding night. Sure, we'd fooled around a little before dinner, but I'd stopped it.

Me.

Not my finest moment.

Of course, I hadn't been expecting my wife to be kidnapped during dinner.

I kissed her lips, her neck, and then undressed myself in record speed and thrust inside her heat.

"Fuck," I growled. "So wet."

She was. So ready for me. Even under the current circumstances, we responded to each other on this raw and primal level.

She was mine. I was hers.

"I'm never letting you out of my sight again." I panted above her, sweat dripping from my brow. "Never. I swear to you, Zee. Never again."

She reached forward and touched my cheek. Damn, it burned. Just a simple touch and I felt it all the way to my soul.

I pumped and pumped, relishing every ridge inside her pussy, every beat of her heart in sync with mine.

I pumped, pumped, pumped. The orgasm didn't even sneak up on me. It was simply there, as if it always had been. As if I'd been denied my love for far too long.

I exploded, thrusting deeply into her, making her mine in the most physical way. I'd have all of her now. She loved me as I loved her, and no one would ever separate us again.

I closed my eyes, letting the explosion in my cock take me to heights unknown. Each contraction spurred me further into oblivion—further into Zee—and I never wanted to leave.

Finally, my body began to calm.

I opened my eyes. Zee was smiling at me, threading her fingers through my hair damp with sweat.

"Baby."

"Hmm?" she asked.

"I'm sorry."

"For what?'

"For being a selfish lover."

"It was perfect."

"But you didn't..."

She giggled. "Do you think I care? This is exactly what I needed and wanted. You. Wanting me. Loving me. I honestly never thought—" She choked up.

I rolled over onto my side and stroked her cheek. "Don't cry, love. I'm here. I'll always be here."

"I never dreamed you could love me."

I laughed slightly. "And I never dreamed you could love me."

"What's not to love?"

The fact that I'm Derek Wolfe's son. But I didn't say it. I simply caressed her cheek once more. "I could say the same."

"I'm broken. So broken."

"You're not," I said. "You're perfect."

"Hardly."

"Perfect for *me*, then."

She smiled. "And you're perfect for me. I don't care whose son you are. I only care that you're *you*. Reid. The man I love."

I brushed my lips gently over hers.

"Still," she said. "So much to get through."

"I know, baby. I know." I drew in a breath and let it out slowly. "But we have some time right now. Time for us. We can think about the rest of the shitshow later."

She smiled weakly. "I like that idea."

"You're going to like my next idea even better. I promise." I rose and went into her adjacent bathroom, wet a cloth with warm water, and cleaned between her legs.

"That's sweet."

"Not really. I have an ulterior motive."

"What's that?"

I threw the washcloth on the floor and bent my head between her legs. "This."

Her beauty stoned me like a drug. Her pussy was pink and swollen, and her clit large and welcoming. I slid my tongue between her folds.

"Oh!" she gasped.

"Mmm," I growled. "Delicious."

"I want..."

I looked up and met her gaze. "What?"

"I want to taste you too."

"I won't say no to that." I rolled up next to her and lay on my back. "Come here." I pulled her on top of me. "Turn around and straddle my face."

"Reid?"

"Sixty-nine, my love. Gives us both the best positioning."

"But I—"

"Hey"—I stroked her lower lip—"you'll be perfect. I promise."

No lie. I didn't care if she was experienced or a novice. I just wanted those lips around my cock and my tongue inside her sweet pussy. Then I could die a happy man.

Fuck! Where had that thought come from?

No one was dying here. Not on my watch.

But...I had no idea what we were getting into. This was Dad's private island. So far, all I'd seen was his first wife—actually, his *legal* wife, if the documents were to be believed—and the dock. The island was large for a private island. Who knew what the rest of it held?

"Enough," I said aloud.

Zee widened her eyes. "Enough what?"

I smiled and pushed all other thoughts out of my mind. "Enough of you not straddling my face, baby. Come on."

She turned around and I helped her get into position. Her beautiful pussy hovered above me. I grabbed her hips and brought her down onto my mouth.

Sweet tang.

"Oh!" She rubbed against me.

"Yeah," I said into her. "Just like that, baby. Ride my face."

She hadn't yet leaned down to take my cock. That was okay. She could go at her own speed. All I wanted was to eat her up.

I dived into her heat.

41

ZEE

Sparks shot through me. I couldn't help myself as my body moved seemingly of its own accord. I slid against his mouth, moving from clit and back again and again and again.

I opened my eyes. His cock was hard. So hard and big. I wanted to make him happy. Wanted that more than anything.

So I leaned forward and took the salty head between my lips.

His growl vibrated against my pussy.

I licked the tip of him, swirled my tongue around it, and then sank my mouth down.

I couldn't take all of him, but I took over half. Then some more. And a little more. The sensations coursing through me seemed to spur me on—as if his work on me made me work on him. I sank down and then up his hard, warm cock.

Again, he growled. Every time I took more of him, he growled, his vibrations flowing into me and out of me and through me.

He tasted of salt and spice and man. Of everything I'd ever dreamed of.

And this made him feel good.

Which meant it made *me* feel good. Everything. Him eating me. Me sucking him. The feel of my breasts against his taut abs. The tickle of his pubic hair against my chin. And his mouth on my clit, his teeth nipping at my labia.

Then—

"My God!" I shattered into a climax when he shoved a finger into me.

I sucked him nearly to the back of my throat, in time with his finger. I sucked him hard and fast as the spasms shot through me, through my pussy and outward into my fingers and toes.

Harder and harder I sucked him. Harder and harder, until—

"Fuck, baby!" He lifted me off his mouth. "Turn around. Ride me."

Still in the throes of orgasm, I obeyed in a haze.

And when I sank down on his massive cock, my clit hit his pubic bone...

And the spasms began again.

I rode him. Not slowly, but hard. Hard and fast. Took him as he'd taken me so many times.

"Yeah, baby. Just like that." His deep voice floated toward me. "Just like that."

When he gripped my hips and forced me down, releasing, I climaxed once more.

Together we rode into bliss. Together.

Always together.

I love you, sweet Zee. I love you so much.

I love you, Reid. So much.

So, so much.

I LAY in my husband's arms. Sated and relaxed but alive. Oh, so alive.

More alive than I'd been in... Ever?

Yes, ever. I never had a normal childhood, with my mother dragging me to auditions, and then of course, I never had the college experience I'd so desperately wanted.

Then my first abduction... The hunt... The escape... The meth years... Rehab... Las Vegas....

Never happy. Never alive.

But now...with Reid... I had a chance.

A chance.

Except my sister-in-law had been arrested for a murder she didn't commit, and my husband and the rest of his family were all still suspects.

Was I selfish to feel happy at this moment?

I sighed against his shoulder.

"What is it, baby?"

"Are you happy?" I asked.

"I am."

"So am I, but I wonder..."

"What?"

"*Should* we be happy? With everything else that's going on?"

"In this room, right now, we can be happy," he said. "We both need it. We deserve it."

"I wish we could stay here forever."

"So do I, love. So do I."

Then a knock on the door.

"Crap," Reid said.

I didn't echo his sentiment, though I felt it. If only...

But too much was still at stake. I still didn't know why I'd been brought here under duress. What the breadcrumbs were that Diamond spoke of. How Reid got here.

So many unknowns, but it was difficult to care while I was in Reid's arms.

But I *did* care. I cared so much. What would it take for Reid and me to have a life happily ever after?

I didn't know, other than it wouldn't happen tomorrow or the next day. Not until Derek's murder had been solved.

And even then...would we still be able to live in peace?

After all I'd been through—all Reid had been through—I had to wonder if it was in the cards for us at all.

42

LACEY

I needed to get in touch with Rock, but he wasn't answering the burner number he'd given me. Which of course led me to worry.

And I didn't have time for worrying. Rock and Reid were God knew where, and I was here, holding the company together. Roy and Riley, bless their hearts, wanted to help, but they didn't work for the company.

Yet they were still suspects, so they had a vested interest in all of this.

Morgan. If I got in touch with him, would he tell me the truth? Did he even know anything more?

Who could I talk to? Terrence was a possibility, but I didn't trust him, of course. Then again, perhaps I could scare him into talking. Scare him into giving up Fonda.

I had Fonda's information, as she'd been at the reading of Derek's will. It was all on my laptop and in the cloud. Technically, since I was no longer a member of my previous firm, I shouldn't access those records.

I laughed out loud. Fuck it all. I was already facing life in prison. What did I care about a slight ethical breach by accessing precious client records? Especially when the client was dead?

I sat down with my laptop and found Fonda's information. She had an apartment here in Manhattan and two phone numbers. Also the number of her agent, Fredricka, the same as Riley's agent.

What the hell? I dialed the first number.

"Hi, darling, it's Fonda. You know what to do!"

I was calling from one of my burners, so there'd be no way to trace the call. I left no message.

Quickly I typed in the second number.

"It's Fonda, loves. You've reached my cell phone. I'm busy at the moment but I'll be sure to return your call as soon as possible. Just leave your name and number. Ta!"

So much for that.

Why not try Fredricka? Fonda was an ageing model, but she still did shoots now and then. I made the call.

"Fredricka Gallant agency."

"Good morning. Lacey Wolfe for Fredricka, please."

"May I tell her what it's regarding?"

"I'm Riley Wolfe's sister-in-law."

Seemed to do the trick. "Let me see if she's in."

I waited a minute, and just when I was sure she wouldn't be taking the call—

"This is Fredricka."

"Hi there, Lacey Wolfe. Thank you for taking my call."

"Is Riley all right?"

"Yes, she's fine. I'm actually calling regarding another of your clients. Fonda Burke. I've been trying to reach her."

"You and me both," Fredricka said. "I've left message after message. She hasn't called me back in almost a month."

Interesting. About the length of time Derek had been dead.

"I'm sorry to hear that," I said. "It's paramount that I speak to her. Does she have anything scheduled?"

"The last thing I have for her is a shoot here in town. It's today, actually, but since she hasn't returned my calls, I've had no choice but to tell the company she may not show up."

"Where's the shoot?" I ask. "And when?"

"I can't divulge that information. I'm sorry."

Crap. "I'll make it worth your while." Since when did I start throwing Wolfe money around?

Since I was looking at frying for a crime I didn't commit. Desperate times called for desperate measures.

"Mrs. Wolfe..."

"I know you're a professional, Fredricka. Riley speaks very highly of you, but hear me out, please."

She sighed. "Go ahead."

I quickly gave her the rundown on being arrested. "Riley and her brothers are still suspects, and believe me, every one of us is innocent. Fonda may have information, and frankly, the fact that she's been MIA since the will reading has me very suspicious."

Another sigh. "All right. I'll give you the information, but like I said, my bet is that she won't show up."

"I'll try anything. Thank you."

I quickly jotted down the info, thanked Fredricka profusely, and promised I'd keep it confidential that she gave me the information.

Chanelle Manhattan headquarters. Apparently they were marketing an anti-aging skincare line to older women, hence hiring Fonda.

I rose and picked out one of my power suits—this one navy-blue wool—from the closet. I dressed, applied some light makeup, and pulled my hair up into a French knot. I was Lacey the lawyer today, not Lacey the wife of Rock Wolfe who was awaiting trial.

If I found Fonda, she was going to answer to me.

43

ROCK

J im: *The hunts we did here in New York. They were tests. For the women who could make it through. Those who did were guaranteed a job for life on the island.*

    Buck: A job doing what exactly?

Jim: A job as prey.

Buck: So for life, you mean...

Jim: Yeah, exactly what I mean. For life...as long as they could stay alive.

    Buck: Time to fess up. I want to know all about those hunts.

Silence.

    Buck: You seem to forget who's holding the gun.

More silence, and then—

Jim: Go ahead. I don't care anymore. Shoot me. Put me out of my misery. I'm done fighting.

    Buck: You sure about that?

Pause.

    Buck: Come on. You've already sung.

Jim: I have, which means even if I get out of here, I'm a dead man walking. I have been for a while now. So go ahead. I've got nothing else to say.

"That's the end of the recording," Buck said. "He clammed up after that."

"Even with your gun?"

"You heard him. He wanted to die anyway. He said I might as well shoot him and put him out of his misery."

"He could have said that all along."

"Exactly," Buck said, "which makes me think he wanted *out* of this all along. Why else would he leave those GPS coordinates in his bible, where you'd find them?"

"Although"—I scratched my head—"It could just be where he kept them. In a safe place. His bible. God knows he probably never opened the damned thing. Not after everything he's done."

"True enough. We'll never know if he meant for us to find them, but we did, and you're there."

"I don't see any hunting ground," I said.

"Look around. It's probably not in plain sight."

Good point. Reid and I knew nothing about the island so far. We'd docked on the west side, because we came from the west, but Buck was right. This place was huge, and nothing as illegal as a human hunt would be out in the open, even on a private island. We had no idea what was on the other side.

"Damn," I said.

"The padre said there's a hunting ground there. He had nothing to lose so I'm betting he's telling the truth. Apparently the elite pay a million dollars a day to go there."

"This is so sick, man."

"Don't I know it, and trust me. I've seen my share of sick as a SEAL and in my private business."

"Fuck it. I don't know if I can do this."

"I can get there in twenty-four hours. Leif and I both. Just say the word."

It was tempting. Having two ex-SEALS here would help, for

sure. But Reid and I couldn't wait that long. "We need you there. I want you to strong-arm Terrence, Reid's assistant. See if you can get him to talk. He's involved in some way." My phone buzzed.

Lacey's burner number.

"Can I call you back? My wife's trying to break in."

"Yeah, sure. No problem. Leif's at your office. I'll have him get with Terrence."

"Sounds good. Reid may have already gotten Leif to approach him." Though he hadn't. Reid's mind had been elsewhere. Now that he knew Zee was safe, he'd get back in the game.

"I'll be in touch." Buck ended the call.

"Hey, baby," I said to Lacey.

"Rock, I've got news. Your dad's girlfriend, Fonda, might be involved."

"Fonda?" I'd only seen her once, at the will reading. She'd been pissed that he didn't leave her anything, but then she left, and no one had heard anything from her.

I listened intently as Lacey filled me in.

"I'm heading to Chanelle now. Fredricka doesn't think she'll show up to the shoot, but if she's there, she's going to talk to me."

"No, baby," I said. "I want you in that suite, where you're safe."

"Rock, how can I just sit here? I'm going to trial for murder. I have to do what's in my power to find the real culprit here."

"I'll send Buck over. Or Leif. You stay put."

"I can't. I just can't."

"Damn." I raked my fingers through my hair that really needed a washing. "Lacey, I can't do what I have to do here if I'm worried about you."

"Reid's doing it, and he doesn't know where Zee is."

"He does now. She's here."

Lacey gasped. "Oh my God. Is she okay?"

"She seems fine. Reid's with her now."

"Then she's fine. You have to trust me, Rock. I'll be fine as well. I can't just sit here and do nothing. I have to prove my innocence."

"Baby, if Fonda's behind this, that means she's a murderer. Which means I don't want you anywhere near her."

"She won't hurt me," Lacey said. "I'm the one taking the fall for her. She wants me alive and well."

I paused a moment to consider her words. She was right, of course, but still...

"Please, Lace. Don't. I'll send someone else over."

"I have to do this, Rock. I love you, and your feelings mean everything to me, but please try to understand."

I sighed. "I do understand, Lace."

"I know you do. And I understand where you're coming from. You want me safe. I need you to trust me. Trust that I won't do anything that will jeopardize my safety."

I exhaled a long breath. "All right. But you call me right after, okay? No negotiation on that."

"You got it. I love you so much, Rock."

"I love you too, baby." I shoved my phone back in my pocket and walked back to the house.

I hoped to God Reid was done fucking his wife, because we needed Remy to take us to the other side of the island.

Even though the thought of what we'd find there made me sicker than I'd ever felt.

44

LACEY

Chanelle Manhattan had a photo studio at their headquarters. I had to wave some cash around to get inside. I was becoming more of a Wolfe every day. If the people whose palms I greased knew I was out on bail for murder, they didn't mention it. Why would they? Green is green.

All I knew when I went in was that a photo shoot was definitely happening. Whether Fonda was taking part, I had no idea.

I stood in the back, out of the way, trying to be invisible. Several photographers were shooting a male and female model.

"Beautiful, beautiful," one photographer said.

"Let's see more of a pout, Genie," said another.

Genie looked like a duck already, but she managed to pout a little more. This was supposed to sell cosmetics? But what did I know?

Click. Click. Click.

"That's a wrap. We got some great shots," the photographer who wanted more pout said. "Take a break, Genie and Herb."

Herb? This gorgeous model's name was Herb?

"Is Fonda ready?" another photographer asked.

My stomach clenched.

"She's in makeup," a young lady replied. "She's almost done."

So she *was* here. Good. Except now I felt like I was going to be sick all over my navy power suit.

I swallowed hard and leaned against the wall. The studio lights were bright, so it was easy to remain in the shadows.

One minute passed. Then another. Three and then four.

Finally, a woman emerged.

Fonda. She was a radiant woman with auburn hair and green eyes. She wore a one-piece emerald swimsuit with a plunging neckline that pushed up her average-sized breasts.

"Gorgeous, Fonda. Let's see some moves."

Someone revved up the wind machine, and Fonda's long hair responded.

Click. Click. Click. "Yes, gorgeous. Tilt your head a little. Lovely."

I scanned the studio. Fonda had emerged from a door off to the left. If I could inch along the wall and get to it, I could be waiting there when she was done with the shoot.

I stepped sideways. Then again. No one appeared to even notice me. Why would anyone, when there was a gorgeous model to look at?

I took another small step.

"Beautiful, darling. Just beautiful. Make love to the camera, Fonda."

Really? Photographers really said shit like that? I had hard evidence now.

I took another step and then stopped to watch the shoot. Fonda didn't look like a person who'd murdered her lover a month ago. Then again, she was playing a part. At the moment, she was a woman on the beach, the wind blowing through her hair. Heck, I didn't look like a person who'd committed murder either, and that hadn't stopped Morgan from arresting me.

"That's it, love. Give me some more shoulder. There you go."

I stepped to the side again. *Stop. Step. Stop. Step.*

Closer and closer I came to the door Fonda had emerged from.

Step. Stop. Step. Stop.

Something hit my left shoulder. I stifled a gasp.

I'd been watching Fonda instead of looking to my left. I'd bumped into another bystander.

"Sorry," I whispered.

Shit, now someone knew I was here. Plus, I'd have to get around him to keep going.

"Who are you?" the man asked.

I pretended not to hear him.

"Hey," he said again, his whisper louder this time. "Who *are* you?"

I didn't have a choice. I turned toward his voice. Even in the shadows, I had to do a double take.

Rock?

Dark hair, a little silver at the temples. Eyes like my husband's. Were they green? Maybe blue. I couldn't tell in the dark.

Whoever this was, he was a dead ringer for Rock Wolfe.

A dead ringer for *Derek* Wolfe.

I flattened myself against the wall and stepped the other way, my heart thundering. Derek Wolfe? Alive? No. Couldn't be. DNA had been checked. His organs...

I was really going to puke.

"Shit," the man said. "How'd you get in here?"

I stepped away again, but he grabbed my arm.

"Help!" I shouted.

The clicking stopped.

"What the hell's going on back there?" one of the photographers shouted. "You okay?"

"No! This guy's manhandling me."

"What the hell?" The studio lights dimmed. "Who are you?"

"I'm—"

"Not you, ma'am. Who the fuck are *you*?"

The man grabbed me and forced me toward the door.

"Help me!" I screamed again.

Once we were out of the studio, he pushed me against the wall. "For God's sake, shut up!"

I squinted, adjusting to the office lighting in the hallway. That voice. That face. My God. It was true.

He was alive.

"Derek?" I rasped out.

"Derek's dead."

"Who the hell are you, then?"

"Damn. None of us wanted this to happen."

"Let me go. I'm Lacey Wolfe. Mrs. Rock Wolfe. My husband will—"

"Shut up." He clamped his hand over my mouth. "We weren't going to let you go down, okay? We weren't going to..." He looked around.

Footsteps echoed.

"Shit." He grabbed me and dragged me to a door at the end of the hallway.

We ended up in a stairwell. I stumbled in my pencil skirt and spiky heels.

"Who *are* you?" I asked.

"Go." He nudged me toward the stairs.

"We're twenty-five flights up."

"You think I don't know that? You got a better idea?"

"Yeah. We go back up there and I have you arrested for assault and battery."

"Nice idea, but *you're* accused of murder. Who's anyone going to believe?"

"Whoever's up there isn't stupid. They heard me scream for help. They're going to know we went for the stairs."

"They're in the middle of a shoot. They're on deadline. Money talks, honey."

"I'm not your honey. Who are you?" I blinked, trying to see him more clearly. But he was already clear in my vision.

He looked exactly like—

"Jordan. Jordan Wolfe."

My jaw dropped. "Who?"

"Jordan Wolfe. I'm Derek's son. His oldest son."

"Irene Lucent." The words seemed to come out of my mouth without any thought on my part.

"Is my mother. Yeah. Now go!"

I started down the stairs, nearly stumbling, but Jordan steadied me.

After a couple flights, he stopped. "Here." He opened the door.

"What floor is this?"

"Shh. Trust me."

"You've *got* to be kidding me."

"I don't want to hurt you," he said, "but I will if I have to. Understand?"

My stomach churned. Crap. Literally. I had to go to the bathroom. I inhaled. Exhaled. Tried to get my body to relax. To chill.

Not happening.

Then I noticed it. The gun. It was strapped to his ankle, mostly hidden by his jeans.

Rock had been right. I couldn't do this. I couldn't—

I retched, and my stomach emptied right there in the stairwell. Right there on the man's shoes.

"Jesus..." he said.

I retched again, but nothing came up.

"For the love of God..." He pulled me into a restroom.

A men's restroom. Urinals lined the wall.

Oddly, the restroom appeared to be empty. Jordan grabbed a handful of paper towels and wiped off his shoes. "Clean yourself up."

I didn't want to obey him, but he was right about getting cleaned up. Miraculously, I'd missed my own clothes when I threw up. I wet a paper towel in the sink and wiped my mouth and face. Then I held my face under the faucet and rinsed out my mouth. Splashed water on my cheeks.

Should I apologize? No. He took me by force. He's lucky all I did was puke on his shoes.

"Listen to me," he said.

"Why should I?" Though I had every intention to, as I eyed the gun once more.

"Because I'm trying to help you, Lacey."

"By assaulting me?" I looked around. "Help! Help me!"

"There's no one on this floor," he said. "It's why I stopped here."

Of course. I should have known.

"Fonda killed your father," I said, "and I'm going to prove it."

"Would you shut up?"

"Help!" I screamed again. "Help me, please!"

"Listen." He clamped his hand over my lips. "I told you once that I don't want to hurt you, but I will if you don't shut the fuck up!"

I grabbed his wrist, attempting to move his hand, but he was too strong for me.

So—

I jammed my spiky heel into his shin.

"Jesus Christ!"

He let go of me, and I ran out of the bathroom. Elevator. Where was the elevator?

I raced down the carpeted hallway, and—

"*Oof!*"

My body was slammed against the wall, and the nose of Jordan's pistol pushed into my chest.

"I warned you, Mrs. Wolfe."

My heart raced. Tears threatened, but I would not beg.

Scratch that. I absolutely *would* beg.

"Please... Rock... I promised Rock..."

"Promised Rock what?"

"That I'd stay safe. For us. For..." My thoughts raced. "For the baby."

He lowered the gun. "Christ. You're pregnant?"

"Yes," I lied. "With your niece or nephew."

"Why hasn't anyone heard about this?"

"I just found out this morning."

"You're lying."

"I'm not! Find a doctor. We'll get an ultrasound. Go get a test and I'll pee on the stick. I'm not lying!"

Would he call my bluff? I had no idea, but any of those things would take time—time that would allow me to figure out how to get away.

"Christ," he said again. "Come with me."

45

REID

I hastily dressed and opened the door to see Diamond standing there. "Yes?"

"I'm sorry to bother you, but your brother is back. He needs to speak to you."

I sighed. Time to get back to real life. At least my sweet Zee was safe and sound. For now, anyway.

"Give us a few. We'll be right out."

Diamond nodded.

I closed the door and turned to Zee. "The carriage has turned back into a pumpkin."

"I guess I always knew it would." She rose from the bed and began to dress in a tropical print number. Damn, she was beautiful.

Once dressed, we left Zee's room and found Rock, Diamond, and Remy waiting for us in the front room.

"I want to prepare you," Diamond began.

"For what?" I asked.

"For what you're going to find on the other side of the island."

"Wait," Zee said. "I was there, wasn't I? When you first brought me here?"

Diamond nodded. "You were. It was the only way we could get you here. That's why you had to be so quiet."

"You keep girls there," Zee said quietly.

"Yes."

My heart began to pound. "What?"

"It's true," Rock said. "Apparently our esteemed father runs a hunting resort here on the island, where millionaire psychopaths can come and live out their sick fantasies."

"They said I was worthy prey..." Zee said quietly.

"You clearly were," Diamond said, "because you escaped."

"But I only escaped because of Roy," she said. "Because of an elevator malfunction. I wouldn't have been able to otherwise. Did anyone else ever escape?"

"No," Diamond said. "They didn't."

"You allowed this?" I demanded to Diamond. "You allowed this to happen? How could you?"

"Please believe me. I had no choice."

"There's always a choice," Rock said. "I've had to make some hard ones."

"But I didn't. He kept me here. I was as much a prisoner as the girls."

"But—"

She gestured me to stop. "Your father wasn't always so corrupt. When he was younger, he was idealistic and loving. He and I were in love."

"Then why did he marry my mother?" I asked.

"You already know the answer to that. For her trust fund."

"Our mother claims she didn't even know about the trust fund until she married our father," Rock said.

"She may not have," Diamond said. "I don't know."

"Then how could our father have known?" Rock asked.

Diamond shook her head. "I don't know. I gave up trying to figure out how he got his information long ago."

"Why?" I demanded. "Why would you stay with a man who married another woman?"

"I don't expect you to understand. I don't understand myself anymore. I can only tell you that at the time I was young, devoted, and in love. I believed in Derek. I trusted him. He said we'd eventually be together here. On the island. But the time got drawn out further and further, and eventually he built the resort."

"Resort?"

"That's what he called it. The Resort. Treasure Island. The hunting ground."

"Money corrupts," Rock said.

"It certainly did in his case," Diamond agreed. "Once he started working on the hunting ground, I decided to leave him. That's when I became a prisoner here."

"A prisoner?"

"Yes. He wouldn't let me leave. He said I was his and I'd always be his, and then he..."

"He what?" Rock asked.

"He brought Jordan into the mix. He said he'd take my son away if I didn't do what he said. That he had the money to do it. My son was everything to me, so I agreed."

"You agreed to stay here as his prisoner?"

"Yes, and to do as he told me." She sniffled.

"What exactly did you do?" Rock asked.

"I took care of the women he brought here. I was the house mother, so to speak, though I never had an official title."

"Oh my God. What did they do to these women?"

"They hunted them. They weren't allowed to kill them, but they could do everything but. Some visitors were true sadists, and they brought their prey to within an inch of their lives.

Some just wanted to catch them to have sex with them. Whatever they did, I took care of them afterward. I made sure they
were clothed, fed, healed in record time, so they could go back to
the hunt."

Zee squeezed my hand. She was pale. Pale and slightly
green. My God. If she hadn't gotten away... If Roy hadn't been in
that elevator that day... If the elevator hadn't malfunctioned...

My poor, sweet Zee would be here. As *worthy* prey.

"I'm going to be sick," I said.

"I may beat you to it, bro," Rock said. "Not much makes me
lose my lunch, but this..."

"I don't know why we're surprised," I said, "after what he did
to Riley."

"As bad as that was," Rock said, "this is on a whole other
level."

"Tell me," I said to Diamond, "how is your son involved in all
this?"

She sniffled. "Derek brought Jordan in once he turned
twenty. He took him on lavish trips and waved money and
women in his face. I lost my son then. Many times I've wondered
why I didn't try harder to escape. I stayed for my son, but Derek
ended up taking him anyway."

"So your son runs this place?"

She nodded. "But now that Derek is dead, and you have all
his assets, we can close it down. We can save those women.
Please. That's why we brought Zee here. So you'd follow. So
you'd—"

"Wait a fucking minute," I said. "*You're* behind this? You
abducted my wife?"

"Yes, but if you'll hear me out—"

"No." I shook my head adamantly. "I don't want to hear
another fucking word."

Zee squeezed my hand then. "Reid."

"I'm sorry, Zee, but they didn't need to take you. They could have picked up a fucking phone and called me. Called Rock. Called any of us."

"Would you have taken the call?" Diamond asked softly.

"Of course! If you'd said who you were."

"Really? A woman you'd never heard of calls you and claims to be your father's only legal wife, who lives on an island you've never heard of. Would you have come, when your sister-in-law has already been arrested? When all of you are suspects? Would you have dropped all of that to come here?"

"I don't know," I said. "But if you'd told us about the hunting ground..."

"I'm sorry," Diamond said. "I couldn't take that chance that you might not believe me. That you might not come. I had to go all in. For the girls."

"So you kidnapped my wife." I shook my head. "How do you expect me to forgive that?"

"Reid," Zee said softly, grabbing my hand.

"What is it?" I said more sharply than I intended.

"Please," she said. "We can *save* them. We can save the women who are here. We have to listen to Diamond."

"She's right, Reid," Rock agreed. "She's right. I don't condone her methods, but Zee is unharmed, and now we can help these women. But I have one question before we go anywhere, Diamond."

Diamond nodded. "Go ahead."

"Who the fuck offed Derek Wolfe?"

46

LACEY

I'd bought myself a little time, but soon Jordan would find out I wasn't pregnant. What did it matter, anyway? I'd either die here, at the hands of my newfound brother-in-law, or I'd die in a prison cell, having been found guilty of a murder I didn't commit.

For the first time, I let the shit of this situation invade my mind. Rock was gone, off on some remote island where I had no idea if I'd ever see him again.

And here I was, trapped on a vacant floor of a building with Derek Wolfe Junior. He'd said he didn't want to hurt me. He'd said he wasn't going to let me go down for the murder.

Who exactly was he? And how were he and Fonda involved?

"Tell me," I finally said. "What do *you* have to gain by doing this?"

He scoffed. "Don't play your legal tricks on me."

"It's a question. You know I'm innocent. You know your brothers and sister—"

"They're not mine. I don't even know them."

"Regardless, you know they're innocent. So who's guilty? You must know."

No response.

"It's a simple question," I prodded.

"Actually," he said, "the answer to that question is anything but simple."

He might be right about that. Already I knew of so many people who were involved. Rock's ex-friends Hoss and Manny. The Romero sisters. Hank Morgan. Terrence. And now Fonda. All I really needed to know, though, was who'd pulled the trigger.

And it dawned on me.

I might be looking at him.

Sure, made sense, right? Derek had completely abandoned Jordan's mother. They might not have any money. Though he had the money to afford a pretty nice gun, from what I could tell. I didn't know a lot about firearms, but this one looked a lot like—

Shit.

It looked a lot like Rock's gun...that was the same model as the one that killed Derek Wolfe.

Damn.

I was face to face with Derek Wolfe's killer.

Maybe.

Would a son off his father? Rock had tried the same thing at fourteen, but he'd been a hotheaded adolescent trying to protect his baby sister.

"Then answer," I said. "If the answer is anything but simple, help me understand."

"Nice try."

"What do you expect me to do? I'm going on trial, and you and I both know I'm innocent. I don't even have a motive, unlike the thousands of others who wanted to see your father dead. Why me? Why *me*?"

"How would I know?"

"You just intimated that you know who killed him. Not that I want to see any of them go down, but all of his children have motives. Why was *I* arrested?"

He didn't reply. Silenced loomed for a few minutes, until—

"Fonda let him stick his dirty dick in her for the last three years, and he didn't leave her anything."

"That's no reason to kill the guy."

"I didn't say she killed him."

"What exactly *are* you saying, then?"

"I'm saying my father fucked us all over, Mrs. Wolfe. Every single one of us, you included."

"Hey, I just wrote his will. He paid his bills. He never fucked me over. Not until he was dead, that is."

"Didn't you think it was slightly odd that he put his estranged son in charge of everything?"

Interesting. *This* son—who, I just realized, was Derek's only *legal* child—knew about the will.

"Yeah, it was more than odd. I tried hard to talk him out of it, but he was adamant."

"Apparently you didn't try hard enough."

"I did my duty, which is to represent my client zealously, whether his desires are in his best interest or not. Did you even *know* your father?"

"Unfortunately, yes, I did."

"Then you undoubtedly know that once he sets his mind to something, there's no changing it. I did my duty. I wrote the will he wanted, and I was compensated for my time. I had no motive to kill the man. Unlike you."

He didn't reply, not that I expected him to. He was clearly smart enough to know I wouldn't believe him if he said he didn't have a motive.

"Put the gun away," I said to him.

"Not likely."

"I'm no threat to you. I'm going down for something you probably did."

No reply. Innocent people usually got real pissed when they were accused of something. Still, this was Derek Wolfe's son. He could be as icy as the man who'd fathered him.

"It was all supposed to be mine," he finally said. "Mine and Mom's."

"What do you mean? All of Derek's assets?"

"Sort of. It's a long story."

"He had four other children, you know."

"Bastards."

"Apparently, but still children of his body."

Jordan pressed his lips together, and his eyes sank slightly. Was he sad? Sad that he'd been denied a relationship with his siblings? That he'd been denied the New York billionaire privilege?

Or *had* he?

"Look," I said. "You've got issues with your father. Who doesn't? He wasn't a nice man."

"He was once," Jordan said.

"Oh?"

"According to my mother, anyway."

"Where *is* your mother?"

He scoffed. "Nice try. I'm not your husband. I'm not falling for your 'I'm a nice and understanding woman' routine."

"What routine? I genuinely want to know."

"My mother had nothing to do with any of this."

"Then you should have no issue with telling me where she is."

"She's safe. Protected."

"Good. That's good. Where?"

"If you haven't found her by now, you never will."

"Don't bet on it. My husband will find her."

Jordan met my gaze with ice-blue eyes. "If he lives that long."

47

ZEE

"**W**ho the fuck offed Derek Wolfe?"

Diamond didn't reply right away. Finally, she cleared her throat. "I did."

My jaw dropped. So did Reid and Rock's.

"You're kidding," Rock said.

"I'm not."

"But you said yourself you're a prisoner here," Reid said. "How could you have gotten to New York, gotten inside his penthouse, and killed him? Do you even know how to handle a gun?"

"And you're letting my wife take the fall?" Rock said, his voice taking on an angry edge. "I ought to kill you right now."

"I wouldn't blame you," Diamond said.

I met her gaze. She was old and tired. Life clearly didn't mean anything to her anymore. She'd lost her husband. She'd lost her son. She'd been forced to take part in this horror for the last—well, only God knew how long.

"I don't believe you," I said softly.

"You should," she said. "I did it."

"You cared for me when I was scared and alone. You said yourself how you cared for the girls here. You're not a killer."

"Zee's right," Reid agreed. "You're not a killer. Give her your piece, Rock."

"Fuck no."

"Give it to her. See if she even knows how to hold it."

Rock sighed and pulled his pistol out of his ankle holster. He handed it to Diamond.

She visibly cringed.

"See?" Reid said. "You don't even want to touch it. You did *not* kill Derek Wolfe, but you know who did, and you're covering for him."

"Your son," Rock said. "It was your son, wasn't it?"

Diamond shook her head vehemently. "My son is innocent."

"Oh? Then who are you taking the fall for? Because you absolutely did *not* pull that trigger. I'm betting you weren't even in the states when the murder occurred."

Diamond said nothing.

"Diamond," I said. "Please. You helped me. Now help my husband and his brother. We need to solve this mystery. An innocent woman is going to go down, otherwise. And if she doesn't, someone else will. My husband and all his siblings are suspects, and they're all innocent." I paused a moment. "Please."

"My son is innocent," she said again.

"Then who *isn't* innocent?" Reid demanded. "You know something, and you need to level with us now."

Diamond sighed, and a look of pure defeat swept over her once fine features. "I will tell you what you want to know, but first, I want you to see what your father was capable of."

"We already know," Rock said.

"You don't, actually." She turned to Remy. "Take them. Now."

48

REID

Two hours later, Remy drove us through a wrought-iron gate into...

Paradise. Not kidding. It looked like fucking paradise. Palm trees, tropical flowers, swimming pools, movie stars. If I didn't know better, I'd think we'd just entered the finest resort on Fiji or Bali. White stone buildings, and in the distance, a gorgeous beach.

But it was all a façade.

Evil loomed before us. My skin prickled. I could feel it.

"I don't get it," Rock said. "Where's the hunting ground?"

"It's all around you," Diamond replied. "Look around. There are myriad places to hide here."

I didn't see what she was talking about, but the place was huge.

"Take them to the dorm," Diamond said to Remy.

"The dorm?" Zee asked. "Is that where I was?"

"Yes. You were in a room tucked away from the others."

"The women are still here?" Rock asked.

"Where else would they be?" Diamond looked out the car window.

"Are there any...hunters here?" I had to ask.

"No. They all left after Derek was killed."

"This is great, then," Zee said. "We can free all the women now."

"Where would they go?" Diamond asked. "They don't know any other life."

"Surely they have families," I said.

"They probably do, but most of them have been gone a long time. Their families have given them up for dead. They'll welcome them home, of course, but these women are not the same people they once were. They're going to need help. Therapy. Some may need to go to a mental hospital."

"We'll take care of them," Rock said. "Whatever they need. We have the resources."

"Of course," I agreed. "Anything they need. We'll get them out of here."

"It's not that simple," Diamond said. "Some of them don't *want* to leave."

"What?" Zee cried out. "That can't be the case."

"Call it Stockholm syndrome." Diamond closed her eyes, frowning. "Or call it life."

"Why the hell would they choose a life of slavery over freedom?" Rock demanded. "That doesn't make sense."

"It doesn't to you, of course," Diamond said. "But to them, this *is* their life. They're fed and cared for. All of their basic needs are provided."

"Except the freedom not to be hunted and raped," Zee said. "This is crazy."

"To you, yes, it is."

"To anyone," Zee said. "Yes, I know I was the lucky one. I got away. Honestly, I always thought the rest of the girls had died. Had been hunted until death. I thought it was a sick game with murderous intent. I had no idea they were still alive."

"Not all of them are," Diamond said. "Some didn't make the cut. They weren't worthy prey."

Zee went pale. "I guess...I didn't think of that. I was just so ecstatic that they were alive."

"A lot of them are," Diamond said.

"Let's get them out of here."

"I already told you that it's not that simple. They're free now. There are no hunts, now that Derek is dead."

"Did you know about his plans to fake his own death?" Rock asked.

"I did. You've probably already guessed that he planned to come here and live out his life doing what he loved best. Hunting women."

"What about Father Jim?"

"Father Jim was supposed to continue finding prey and then send them here."

I wanted to puke. Really puke until I was inside out.

"And you... Your son..." I prodded.

"Derek said we would finally be together, but I lost any love I ever had for him long ago, once he showed his true colors."

"How did he run this place?" Rock asked. "All his assets were left to us in his will."

"Except those weren't all his assets," Diamond said. "This place has netted Derek millions over the years. Probably billions, not that I'd know. He didn't share those things with me. He shared them with Jordan, though, and Jordan knew he'd be a rich man once his father died."

"Rich on dirty money," Rock said.

Diamond shook her head. "Derek was a master at laundering. All Jordan's money is clean and crisp."

"Fuck." I shook my head. "Fuck all of this."

"That gives your son a huge motive," Rock said. "Don't try to protect him."

"I'm not. I don't believe my son killed his father. Why should he? He was already the beneficiary to this place."

"Maybe he wanted it all," I said.

"My son only had one Achilles heel," Diamond said, "and it wasn't his father. Or me."

"Who was it, then?"

"Derek's girlfriend. Fonda Burke."

"So it *was* her," Rock said. "Lace was right."

"Why would you try to protect her?" I asked.

"I'm not protecting anyone," Diamond said. "*I* did it."

"Are you really still selling that story?" Rock asked. "No one's buying."

"You're not a killer, Diamond," Zee said. "You'll never get me to believe it.

"Fine," she said. "Don't believe it. But you can at least believe this. I'm not sure who did it."

49

LACEY

"What's that supposed to mean?" I demanded.

My heart raced. I already knew Rock was in danger, but Jordan made it that much more real.

"It means I'm not going down for any of this. And neither is Fonda."

"Oh my God." Recognition dawned on me. His eyes told the tale. "You're in love with her."

"She was too good for him."

"I don't deny it," I said. "Everyone was too good for Derek Wolfe. Even Connie."

"Bitch," he said.

"Your father was the bigamist, not Connie. At least not knowingly."

"She's still a bitch."

Knowing what I knew, I couldn't deny it. Any woman who let her children be abused was definitely a bitch. But did Jordan even know any of that?

I'd inadvertently found Jordan's weak spot. Now I had to figure out how to use it.

He held his gun nonchalantly in his right hand. I looked down the hall. Now or never. I had to try.

"Fonda!" I called.

He turned swiftly—

And I made my move.

I knife-handed his forearm, the gun slipped, and I dived toward it, grabbing it. Without thinking, I turned toward him and pointed it at his head. "Don't you fucking move."

The gun was hot against my palm. Was it even loaded?

Yeah, it was, or Jordan would be hightailing it out of here or trying to overpower me.

It was definitely loaded. I was holding a *fucking loaded gun*.

I had no idea what I was doing, but I had to make him think I did. I was a trained attorney. I could make him believe anything I wanted.

Right?

"You're going to start talking," I said through clenched teeth. "Or I'm going to blow your fucking head off and then Fonda's. No. Scratch that. I'm going to make you watch while I blow Fonda's head off. Then I'll take care of you. The two of you can be soul mates in hell."

My words surprised me. I was ruthless. This was what being wrongly accused had done to me. I flashbacked to Rock pulling a gun on the dirty cop in Montana who threatened to arrest me for murder.

I was doing the same thing.

Jordan was good. I'd give him that. His features were icy and cold. I couldn't tell if he wasn't scared at all or if he was secretly pissing his pants. I didn't dare look down. My gaze remained firm on his.

I walked closer to him. "Maybe you didn't hear me, asshole."

Finally, he raised his hands. "Okay, okay. Ease up."

"Ease up? Really? After you've been dragging me around and holding me at gunpoint? I don't think so."

"I told you. Fonda and I weren't going to let you go down for this."

"Really."

"Yes. We never wanted that. Our plan was to…"

"To what? Your plan was to what?"

"To let his other kids go down. They got all his assets. I got…"

"You got *something*," I said, "or you wouldn't be here."

"Never mind that. I never wanted any of it. Not after I met Fonda. I made sure every one of my half-siblings had a motive and that evidence pointed at each of them. *You* weren't my idea."

"Then whose idea was I?" I stalked up next to him and touched the nose of the gun to his temple. "Who stole the surveillance tape from my building that would have proved my innocence? Who planted my belongings?"

"It was… It was the cop. The dirty cop. But that was before…"

"Before what?"

"Before you went and married my brother. For God's sake. You ruined *everything*."

"*I* ruined everything? You've got a lot of nerve."

"I wanted one of my half-assed siblings to go down."

"But they're innocent."

"Are they? Are they really? They got the high life, living in New York as Derek Wolfe's *real* children. For all I know they actually *are* behind his death."

"You don't know anything." I shook my head. "He abused every single one of them. Seems to me *you're* the lucky one."

"I know what he did to them. What makes you think he didn't do the same thing to me? To Fonda? Why the hell do you think we wanted him dead?"

"At the cost of one of your brothers? Your sister? Me?"

"I don't know any one of you from Adam, and I've already

explained to you that we never wanted *you* to go down. We've got no beef with you, other than the will you wrote."

"I've already told you I tried to talk him out of it."

"I get it. Fonda and I both do, okay? You were never on our radar. It was the cop's idea."

"And now? What are you going to do about it?"

"We've got the dirty cop dead to rights. We know he went to you asking for a bribe. He's the one who tried to pin it on you. He set it in motion before you married Rock, and it was too late to do anything about it *after* you married him. He didn't want to pin it on a Wolfe, even though the evidence was there."

"Let me guess." My mind raced. "He saw the Wolfes as a paycheck."

"I'd say you're smarter than you look," he said, "but you might take that the wrong way."

I pushed the nose of the firearm further into his temple. "Nice. Are you forgetting who's holding the gun here?"

"No, I'm not. But if you pull that trigger, all the information I have will be down the freaking toilet."

He wasn't wrong. He had me at metaphorical gunpoint while I had him at actual.

"I can always go after Fonda," I said.

He winced. Only slightly, but I noticed. That continuing legal education class on body language I took last year had definitely paid off.

"How'd you find out your father was faking his death?" I asked.

"He told me."

I nearly dropped the gun. "*You're* the leak. It wasn't Derek. It was you. *Your* voice. You sound just like the others. *You* made that call to Rock in Montana. From Reid's office. It wasn't Derek at all. Then you called Nieves Romero, saying you were Roy."

"Give the lady a gold star." Jordan chuckled.

"But why? You *knew* what would happen."

"Hell, no, I didn't know what would happen. I thought it would implicate Reid and Roy. Rock and Riley already had reason to be implicated. Reid was my father's right-hand man, and I didn't know about Roy and the elevator at that time. I needed all four of them in the mix. I had no idea the Romero woman would intercept the message to Rock and tip off the cops, but I used it to my advantage to bring Roy into the mix."

I shook my head. "We had it all wrong. We thought Derek was trying to take his children down."

"Dad did a number on them with that will he had you draw up. Why would he try to send them all to prison? Who'd run his billion-dollar enterprise then?"

I picked my jaw up from the floor. How had we gotten this so wrong?"

We hadn't known Derek had another kid, for one thing. But we'd overlooked Fonda from the very beginning. If Derek had treated her the way he treated Connie, his kids...

Damn. We should have known.

"Which one of you did it? You or Fonda?"

"Listen. If I tell you... If I give you proof that implicates the two of us, you have to do something for me."

"Not likely."

"Then kill me. Kill me and kill her. That information dies with us, and you go down."

50

ZEE

"Then we're back at the beginning." Rock paced across the floor.

"You just claimed your son was innocent," Reid said. "So we know it wasn't him, right?"

"I meant innocent in the way a mother will always see her child. As innocent as the day he was born. His father tainted him, corrupted him." Diamond sniffled. "I'll always believe he's the baby I carried."

Diamond had taken care of me. She took care of the girls. She was first and foremost a mother.

And a mother would always believe in her child.

A good mother would, anyway.

"You also just said Derek corrupted your son," Rock added.

"He did. He took Jordan from me. The one thing I loved more than my own life."

"You're not ruling him out, then," Reid said. "He *could* be the killer."

Diamond said nothing.

She didn't have to.

Everything became clear to me then. Why Diamond hadn't

tried to leave the island. Why she stayed. It wasn't just because the women needed her. It was because she no longer had a life outside this place. She had no motivation to find something better once her son had been taken from her.

"Take us to the women," I said. "We have to get them out of here."

"I just told you—"

"You heard my wife," Reid said through clenched teeth. "She wants to see them, and I do too."

A LITTLE WHILE LATER, we arrived at what Diamond called "the dorm." Where I'd been held when I first got here.

"Some of them are in the common area," Diamond said. "Others won't leave their rooms."

"I understand," I told her.

"I believe if anyone here understands," she said, "it's you."

Reid went rigid next to me, but thankfully he didn't say anything. Diamond was right. He couldn't possibly understand what the women had been through.

We entered the building. Diamond punched security codes into not one but three different panels. These women were definitely kept prisoners.

Once inside, we stopped at a reception desk, which was unmanned. Diamond punched in one more code, and the clear door clicked. Beyond the door, a few women sat in a large area. A television was on, playing what looked like an old black-and-white sitcom.

"What are they watching?" I asked.

"*I Love Lucy.* It's from the fifties. That's all that streams in here. Old movies and shows. No news. Nothing contemporary."

"Nothing that would show them what they're missing," I said quietly.

"Exactly. It took years for me to get Derek to allow this one television, and he allowed it only on the condition that it stream nothing to get them thinking."

"So you did have some pull with him," Reid said.

Diamond scoffed. "Very little. But he listened to me when it came to the girls. He wanted them healthy and pliable. I kept them that way, so he took what I said seriously."

"God, this is sick," Rock muttered.

"Can we...?" I lifted my eyebrows toward the girls in the room.

"Go ahead. If they wanted to leave, they would have when they saw us. The more frightened ones won't come out of their rooms."

"How many women live here?" Reid asked.

"Right now we have twenty-three. At times we had over thirty, but in the last year no one new has come in."

"Because Derek was busy plotting his own fake demise," Rock said.

"Most likely." Diamond nodded as we all walked toward the women. "Girls, I've brought some people to meet you. They're nice people and they won't harm you."

"We want to help," I said.

One of the women looked at me, cocking her blond head. "Have we met?"

I shook my head. "No. I've never been here before."

"But you... You look familiar to me. Like I saw you in a dream once, or something."

I walked toward her, her voice spawning a decade-old memory.

I dropped my mouth open. I'd last seen this young woman

lying on the floor with both shoulders dislocated, her head shaved.

"Kill me," she'd said. "Please.

I'd refused, of course.

But I knew her.

"Katelyn?" I said hesitantly.

"Was that my name?" She squinted slightly. "Yes, I think it was."

"Oh my God! I thought you were—" I stopped myself from continuing. I also had to stop myself from running toward her and grabbing her into a hug.

She was alive! Katelyn was alive!

"My name is Moonstone," she said. "That's what I'm called here."

"You're Katelyn." I turned to Diamond. "Moonstone. Diamond. Why?"

"Derek gave them all names of gemstones. It was part of the lure of this place. He called it a Treasure Island. It was a treasure hunt."

An unwanted thought speared into my head. What might my gemstone name have been? Sapphire, for my eyes? Or something else?

"Why do you have a gem name?" Reid asked.

"Because I was their mother. Diamond. The mother of all the gems."

"You were never..." Rock cleared his throat.

"No. I was never hunted, though there were times I wished I were. I wanted to take the pain and humiliation away from these women. They became like daughters to me." She gestured to the other two women. "You've met Moonstone. This is Garnet and Onyx."

Onyx had black hair and dark skin. Garnet... I couldn't see the connection.

"We're going to help all of you ladies," Reid said. "You'll have the finest healthcare and emotional support. Your life here on the island is over. No one will ever harm any of you again."

Diamond was right. Not one of them leaped up in joy.

They'd been brainwashed. Katelyn had even forgotten her real name.

"We could bring the help here. To them," I said. "They don't have to leave."

Rock shook his head. "We could, but they'll be better off at home." He turned to Diamond. "Do any of them remember their former lives? Their former names?"

"I do," came a meek voice. The woman named Garnet stood.

"What can you tell us?" I asked.

"My name is Aspen Davis. I'm from Colorado."

"I'll have Buck check it out," Rock said.

"And you," I asked Onyx. "Do you remember how you came to be here? What your name was?"

"I've always been here," she said.

I glanced at Diamond. She shook her head slightly at me.

Some would require more help than others.

I feared some might be beyond help.

But at least they were free now.

And we'd see that they got whatever they needed.

Was he calling my bluff?

I couldn't read his body language. So much for that class now. He was eerily calm for a man with a gun at his temple. Almost too calm.

I cocked the trigger. "Have it your way, then."

He went rigid. "Please," he said softly.

Yup, this gun was definitely loaded. If I'd been unsure before, no longer.

"Start talking, then," I said.

"I'll give you what you need to implicate us, but you have to help us disappear."

"What makes you think I know how to do that?"

"Your husband does."

"My husband's a biker from Montana."

"Your brother-in-law, then. Reid. He can do it."

"What makes you think that?"

"He learned at my father's side. He can make anything happen that he wants. Get Morgan in on it, and it will happen."

"Morgan's a tired old detective who wants money to disappear on his own."

"He is that, but he's also part of a syndicate inside the NYPD that was on my father's payroll. I can get you those names. In fact, we can implic—"

"No. No more implicating someone who's innocent. We're done with that."

"Hey, those guys may not have pulled the trigger, but they're far from innocent."

His idea was tempting, but, "No. Only the guilty party goes down for this murder. If that's you and your girlfriend, so be it."

"You have nothing without the evidence tying it to us. If you had anything, Fonda would have been hauled in before now."

I couldn't fault his statement. He was right. We had nothing.

"What about your mother?" I asked. "You're just going to leave her?"

"My mother wrote me off long ago."

"Why?"

"She thinks my father corrupted me."

"Didn't he?"

"In some ways, yes." He suppressed a shudder. "When he first introduced me to what he had planned for the island, I was sickened. Really disgusted. I wanted no part of it."

"But..."

"But...I got seduced by the money. Seduced by everything about it. My father was...hypnotic, almost. As icy as they came, and I swear to God he could make anyone believe the most heinous thing in the world was for the common good."

"How in the hell did he make you believe *any* of this was for the common good?"

"Honestly, looking back, I have no idea. But once you start doing something bad, it becomes easier and easier. I know you won't believe this, but I wish I could take it all back."

"Some things can't be taken back."

"Don't I know it. The whole thing was supposed to be his legacy, and my future. And I was okay with that...until Fonda."

"You fell in love."

"Yeah. He brought her to the island. Not the hunting ground, but to the other side of the island, and the two of us... We just clicked."

"She wasn't in love with Derek?"

"Hell, no. She was with him for the same reason any model dates a billionaire. He was a sugar daddy and she was his arm candy."

"How do you know she loves you, then?"

"Because she committed murder with me. I knew I'd never be free to be with her until my father was gone, and there aren't a lot of people in the world who wouldn't say the world is a better place without him."

The gun was growing heavy in my hand. "I don't disagree, but that doesn't give you the right to play God with someone else's life."

"Yeah, yeah, yeah. I've been through every moral argument, believe me. I've done a hell of a lot of shit I regret. It's because of Fonda that I've regained my conscience."

"People with a conscience don't kill their fathers."

"They do if it's the only way they'll be free. The only way the woman they love will be free."

"How were you planning to get out of all this?"

"Fonda and I were leaving after today. She arranged to get paid in cash for today's shoot, and we've got cash stashed here and there. But now, with my half-brothers' help, we can truly disappear."

"Wait, wait, wait. There are still unanswered questions. Father Jim? Did you kill him?"

"No."

"Do you know who did?"

No response.

I shoved the gun into his temple, making a dent.

"I don't know, but my guess is someone at the NYPD."

"Part of the Wolfe brigade."

"It's a guess, but it makes a lot of sense. I had no beef with Jim. I thought he was a psycho, but so was my father."

"Still, you let it all happen."

"I did."

I shook my head and groaned. "You're as sick as the rest of them. I should just end this now."

"You can. I can't stop you. But if you get Fonda and me off the grid, I'll give you all you need to close this case. For good."

"Reid isn't around," I said, "and I have no idea how to do any of that."

"Not my problem."

"Well, yeah, it kind of is. You just confessed to me."

"You know as well as I do that it's hearsay."

"Sure, I do, but it's more than they've got on me, and somehow *I* got arrested."

He went rigid for a second before resuming his cool stance. Yup, that had scared him.

"I doubt you're wired," he said. "And even if you are, it's not admissible."

"That's where you wrong." I smile. "I *am* wired. And you're going down now. Both you and Fonda."

"You bitch."

"Don't you fucking move," I said. "I've got you dead to rights. You, Fonda, and Hank Morgan. And you're *all* going to pay for putting me through this shit."

"You're bluffing."

He was right, but I was all in now. "You want to take that chance? My husband has our entire suite wired. We're watching everything. How do you think I knew Fonda would be at that shoot today?"

"Fuck," he said. "What do you want, then? What will it take for you to let us go?"

"The evidence. Right here. Right now."

"It's not here."

"Then take me to it."

"But Fonda's almost done with her shoot. I'm supposed to meet her afterward."

"I guess she'll just have to wait, won't she? Where's the evidence?"

"Please." He stayed still, but his muscles tensed even further. "You'll get us out of here. You have to."

"Right now I don't have to do anything except decide whether or not to pull this damned trigger. I'm not making any promises until I see what you have. Scratch that. I'm not making any guarantees until all the Wolfe siblings and I are cleared of this murder."

Nothing for a few minutes.

Then he finally nodded. "You win. I'll take you to what you need."

REID

Zee and Diamond stayed to deal with the women while Rock and I tore through the files and computer in the reception area, looking for evidence.

"Bro, we need a hacker," Rock said.

I nodded. "We need Leif, but he's not here. I know a little bit, but this code is encrypted and it's different from anything I've seen."

"You think Diamond knows?"

"I think she would have told us if she did. She already said the money is clean when it filters into the US."

"Do you think any of the Wolfe Enterprises money is dirty?" Rock asked.

I shook my head. "It's not. I have access to all those accounts. His dirty money comes from this enterprise, which, I'm happy to say, I knew nothing about until now."

"Fuck. Is anyone going to believe we didn't know anything about any of this?"

"They have to. We didn't. We didn't even know about Dad's first wife. Mom never knew. He's kept all of this tightly veiled over the years. I suppose we'll never know why."

"Yeah. Like why he'd drag his first-born son, his only legal child, into this mess but give *us* the legal enterprise?"

"He fucked us over in his own way."

"Right. By making me move to New York and giving me what should have been yours."

I sighed. "Yeah. I'd like to say I'm over it. I am getting there, and you're doing a bang-up job. Better than I thought you would."

He smirked. "Turns out I kind of like it. I never thought I would, but running a business is a challenge. I'm learning a ton. Thanks to you."

"We can do great things together, Rock," I said earnestly. "We'll take Wolfe from a three-billion-dollar enterprise to a one-hundred-billion-dollar enterprise. I've got lots of ideas."

I continued tapping, entering code, trying my best to decipher, when I made it through the first door. "Bingo!"

"You got it?"

"Yeah. Except now it wants a password." I turned the keyboard over.

My father would never be stupid enough to leave a password in plain sight. So of course there was nothing taped to the bottom of the keyboard.

I started typing furiously. Rock. Reid. Roy. Riley. Princess. Princesstrips. Irene. I tried all our birthdates.

"Fuck." I scratched my head. My scalp itched. I still hadn't had a shower in days.

"I can't think of anything," Rock said. "You want me to call Leif?"

"He'd have to get here. He can't hack a computer over the phone."

I typed in Diamond. Moonstone. Garnet. Onyx. Treasure-hunt. Treasureisland.

Nothing.

"Try Fonda," Rock said. "Try Jordan. Connie. Constance. Larson. Lucent."

I tried them all.

Nothing.

I tried all the combinations of all the words I'd already tried. As many as I could think of.

I typed until I was sure my fingers would fall off.

And then—

"What about..."

I typed in the numbers slowly.

The date of my father's death.

The date he meant to disappear, only to die instead.

I tapped each one, letting my finger hover over the last digit for a few seconds before—

Tap.

And the screen opened.

"I'll be damned, bro," Rock said.

"It was the date he thought he'd be free to live out the rest of his life here."

"Do you think he was running from something? From us? From Mom?"

"He unloaded Mom years ago, and he was still abusing Riley. But he was looking forward to this for some reason."

"Maybe he really loved Irene."

I scratched the outer shell of my ear. "If that were the case, why Fonda? Why all the other women over the years? Why Riley?"

"I don't know, man," Rock said, "but take a look at those fucking numbers."

My eyes went wide. "Oh. My. God."

Account after account. Some in Switzerland, others in the Caymans. A few in the continental US, even. Together totaling billions.

"He made more billions here," Rock said. "And it all looks clean."

"We can't tell from this, but at first glance, yeah, it does."

"Jordan's name is on all these accounts," I said, "and..." I tapped furiously. "He made a withdrawal from the bank in New York." I paused. "Yesterday."

"For how much?"

"Five hundred grand."

"That's it?"

"Makes perfect sense. Such a small amount wouldn't look odd to anyone going through the accounts."

"He's in the US, Diamond said." Rock wrinkled his forehead.

"Yeah. He is." I groaned. "He's going to run."

53

LACEY

Jordan and I walked a few blocks to another building.

"Fonda's apartment is here," he said. "Come on."

I followed him, his pistol securely in my purse with my hand still on it. He nodded to the doorman and then walked in. We took the elevator to the seventeenth floor and he slid a keycard through the door of apartment 1765.

"You kept evidence here? At Fonda's?"

"Yeah. We made sure she couldn't be implicated. They wouldn't come here without a warrant, and they couldn't get a warrant. Besides—"

"You made sure all your siblings looked guilty."

"Right on. I learned from the best. My father himself."

"Yeah, yeah, yeah. Just get the evidence, and then I'll decide whether it's enough to help you and Fonda hightail it out of here."

"So you're considering it."

"Of course I am."

But I was lying. If he and Fonda had truly killed Derek, they were going down. Hank Morgan was going down. Everyone behind this scheme was going down. And yeah, I was feeling particularly vengeful after being dragged away in handcuffs and stuck in a holding cell for hours.

"It's in a safe hidden inside a book." He walked toward a small bookshelf on one wall.

I stepped closer, still training the gun on Jordan.

The contents on the shelf were interesting—a mixture of romance novels and hardcover classics. Jordan pulled out a leather-covered copy *Moby Dick*. He opened it, and inside was a tiny safe. He entered a combination. was a thumb drive, a glasses case, and a manila envelope. He pocketed the envelope and handed me the thumb drive.

"This will show you what really happened."

I shoved it in the pocket of my navy blazer and then eyed the glasses case. "What's that? And what's in that envelope?"

He turned toward me and opened the glasses case. "Fonda's readers." He pulled out a pair of glasses.

"She keeps reading glasses locked in a safe?"

"These are special readers," he said. "Really expensive."

"What?"

But that was all that came out of my mouth as Jordan lunged at me and pushed one of the temple tips into the side of my neck.

Sharp? The temple tips of eyeglasses.

"I'm really sorry about this."

Words. From Jordan.

I dropped to the floor, losing hold of the gun.

In a haze, a blurry image moved around me. Making sounds.

A loud noise.

A gun firing.

No! No! No!

And then...

Nothing.

54

REID

Files led to more files. "There's enough here to implicate Dad and our half-brother for about fifty lifetimes."

"Anything on Irene?" Rock asked.

I shook my head. "Her name is nowhere to be found. He kept her out of it."

"Amazing. You think maybe he truly loved her?"

"Nah. Derek Wolfe didn't love anyone but himself. He didn't love his kids, not even this Jordan dude, or he wouldn't have dragged him into this mess."

"I don't get it." Rock shook his head. "He had everything. Every-fucking-thing. Why would he do something like this?"

"Because he could."

Rock and I both jerked upward at Diamond's voice. She'd sneaked into the small cubicle without either of us noticing.

"It's just a theory," she continued, "but I think your father, after he made a legal business out of your mother's trust fund, realized that criminal activity paid a lot better. He took a look at where the money had come from. Your mother's money was clean, but only because it had been laundered three or more times to get it there. It had originally come from crime, and he figured he could do the same thing. Plus, with the billions he'd already made legally, he could finance just about anything."

"But a hunting ground." Rock shook his head. "Who the hell comes up with that?"

"We'll never know the answer," Diamond said. "God knows I could never get it out of him."

"Father Jim," I said.

"Is dead," Rock replied. "Sorry. I didn't get the chance to tell you about my call with Buck. You were...indisposed."

My cheeks warmed. What the hell? No reason to be embarrassed about making love with my wife.

"So Jim's dead. Jordan's gone. Morgan's dirty." I rubbed my jawline. "And we still don't know who the hell offed our father. How are we going to get Lacey out of this? Get ourselves out of this?"

"This place goes a long way toward that," Rock said. "None of us are implicated in any of it. Only Jordan."

Diamond's face fell.

"I'm sorry," Rock said, "but if he did it, we need to know. My wife is innocent. So are the rest of us."

"Someone out there knows the truth," I said. "I think we start with Terrence. He got himself inserted in this somehow."

"You think he killed our father?" Rock asked.

"I have no clue, but we're going to find out what he knows. I'll have Buck and Leif rough him up."

Rock's burner phone buzzed. "Hold on. I don't recognize this number."

"Don't answer, then."

"What if it's Lace?"

"She wasn't supposed to leave the suite."

"Except..."

"What is it, Rock?"

"She went out. To find Fonda at a photo shoot."

Diamond raised her eyebrows. "Fonda?"

"Yeah. Fonda Burke. She was dating our father."

"I know who she is," Diamond said, "but she wasn't in love with your father."

"Of course she wasn't," I said. "Who would be?"

Diamond bit her lip.

"I meant...who would be *now*?"

She nodded. "I know. Still... But that's in the past. He was a good man once. Or maybe he never was. I don't know."

"What about Fonda?" Rock urged.

"Right. She wasn't in love with Derek. She was in love with my son. With Jordan."

Rock's phone call stopped.

"Fuck. I should have answered."

"Call back, then."

"This burner doesn't keep numbers."

"If it's important, whoever it was will call back."

"God willing. Fuck." He raked his fingers through his hair. "We have to stop him. Jordan."

"How? He's gone and he's carrying around a load of cash. Diamond, do you—" I turned, but Diamond had gone back into the common area with Zee and the women.

"Five hundred grand won't last too long if he has to lie low," Rock said.

"He may have more. He's probably been stashing money in various places for years." I tapped more code into the computer.

"This is crazy," Rock said. "How are we supposed to find him?"

"We find Fonda. Apparently she's his weakness."

Rock rubbed his forehead and then grabbed his burner phone. "Lace. I should have answered. It had to be Lacey."

My heart raced. Yeah, I was worried for Lacey, but it beat

even more rapidly when I hacked into a new document. "Oh. My. God."

"What? What is it?" Rock was rigid next to me.

"It's a list," I said quietly. "A list of visitors to the island."

I stared, numb.

Rock stood behind me. "You're fucking kidding me. The governor? Two former presidents? A crown prince of the principality of Cordova? This has to be fake."

"It's not," I said softly, my stomach clenching in disgust. "If it were fake, he wouldn't have hidden it so well."

"My God," Rock said. "Celebrities. Politicians. Royals. How did they even know about this place?"

"I don't know." I swallowed hard. "I don't *want* to know."

"This is nuts." Rock continued looking over my shoulder. "So many names I recognize. So many I don't. Except... Jonathan Leopold. That name sounds familiar for some reason."

"It should." I swallowed once more against the nausea. "He's the DA who had Lacey arrested."

Rock was behind me, but his tension flowed into me. Though I couldn't see him, I knew he'd gone rigid. Completely granite. His knuckles went white against the edge of the desk.

"I'll kill him," my brother said.

"Get in fucking line."

"How could a DA afford to come here, anyway?" Rock asked.

"Payment," I said. "It was payment for a favor. That's how business works."

"I know how business works. I get the whole favor thing, but this? How are people so sick?"

"Beats the hell out of me."

"I think," Rock said, "it's time we go home. I have a few *favors* to collect myself."

~

ZEE, Diamond, and Remy sat with Rock and me back at the mansion.

"We can't," Zee said. "Diamond will be charged as an accomplice to all this."

"It's no less than I deserve," Diamond said quietly. "I *was* an accomplice."

"You did what you had to do. These women are alive because of you. Please, Reid." Zee met my gaze. "Please. Don't do this to her."

Those damned blue eyes. How could such beauty exist in this treacherous world?

"I can talk to our attorneys," I said. "If you cooperate, Diamond, they might be able to get you immunity or at least a commuted sentence."

"I'll do whatever I have to do to make sure this place is shut down." Diamond stared into her lap. "Even if it means I spend the rest of my life in prison."

"Diamond..." Zee said.

"It's okay." Diamond nodded to Zee. "Really, it is. My son will get a lot worse."

"Your son *did* a lot worse," Rock said harshly.

Zee's eyes met mine once more, but I couldn't go soft. Rock was right. Our half-brother had to go down, and if he took his mother with him, so be it.

Rock clenched his burner phone in his hand. He still hadn't heard from Lacey.

I understood exactly how he felt. A day ago I'd been in the same spot—not knowing whether the woman I loved was safe. I didn't envy him.

"We're going home," I said. "All of us."

"But the women..." Diamond whispered.

"If they don't want to leave, we'll set up medical and psychological help for them here. Get them ready. Believe me, they'll have everything they need."

"The cost will be exorbitant," Zee said.

"We have access to Derek's dirty accounts," I said. "I can't think of a better use for that money. I've already begun a transfer to a secure location outside the US."

"That's Jordan's money," Diamond said.

"Seriously?" Rock shook his head.

"You didn't let me finish." Diamond clasped her hands in her lap. "I don't want any of it, and I don't want him to have any of it. I'd rather it all go to the women."

"The Feds will probably confiscate a lot of it, anyway," Rock said.

"No doubt," I said, "but I made sure there will be enough to take care of the women, freshly laundered and outside the US. Dad taught me well."

The words made me sick. My father had taught me about money laundering when I was a mere eighteen years old. Said his company didn't do it, but it was a good skill to have.

Should have been my first clue.

I turned to Rock. "Zee and I can make the arrangements for the women. You get off this island now. Go find your wife."

Rock nodded. "Thanks, bro."

55

LACEY

"**M**a'am. Ma'am. Are you all right?"

Headache. Bad headache. My eyes cracked open. Oh my God. *Where am I? What am I doing here? Whose place is this?*

Blurred images came into view slowly. I still didn't recognize the place, until—

I sat up, rubbing my temples. On the floor next to me was what looked like a book, only it was open, and inside was a safe. An empty safe.

Images came back to me then. This was Fonda's place. The safe. The eyeglasses. With a pointy temple tip. I touched my neck. Yes. He'd injected me. Derek's son Jordan had drugged me with something. How much time had passed?

I tried to stand, but dizziness took over. Not a great idea, at least not yet.

"Easy, ma'am. I've got you."

My vision was blurry, but he was...a police officer?

Great. And I was out on bail for murder.

The safe...

What had been in that safe? The glasses. Their case sat on

the floor next to the open copy of *Moby Dick*. An envelope, manila. Nowhere in sight, at least that I could see from where I was sitting. And...

A thumb drive.

He'd given me a thumb drive. Who? Jordan. Jordan Wolfe.

Where was that thumb drive?

I looked around as the cop helped me to my feet.

"Someone called about a gunshot. Your door was unlocked. You should be more careful, ma'am."

I listened with only one ear as I patted the pocket of my blazer. Shit.

No thumb drive.

It was supposed to be evidence exonerating the Wolfes and me. Implicating Fonda and Jordan. Where had Jordan gone? Had he been playing me this whole time?

I'd had a gun.

A gun.

I peeled my eyes...

No gun.

The firearm was gone.

Just as well. I didn't need the cops to find a gun with my fingerprints all over it.

But a shot *had* rung out. I remembered now. I squinted, willing my vision to focus. Something gold caught my eyes.

A casing. The shell from the gunshot. I'd thought he was shooting me, but I was fine. Jordan couldn't have been that bad of a shot.

Why did he shoot the gun?

"Do you have any ID, ma'am?"

"Uh...yeah. I do."

I hadn't brought my purse to the shoot. Quickly I checked the pouch strapped underneath my blazer. My ID was there. My credit card. The hundred bucks in cash was gone, and so was my burner phone.

Strange. He took the phone and the cash but not my credit card?

What was Jordan's game plan?

I had no idea what time it was, how much time had passed since I'd been here.

I fumbled with my driver's license and handed it to the officer. Within a minute, he'd be hauling me to the station. But what other choice did I have? The gun was gone, and it wasn't like I'd actually hold a police officer at gunpoint, even though I'd witnessed my husband do the same in Montana.

I stood, keeping my balance as best I could as I scanned the place for the time. Didn't anyone keep clocks at home anymore? Did the whole free world rely on cell phones to know what time it was?

A couch sat against the far wall. It beckoned. I could lie down until my head stopped pounding, until the vertigo went away.

If Rock were here, he'd insist I get checked out.

As much as that sofa called to me. I had to get back to the suite. Thank God Jordan had left my credit card. I'd get a cab.

"Lacey Wolfe," the cop said. "That name sounds familiar."

I sighed. What was the use? "I'm the wife of Rock Wolfe, CEO of Wolfe Enterprises. I'm out on bail for Derek Wolfe's murder. And I'm innocent."

"So this isn't your place?" He grabbed his cuffs. "Looks like I've got you for breaking and entering."

"No, no." I shook my head. "I was brought here. This is Fonda Burke's place."

"The model?"

"Yeah, the one and only. Her..." What was Jordan Wolfe

anyway? "Uh...significant other brought me here. He had evidence to exon—"

My gaze zeroed in on a cardboard box on top of the coffee table. "For Lacey" was written on the side of it in black marker.

Had that been there before? Surely, I would have noticed it.

I walked slowly—I was still a little dizzy—toward it and looked inside. Several thumb drives. One had a label identifying it as the missing timeframe from the surveillance at my apartment building.

I grabbed it. "I need to see what's on this. All of these. Please. Now."

"Ma'am, we're going to have to take you in."

"Please. You know I'm innocent. If you know anything about this case, you know the evidence against me is purely circumstantial. It was all planted. This will exonerate me. I swear it."

"We'll let the DA be the judge of that." He picked up the box.

"No! That belongs to me. It has my name on it. It's mine."

"But this isn't your place."

"Yes, but I didn't break in. I swear to it. I'll tell you everything, but I need my lawyer present. And..."

"And...?"

"My husband. I need to contact my husband."

"Where is he?"

I opened my mouth and then shut it. Rock and Reid weren't supposed to leave the state of New York. I couldn't tell this officer that they were somewhere in the Pacific.

"I'm sorry, ma'am. I need to call this—"

The officer nearly jumped out of his blues when a burly man plowed through the door. "Lacey! Thank God. Rock will be so rel—" He spied the cop. "Fuck."

My mouth dropped open.

"Who the hell are you?" the cop demanded.

"Buck Moreno. I work for the Wolfes. Rock asked me to find his wife."

"His wife is coming with me," the cop said.

"Fine. As long as you play by the rules." Buck pulled out a cell phone and sent a quick text. "I'm calling her lawyer. He'll meet us at the station."

"Grab that box," I said to Buck. "I have a feeling it contains everything we need."

56

REID

The files Jordan left with Lacey managed to exonerate every one of us.

Apparently my oldest brother had been surveilling all of us, and the evidence showed all of our whereabouts the night of the murder. We all got over the privacy violation quickly, as it proved our innocence. After we proved Derek had set out to fake his death and that Nieves intercepted Jordan's faked call, the rest fell into place.

As for who fired the fatal shot?

It was either Jordan or Fonda. We'd never know for sure. Neither of their prints were on the murder weapon, although Rock's were. The authorities had finally traced the weapon to a gun show Rock had attended. He'd used the firearm at the shooting range before choosing to purchase an identical one. Somehow, Jordan had obtained the gun with Rock's prints.

Rock and I gave the files we'd found on the island to the FBI and the NYPD. DA Jonathan Leopold was arrested, and the NYPD did some serious housecleaning. Lacey's tape of Morgan got him arrested. He'd cried like a baby when he was hauled in.

Terrence bawled like a baby, as well. Seemed he wasn't as

tough as he wanted people to think he was. All he'd done was doctor a few office records and try to goad me into believing an office security breach was imminent. Turned out Dick Fallon, head of security was clean. Terrence got off with a slap on his wrist.

Hoss, Manny, and Nieves told their story and somehow evaded arrest as well. Leta was still recovering, and the other three testified that she wasn't very involved, anyway. We'd been able to trace her attackers through the NYPD, who were angry that she'd met with Roy and Charlie.

No prison time for any of them.

Father Jim was, of course, dead. We'd never know the extent of his involvement, or if he'd truly wanted to get out after my father was killed.

Good riddance.

I was beginning to truly detest the system. Would anyone pay for all this shit?

Apparently not.

The true culprits, Jordan and Fonda, had disappeared.

"JORDAN SWORE they weren't going to let me go down for this," Lacey said a few days later, when we were all together in the conference room at the office. "He wanted it to be one of you. But in the end, he did the right thing."

"A good woman helps even the most corrupt see the light." Rock smiled at his wife.

"Except for our father," Riley said. "Irene couldn't do that for him."

"No," Rock said. "He was apparently beyond help."

"I still feel bad for Diamond." Zee squeezed my hand.

"We did all we could," I assured my wife. "She'll be in

minimum security, and after a year, she'll be eligible for release. We'll take care of her."

What Zee didn't know was that Diamond had agreed to plead guilty to accessory to kidnapping so that the government would release the island funds for the benefit of the women who'd been held there. The Wolfe Foundation was already setting up treatment for them, along with all other needs. They'd be taken care of for life.

Diamond had begged me not to tell Zee or the other women. She didn't want any of them feeling guilty. I hated keeping it from Zee, but I didn't want to add to her burden.

What my father had ever done in his life to deserve a woman like Diamond was beyond me.

"So...the island," Rock said. "Now that Jordan's gone, it's ours."

"How is that?" Roy asked.

I cleared my throat. "The deed was held in joint tenancy between Dad and Jordan. After Dad died, Jordan put Rock's name on the deed. We have no idea why, but it's his now."

"And as far as I'm concerned," Rock said, "anything of mine belongs to all of us."

"You're very generous." Riley smiled.

"Lace and I both agreed," Rock said. "Any one of you would have done the same."

"True." Roy nodded. "We're all in this together."

"So..." I drew in a breath. "To that end...we have an island. A gorgeous tropical island with a built-in resort."

"That was used to hunt women," Zee reminded me.

"Yes." I sighed. "It was. But we can change its course. Do something good with it."

"Or sell it to the highest bidder," Roy said.

"We can," I said, "but I'm the COO of this business, and my instinct says it's a valuable asset and we should keep it."

"I don't know, bro," Rock said. "Part of me feels like this is a bad idea. Our whole company was founded on dirty money from our great-grandfather."

"True." I nodded. "We can't get away from that. But it's ours now. And we can use it to do a lot of good in this world. Dad may have set all this shit in motion, but we can reverse its course. We have the power now, Rock. We need to use it."

"I want to help," Riley said. "Matt and I have been talking, and we want to help with the foundation. I want to help survivors of sexual abuse. Of any kind of abuse, and I want to start with Dad's victims. What if we made the island a retreat or something? Where victims can go to get therapy? A healing place? Where better to heal than a beautiful island?"

"I love that idea," Roy said. "Charlie and I have been talking as well."

"About what?" I asked.

"We'd like to set up an art colony on the island."

"I love that!" Riley nearly jumped. "We could work on it together. Our two visions could overlap. Healing through art. Or just art. Or just healing."

I wasn't sure I'd ever loved my brother and sister more than at that moment. "That's a great idea. Rock and I have been talking as well about what to do with the property."

"How to make the most profit, I'll bet," Roy said dryly.

"What's wrong with profit?" I said. "Without the ability to profit, none of us would have the kind of money we do. The island's big enough for all three of our ventures. Roy and Charlie, you can have your art colony. Riley and Matt, you can have your retreat. And Rock and I are going to build the most luxurious resort, casino, and spa in the world!"

"One problem," Rock said. "What do we call the island? Not Wolfe Island."

"Why not?" I asked.

"The Wolfe name is dirty."

"The Wolfe name is *ours*," I retorted. "Dad didn't use the name on the island. The hunting ground was called Treasure Island."

"Still..."

"It's *our* name, Rock," I said. "We need to take it back."

"Name it after your wife," Rock said. "Zinnia. It's a beautiful name of a beautiful flower."

I cocked my head as my gorgeous wife blushed. Not a bad idea at all. But, "This is *our* enterprise. The Wolfes. Rock, Roy, Reid, and Riley. Not Derek. We need to take back our own name."

"Why?"

"Because unless we change our names legally, it's still our name. It still has recognition. Dad did a lot of things wrong, but his branding was good. We've got our real estate. Our luxury hotels and golf courses. Our wineries. Our...everything. Rebranding would be huge, and frankly, we've spent a fucking buttload of money clearing our names. Well worth it, of course, but rebranding will cost hundreds of millions, and it's money we don't have to spend."

"But it's the bastard's name."

"It's also *our* name. I know you're not a businessman at heart, but surely you see the benefit of keeping the brand."

Rock finally nodded. "Okay. It's just... I hate that mother-fucker so much."

"So do I. That's why we take back the name, bro. We fucking take it back and make it great."

He nodded. "Wolfe Island it is, then, assuming the rest of you approve?"

"I'm good," Roy said.

"Me too," Riley said. "Maybe for once I can be proud of my name. Though I'm still taking Matt's."

"Wolfe Island, then," Rock said. "Wolfe Island Luxury Resort and Casino. Wolfe Island Art Colony. Wolfe Island Retreat Center. It actually has a nice ring to it."

"Remember," I said. "Derek Wolfe is dead. He no longer matters. The Wolfe name is about us now. The eight of us."

～

A MONTH LATER, we all gathered in the now-cleared top floor penthouse. Rock and Lacey's belongings were still in boxes, but we had a makeshift meeting with good old New York-style pizza and cheap chianti from the liquor store on the corner—Rock's request.

"To Wolfe Island." I held up my glass of wine.

"We'll have to make getting there easier," Riley said.

"We will," I agreed. "I've got transportation engineers working on those details. Architects and design engineers working on the plans. My plan is to get it opened in a year's time."

All eyebrows except Rock's shot up.

"That's impossible," Roy said.

"It's definitely possible for the art colony and retreat." I cleared my throat. "The resort will take a little more effort and we'll be greasing some palms, but I *will* get it done. We're taking back everything Dad stole from us and all of his victims. We're going to make this work." I grabbed Zee's hand and caressed her palm with my thumbs. "We can't change what he did to you, my love. Or to Riley. Or to the rest of us. What we can change is how we deal with it. We're going to turn his legacy into a legacy of love."

"And profit!" Rock laughed.

I laughed and nodded. "Profit creates jobs. Profit means we can help those who need it."

"And it works pretty well for the rest of us," Roy said jovially.

I looked around.

Roy, no longer a recluse. Happily married and moving to a beautiful island to run an art colony. He and Charlie could paint to their hearts' content and mentor other artists.

Riley, still a supermodel, now styled as Riley Rossi. She'd continue to grace the runways wearing the newest fashion, and she'd also help Matt run the retreat from offices on Wolfe Island. She'd decided only to travel for the best shoots. Otherwise, she'd be doing the work of her heart from the island.

Rock, my big brother, would stay in New York with Lacey to run Wolfe Enterprises. Our attorneys had advised us that the newfound information regarding our father's exploits was grounds to petition the probate court to nullify the portion of Dad's will requiring Rock to stay, but he and I agreed we both needed to be in Manhattan.

We worked well together, and our personalities and business senses seemed to complement each other. Lacey would take over the Wolfe legal team once Lester retired in a couple months.

Our long lost brother, Jordan. On the run as a fugitive. No one had put up any roadblocks, though. In the end, once we were all exonerated and the bad cops were behind bars, no one seemed to care so much that Derek Wolfe was gone. Our half-brother had put us through this, but in the end, he'd saved us.

In my way, I wished him well.

I stared at the beauty next to me. My Zee. Where would she end up?

She hadn't made any decisions yet.

Perhaps she'd decide to work for the company. Perhaps she'd go back to dancing. Perhaps she'd go to college and then medical school and finally realize her dream of being a doctor. Or perhaps she'd stay home once the little bundle percolating inside her arrived. Turned out she didn't have her pills on the island.

Not a bad thing.

I smiled and squeezed her hand.

We'd all been through our personal hell.

There was nowhere to go but up.

CRAVING MORE WOLFES?

Here's a sneak peak of *Escape*, a Wolfe Island Novella. Available only for a limited time!

EMILY

I stop looking over my shoulder on the fourth day.

I don't notice this until the evening, when I sit down by myself at the bar. I've been at the Wolfe Island Art Colony less than a week, but until today, I've been watching my back.

When you're hiding from the devil himself, you don't let your guard down.

A second after sitting down on the wooden stool at the beachfront bar, I look behind me.

That's when I realize it's the first time I've done it today.

Whether that's good or bad, I can't say. I shouldn't be getting too comfortable.

"What'll it be, pretty girl?"

I shift my gaze toward the bartender's deep voice—

And nearly drop my jaw onto the counter. His eyes are such a gorgeous mixture of emerald and cognac. Most would simply call them hazel. I see a swirl of Prussian Green and Olive Green with hints of Renaissance Gold.

And believe it or not, those amazing eyes pale in comparison to the rest of him.

I smile shyly. I've kept to myself since I arrived on the island, spending most of my time painting the scenes outside my hut. This is the first time I've ventured to the beach.

"You going to answer me?" Hunky bartender raises his dark brown eyebrows.

"Yeah. Sorry." My cheeks burn. "Just some water, I guess."

"You guess? You can do better than that, pretty girl."

Pretty girl. The second time he's called me that in the span of two minutes. I don't feel pretty. On the outside, I suppose I'm okay. On the inside, a disaster.

"Cat still got your tongue?" He smiles a lazy smile, that makes him even better looking. "Trust me?"

I part my lips and lick them. Trust him? I trust no one. No one. He has no idea what kind of can of worms he's opened.

"I'll take that as a yes." He reaches under the bar and pulls out a martini glass.

I hate martinis, but still I say nothing.

"Try my specialty. Virgin?"

My jaw drops. "Of course not!"

He laughs. "I mean do you want the virgin version of my specialty?"

"Oh." God, my cheeks can't get any hotter. I can only imagine what they look like in the light of the setting sun. "That's what I meant. I don't want the virgin one."

"Got it." He smiles.

Yeah, he doesn't buy it, but I give him credit for letting me try to weasel out of my embarrassment.

He turns toward the back of the bar and pulls three different bottles from the myriad options.

Three bottles? Maybe I should have gone with the virgin.

He fills a stainless steel shaker with crushed ice and adds a stream of the golden, the yellow, and the hot pink. I eyed the bottle closest to me—the pink one. Crème de Noyeaux. Never heard of it.

Next he adds what appears to be orange juice and then pineapple. A Mai Tai maybe? No, he said it was his specialty. Surely he didn't invent the Mai Tai. Or maybe he invented this particular version.

He adjusts the lid and shakes several times. Once he's done, he slides a slice of lime around the rim of the martini glass, dips it in sugar, and then strains the contents of the shaker into the glass.

I notice the color first. It's a lovely pinkish-orange, the shade of last night's sunset that I tried to capture on canvas but couldn't.

He pushes the drink toward me and sets a cocktail napkin next to it. "Tell me what you think."

Good enough. I inhale and pick the martini glass up by its stem. I sniff. Nice fragrance. Orangey and almondy. Very tropical.

"Well?" he says. "Are you waiting for a little umbrella?"

I can't help myself. I laugh. I laugh like I haven't in a long time, and it feels good. Really good.

"You got one?" I ask.

"Your wish is my command." He reaches under the counter and then pops a tiny pink umbrella into my drink.

If I had my phone, I'd shoot a pic and post this on Instagram.

I don't have my phone, though, and I deleted all my social media accounts.

In fact, the only person who has a clue where I am is my brother, Buck, and he's sworn to secrecy. He helped me get the invitation to the colony when I needed to leave town in a hurry. The person I'm running from can't touch Buck.

No one can.

WANT the rest of Emily's story?

Escape is available in *Cocktails on the Beach*, a limited run anthology featuring Helen Hardt, Leah Marie Brown, EmKay Connor, and Lyz Kelley. Preorder your copy now for only $2.99! The price will increase after release.

Also coming soon...two new series! *Wolfe Island* and *Gems of Wolfe Island*. Stay tuned!

A NOTE FROM HELEN

Dear Reader,

Thank you for reading *Reckoning!* If you want to find out about my current backlist and future releases, please visit my website, like my Facebook page, and join my mailing list. If you're a fan, please join my street team to help spread the word about my books. I regularly do awesome giveaways for my street team members.

If you enjoyed the story, please take the time to leave a review. I welcome all feedback.

I wish you all the best!

Helen

Facebook

Facebook.com/helenhardt

Newsletter

Helenhardt.com/signup

Street Team

Facebook.com/groups/hardtandsoul

ACKNOWLEDGMENTS

Thank you so much to the following individuals who helped make *Reckoning* shine: Christie Hartman, Martha Frantz, Karen Aguilera, Angela Tyler, Linda Pantlin Dunn, Serena Drummond, Kim Killion, and Marci Clark.

ALSO BY HELEN HARDT

Standalone Novels and Novellas

Reunited

Misadventures:

Misadventures of a Good Wife (with Meredith Wild)

Misadventures with a Rockstar

The Cougar Chronicles:

The Cowboy and the Cougar

Calendar Boy

Daughters of the Prairie:

The Outlaw's Angel

Lessons of the Heart

Song of the Raven

Collections:

Destination Desire

Her Two Lovers

Non-Fiction:

got style?

ABOUT THE AUTHOR

#1 *New York Times*, #1 *USA Today*, and #1 *Wall Street Journal* best-selling author Helen Hardt's passion for the written word began with the books her mother read to her at bedtime. She wrote her first story at age six and hasn't stopped since. In addition to being an award-winning author of romantic fiction, she's a mother, an attorney, a black belt in Taekwondo, a grammar geek, an appreciator of fine red wine, and a lover of Ben and Jerry's ice cream. She writes from her home in Colorado, where she lives with her family. Helen loves to hear from readers.

http://www.helenhardt.com

CPSIA information can be obtained
at www.ICGtesting.com
Printed in the USA
LVHW041505220721
693425LV00002B/191

9 781952 841040